ALARIC'S OBSESSION

AN ETERNAL GUARDIAN NOVEL

TASHA M TAYLOR

This book is for all the fantasy/paranormal and erotica lovers across the globe. If you fell in love with Rome and Alara, then hopefully, Alaric and Na'tori make you fall even harder. Dive in and enjoy Lovies.

PROLOGUE

Rome stood at the opening of a doorway as the sun dropped from the sky, casting darkness and shadows into the bedroom before him. The form within the bed thrashed and turned beneath the sheets, the smell of sweat and sickness filling the space along with the scent of desperation. It was pouring from Alaric's pores as he continued to toss and turn beneath the sheets, his cracked voice grumbling incoherent words that Rome couldn't quite make out even with his supernatural hearing. He could also feel Alaric's telepathic abilities filling the air as they searched for a weak mind to probe and corrupt. This phenomenon was something that had been happening recently. Since his mental decline had accelerated, his inability to control his gifts while he slept was becoming a danger to others around him. No matter how many times Alara attempted to heal her brother's mind, it was evident that their healing sessions simply stopped the virus for a week or so before it ate away at him once more and sent his mind into utter turmoil.

Since the moment Alaric had been shot with the virus that was capable of killing Rogues and incapacitating Eternals, his cells had been eating away at themselves in a way that had everyone questioning why the virus affected him so differently. He should have been dead, considering the months that had come and gone with it spreading throughout his body. With each healing session, Alara—his mate—walked away feeling worse and worse about the situation because, without her blood, the virus that was running rampant among her brother's cells wouldn't even be possible.

Rome erected a bubble around the room with his own telepathic abilities, all in an attempt to keep Alaric's mind from diving into another's, when a silent figure approached him from behind. He glanced over his shoulder and met the mismatched blue and green eyes of one of his closest friends and trusted guardians before his eyes flew back to the bed.

"He's getting worse." Silas frowned as he stared into the bedroom at Alaric's thrashing form. "What are we going to do about him? If we continue to do nothing, then he will die. I've seen it, sir, and his death will not be pretty."

"We still have time to find this doctor and get answers. Alara will heal him again once he wakes, and we shall go from there." Rome replied even as dread began to swirl within his gut and Alaric's power fought to break free from his hold.

They needed to figure out something soon. Not just to save Alaric's life but also to save the minds around him that had the potential to be twisted and even erased due to his inability to control his abilities. Rome needed to figure out a way to protect the people under his direct care and come clean to his Guardians and Alaric that there was a way to save him from the virus slowly killing him. The way to save his mate's brother was simple, but whether it would actually cure him of the thing that was killing him was an answer he didn't have. He did know that the people who had come to trust and believe in him for so many centuries might no longer do so after they heard what he had to say in tonight's meeting.

"Begin to gather the others," Rome commanded as he stepped over the threshold into his brother-in-law's room. "I'll wake the sleeping giant."

. . .

ALARIC SAT JUST AS STILL and unmoving as the rest of the people he had gotten to know over the last eight months as Rome dropped a bomb on them that no one had been expecting. The only one who seemed unbothered by his secret was his mate, Alara. In fact, her expression looked just as put together as her counterpart.

How long had she known?

His suffering could have ended, and a new life could have begun had they been more transparent with the truth. For the entirety of his life, he'd moved in shadows and lies, keeping things from people, convincing himself that it was for the better, but now he knew that to be a lie. It wasn't for the best, and now fate was telling him that he had made many mistakes and had to pay for them. He didn't believe much in a higher power, but his imminent death convinced him otherwise. Only fate could be so cruel. The newfound freedom he had gained after getting his family away from Titan was now short-lived if he didn't take the opportunity that Rome was attempting to hand out to him. Would he take it? Did he want to risk what he would then become?

His voice cut through the silence that stretched within the cozy living room that he had begun to consider home and waited with bated breath. "How long?"

Alara's eyes swung to him; misty gray with a tinge of light blue stared back at him as guilt crossed his sister's face. "It's been a few weeks since I found out. I wasn't sure how to bring it up to you, and Romulus thought it would be best if everyone learned the truth once everything had settled down."

"Let me guess…" he spread his arms out to draw attention to the six Eternal Guardians that were still strapping on their weapons for their hunt for the night, "this is what you consider settled down? We still don't have answers, Alara. We're still chasing rumors, hoping to locate Titan's new base of operations and the doctor responsible for creating this virus in the first place, yet here you both are telling me that you've had a cure this whole time. There's been a way to save me, and you've been sitting on the information."

"Alaric is right," Amirishka stated. "What exactly can you do to save him? Would it actually work? And if it does, why did you keep this information from us?"

Rome squared his shoulders and stared directly into Alaric's eyes. "I don't know if what I'm suggesting would actually work or if it would only speed up the process of the virus. It's why I didn't consider bringing this to you as an option. You would be changed on a genetic level that cannot be undone once the process has started." He paused, his gaze running over each of his warriors before it once again rested on his brother-in-law. "If we do this, you'll no longer be a Kindred, but instead, you'll become like me and my brethren. You'll be an Eternal, and there's no telling what that change would do to you."

"That's why we've always been forbidden from sharing our blood with a human, isn't it?" Cairo questioned, anger lacing his tone as he glared at their leader. "It's our blood that makes an Eternal possible."

Rome neglected to respond, his eyes still drilling into Alaric as he waited patiently for a response to the information he'd provided, but no answer came. Instead, Alaric stood and quickly exited the room with his hands clenched into fists at his sides. He refused to say a word. He wanted to lash out, rage even, but what would that do for him? Probably nothing, and expending energy he couldn't dare risk was a no-brainer. He needed to calm down, think rationally, and figure out what to do.

Regardless of this new information, Alaric knew he was dying, and this virus was progressing a lot faster than anyone thought possible. He didn't have much time to make a decision that could forever alter his life, but he needed to figure it out quickly before it was too late.

CHAPTER
ONE

Four Months Later

The music and bass pulsed and throbbed within the air around him as the scent of sweat and sex filled Alaric's nasal passage. His eyes continued to scan the area in search of the Rogue vampire he and Silas had followed into the club only moments before. Bodies shoved against him as they swayed to the beat of the music. The place was packed like a can of sardines, giving you no room to really move around or maneuver if anything should happen within the walls of the establishment. It was the perfect place for a Rogue to look for their next victim. Here, people drank excessively, and no one paid attention to their surroundings. With the dimness of the lights, a human would never realize that some of the occupants within the room sported fangs and glowing eyes. They never knew that they were being hunted by beings that would like nothing more than to bleed them dry.

Alaric searched for the tall immortal he'd been paired with since he began hunting with the Eternals and paused when Silas's six-foot-eight frame stepped from the shadows across the club from him. He couldn't read his expression, but by the stiffness in his shoulders and the tightness in his jaw, Alaric could tell that something was wrong. The feeling of someone trying to penetrate the barriers of his mind reached him, and he knew without question that Silas was attempting to speak with him. Over the months of working exclusively with each other, he'd become incredibly familiar with Silas's unique mental imprint, and he allowed his shields to drop and grant him access.

"Someone else is here."

"Another Rogue?" Alaric questioned as his eyes began to scan the room in search of another enemy, yet he came up with nothing. *"Where are they?"*

Silas was silent for several moments before he spoke again. *"It's not a Rogue, I'm not sure what the scent is, but it's unusual…intoxicating and distracting. I can't get a bead on where it's coming from, and I've lost sight of our prey."*

"I don't have your sense of smell Si, so I don't know what you're going on about. Forget it and locate the Rogue."

"If you would take Rome up on his offer, then maybe you would have my heightened senses."

Alaric slammed down on the barriers of his mind, effectively blocking Silas as he snarled in annoyance and pushed his way through the crowd to search for the vamp he'd followed inside. He looked into the mind of every human he passed, all while pushing down the throbbing pain that began to pulse through his brain and irritate his gaze. He couldn't help but think that Silas was right. He should have taken Rome up on his offer to go through the process of becoming an Eternal, but he couldn't help but feel like he still had a chance to find the doctor who had created the virus that was coursing through his blood and rewriting his cells in the worst way possible. He didn't want to drastically change his genes if he didn't need to. If there was a potential way of reversing what had already been done to him, he would gladly take it over, becoming Immortal.

Immortality seemed like a lonely life to live.

Watching and spending time with the Guardians day in and day out had shown him a new way of life, and it was one he wasn't interested in living. With Rome the only Eternal in several centuries to ever find the other half of his soul, it didn't give him much hope for finding his own. Not that he was actually interested in a mate, but if he was going to live forever, he would at least want someone to live it with. Life could be lonely as a human; he couldn't imagine the loneliness that ensued for those whose lifespans were never-ending unless they were killed.

He was moving for the bar, eyes still scanning for the Rogue, when his gaze landed on platinum blonde hair that stood out against the sea of blackness and strobe lights that filled the room. Her hair fell in a straight waterfall down her back, nearly to her ass. He'd always had a fascination with long hair on women. The idea of holding all of those long strands within his fist made his heart thunder in his ears. Alaric couldn't see exactly what she looked like with her back to him and bodies between them, but he could just barely make out her thin frame beneath the light blue skin-tight dress that hugged the curves of her hips and ass. His gaze was moving back up to the crown of her hair when a figure approached her and whispered into her ear.

Alaric froze. He knew that face and profile. It was the Rogue he'd followed into the club to begin with. He reached down and palmed the hidden blade within his jacket as he started to work his way through the crowd. The closer Alaric got to them, the more he noticed their familiarity with each other. The vamp stood close enough to kiss her, his hand resting lightly upon the small of her back as she seemed to turn into him. Was the Rogue compelling her? Had he already bitten and injected her with the venom that made humans pliable to their advances? He was several feet away when he attempted to breach her mind and was once again frozen in shock when a mental barrier like a diamond greeted him.

Her head swung around, and opalescent eyes gazed back at him in what could only be described as shock. Her pale skin was sprinkled with freckles that looked as if they were dancing beneath the lights. Her nose was upturned with sculpted model-like cheeks, a pointed chin, and full bow-shaped lips that commanded attention. Her beauty was ethereal, a thing of dreams and wonders that made the breath in his lungs stall out. He was moving for her when he recalled the Rogue and snapped his gaze towards the six-foot-three figure standing at her back. His eyes were blood red, lips drawn back in a snarl that would make a lesser man piss themselves in fear. He circled his arm around the female's neck and jerked her backward and into his body before moving for the exit door behind him.

Alaric sent a telepathic shout to Silas to meet him outside before following the Rogue and the woman out the door and into a side alley. Without taking his eyes from the vamp, he drew his blade from his jacket and shadowed him with every backstep he took.

"What are you?" The Rogue hissed through his teeth as his sandy brown hair hung loosely around his face. He inhaled repeatedly in an attempt to lock onto Alaric's scent.

"I'm the man sent to kill you and your kind," Alaric responded, "now let the pretty woman go, and we can hash this out alone."

"If you know of my kind, then that means you work with my enemy. I can smell a taint within your blood. You're sick." He ran his nose and then tongue against the base of the woman's throat and smiled sharply, "She, on the other hand, smells like every fantasy I've ever desired wrapped in one, and I intend to get my taste of her."

Her voice was soft and angelic yet absent of the fear most humans used when being held against their will. "Don't I get a say in the matter?"

Alaric opened his mouth to speak and de-escalate the situation but instead was stunned into utter silence when she moved quick as lightning, jerked out of his arms, and turned around to stab the Rogue directly in the heart with a dagger he never saw her pull out.

Rogues weren't like Eternals, where they needed to be buried and their bodies preserved beneath the layers of the earth with boundary spells. Instead, they simply became ash upon death. Their ash would then scatter in the wind, leaving behind clothes and whatever blood had been spilled. So, in a matter of moments, the Rogue was gone, and clothing and ash remained in his place.

Alaric watched her replace the dagger in the side bag he hadn't bothered to notice slung across her ample chest before her unusual gaze met his. He took determined steps forward until he was only a few paces away as his mind attempted to probe hers and those around them. He continued to meet that diamond resistance within her mind, and he could tell she felt him trying to worm his way through her barriers by the tightening of her features. When his mind brushed against Silas's, he relayed another message just for him.

"The Rogue has been indisposed. If you can keep all humans from the side alley while I do clean up, that would be appreciated."

"What needs cleaning? Is there a problem?" Silas sighed heavily before he spoke again, *"I was on my way to you when I had to dispose of another Rogue feeding within the men's room. I can be there in five minutes. I need to wipe the minds of those involved on my end."*

"Take your time; everything's fine out here."

Alaric removed himself from the Eternals' mind and focused once more on the woman before him as she searched the pockets of the dead Rogue before she threw the clothes in the dumpster and headed towards the alley entrance. He didn't stop to think about his actions and reached out to grasp her elbow before she could walk away. Usually, he would never touch a woman without express permission, but he couldn't just let her walk away without explaining herself. This was unusual on all levels, and it was evident that she was a Kindred, but that didn't explain how she was aware of Rogues and why interacting with one hadn't fazed her in the slightest. It almost appeared to him as if this was a regular occurrence for her, and if it was, then how had she never landed on the Eternal Guardians' radar?

Her gaze snagged on his hold on her arm before her eyes narrowed on his face, "Release me." Her voice still carried that angelic sound, yet he heard the anger within her tone.

"I can't do that," he replied, "How do you know about Rogues? You're a Kindred, aren't you? Another telepath? Or are you a shield, and that's how you're blocking me from your mind. A regular human wouldn't be capable of doing so."

"I won't repeat it."

Alaric's expression morphed into a frown. "Will you run if I do?"

She seemed to mull it over as she looked him up and down

before she shook her head slightly. "I won't if you tell me what you want."

To believe her or not is what he struggled with for several seconds before he loosened his grip and dropped his arm. Standing close enough to kiss, Alaric towered over her five-foot-six frame at six-foot-three, just as the dead Rogue had. She looked minuscule beside him and caused his mind to wander into dangerous territories. It took effort on his part to focus on what was truly important in this moment.

"Well?" She snapped. Her unusual opal eyes seemed to swirl with purples, blues, and pinks as the smell of honey drifted from her skin like a cloying lotion. "What do you want?"

"Your name, what is it?"

She crossed her arms over her chest in a defensive posture, causing her 34b breasts to rise slightly beneath the thin fabric of her dress. A soft wind chose that moment to drift by, bringing with it the cool autumn air that caused her nipples to stiffen. His eyes drifted once more to her chest and held just as a pounding headache began to press against his mind, along with voices he didn't recognize. Alaric grimaced against the pain and glanced up to find her staring over his shoulder. Her pale skin went several shades paler as her eyes widened in surprise and fear before she took several steps back. He knew that Silas had just stepped into the alley without having to look.

He normally got that reaction due to his larger size and unusual look. Straight black hair fell to his waist with streaks of white within the strands. His right eye was dark green while the left eye was a dark blue, yet with heightened emotions, they were known to brighten unless he fell into a premonition that caused them to bleed into a milky white sheen that freaked even Alaric out. His body was packed with muscles, yet his build was lean and thin. The scar that crossed over his right eye and his thin lips gave most people pause, yet he was one of the nicest people Alaric knew.

"I said everything was fine." Alaric glanced over his shoulder to meet the Eternal's stare but found him staring just as intently at the woman. "What's wrong?"

"She's a Kindred," Silas replied. He crossed the alleyway in several steps and came to stand beside his brother-in-arms before he spoke again. "I can't read her, can you?"

"No, but we were just getting to introductions until you interrupted us."

Silas grunted and inhaled deeply before stiffening in shock. His head cocked to the side, and he watched her even more closely. "Your scent is…off. What exactly are you? You can't just be a Kindred; you're more."

Her gaze flew between them in fear as her hand dug into her purse, and she pulled out a small vial that she dropped onto the floor. They stepped back from her as gas filled the space between them and blinded them to the woman making a hasty getaway.

CHAPTER
TWO

N a'tori ran as fast as she could within the three-inch heels she'd decided to don for the night and cursed her stupidity for stopping to entertain the man that had attempted to save her from the Rogue she'd been hunting. She stuck close to the shadows and meshed easily with the traffic of people walking the streets as she maneuvered to the car she'd left parked several blocks from the club. As soon as she slid into the leather seat of her black Audi R8, she released the breath she hadn't known she'd been holding and quickly checked the mirrors as she started up the car and peeled away from the curb.

Her breaths came in quick, short pants as her hands shook against the steering wheel. Running into an Eternal had not been on her list of things to do for the night. Even running into the man with the familiar misty gray and light green eyes hadn't been on her agenda, but new ideas flowed through her head rapidly now that she had. She'd never met Alaric before today, but she would recognize his harsh features anywhere. With a pointed nose, rounded cheeks, and a five o'clock shadow that surrounded unevenly plush lips, he made her think of sinful nights with him starring in every single one of her fantasies. From pictures and videos she'd previously seen, Na'tori knew that Alaric's body was muscular with a 12-pack that defied every law in the book, along with graphic tattoos he'd received over the years he'd been employed through Titan.

She definitely hadn't been expecting a run-in with one of the men who was on the top of her brother's kill list, and now that she'd seen him, she was obligated to tell her family. She slammed her hand against the steering wheel and constantly checked her mirrors to ensure she wasn't being followed as she returned to her apartment. She should have been heading to the warehouse to update her family, but she needed a moment to think. Na'tori needed a plan, or her actions tonight could bite her in the ass. She'd killed the Rogue when she should have been doing the opposite. She should have brought him in, but being held and threatened hadn't convinced her to let him live.

She was pulling into her parking spot when her phone rang in her purse. She pulled it out and glanced at the caller ID to see her brother's name flashing across the screen. Dread swirled in the pit of her stomach, but she picked it up anyway, knowing she couldn't ignore it or act as if she hadn't received the call. He would know. He always knew.

"Where the fuck are you?" Lukas Titan screamed through the receiver the moment she picked up.

Leaning her head back into the seat, Na'tori fortified her breathing before she replied. "I just pulled in front of my condo."

"Why the hell are you there when you should be in the lab with my man in tow? Do you think I allow you the freedom you have from the kindness of my heart? News flash, I do not, so get here now and bring me my man."

He never did anything out of the kindness of his heart—if he even had one to begin with—but she couldn't tell him that. She had to take his words on the chin and never respond in anger, or that freedom he spoke of would be non-existent, and she would end up just like one of his many volunteers.

"Bringing him in will be a problem," she sighed heavily, "He tried to kill me and I was left with no choice but to ash him."

"You killed him?" He snarled, "And when exactly did you plan on telling me he was dead?"

"I planned on telling you tonight as soon as I changed clothes and came in. I followed him into a club and needed to dress the part to attract him. They prefer it more when a woman looks the part of a slightly intoxicated victim with little to no clothing. Luckily, I had a dress just for the occasion in my car." Na'tori double-checked her purse to ensure she had everything she needed before climbing out to get into the safety of her home. "As soon as I change, I'll be right in."

"We'll be waiting for a full report, but don't keep us waiting long, little sis, or you won't like the consequences."

She sighed in relief when he hung up before she unlocked her front door and closed it once she was inside. She inhaled and smiled when the smell of honey and elderberry flowers tickled her nostrils. The scent always brought with it a wave of relief, yet she never knew where it came from, only that it brought her the comfort she needed. Most often, it clung to her skin even after she showered, but right now, she could only smell the stench of the club.

Na'tori dropped her bag and keys by the entryway table after double-checking her locks before she headed for her bedroom. She hadn't lied when she told Lukas that she needed to change clothes. Being around so many people as they brushed up against her within the club, the scents accompanying them seemed to cling to her skin like a scarf she didn't want to wear. She needed to wipe their energy off as quickly as possible, so she undressed and jumped into the shower to wash the night away. She stood beneath the spray of the water as her mind milled over the events of the day.

Working all morning only to be sent out to hunt down a Rogue once the sun had set had not been on her list of things she'd wanted to take care of, but when her brothers ordered her to do something, she did it without question. Since she was a child and her family had learned the truth about her, she was looked at as less than them, yet she was a helpful tool when they needed her. Like hunting down Rogues and searching for Kindred. Her ability allowed her to discern whether a person was human, Kindred, or a Rogue, so seeing Alaric and the Eternal tonight had shocked her. Na'tori had never encountered an Immortal until tonight, but now that she had, she would forever remember what an Eternals' aura looked like. The pure white energy that had encased his body had shocked and terrified her to the point of retreat.

Her brothers' stories about their kind were enough to know that she never wanted to be alone with one of them. They were supposed to be bad news. Apparently, they killed without mercy, and as their enemy, she wouldn't be given an opportunity to speak once they realized who she was. Instead, she would be killed on sight, which is why tonight was such a big question mark for her.

Had the Eternal not recognized who she was?

She rushed through her shower in record time and dressed in a pair of black slacks, a cream blouse that brought out the swirl of colors that took place in her eyes and pulled on a pair of short black stilettos that pinched her toes, but if she was caught in anything else than what was considered her 'uniform,' she would never hear the end of it. She touched the skin of her neck and shuddered when she recalled what it felt like to wear one of those terrible gold collars that Lukas had forced around her throat on numerous occasions. It had been to 'keep her in line'—according to him—but it had been an unjust punishment to her. He had wanted to strip her of the power she had grown to love. She wasn't even sure how he had developed such a thing without her knowing, but Na'tori had promised herself after the last time that it would never happen again. She would do as she was told and avoid all negative interactions regarding her family. She needed to find the proof she sought because everything was not as it seemed. Her brothers were hiding something from her, and she intended to discover what that something was.

She grabbed her purse, keys, and jacket on her way out the door but paused when her phone rang, and Lukas's name flashed across the screen. The temptation was there not to answer and simply speak to him when she went in, but the phone was flashing like a neon sign. She picked up the call, but she so reluctantly.

"Yes, Lukas?"

"There's been a change of plans. Don't come to the warehouse. You stay inside until you hear from me or Zeke. Evan is AWOL, so if you hear from him or see him, let me know immediately. Do you understand?" His voice was harsh and filled with the tone she was all too familiar with.

"What happened now?" Na'tori questioned as she made her way back toward the living room. She took a seat on her couch with a frown.

The only thing that would cause him to be so hyper-vigilant was if another one of his Rogues had left the facility without making prior arrangements with him. You see, working for Titan meant being under surveillance 24/7, and if you were unaccounted for, you were considered AWOL and a threat to the company. It didn't mean that Lukas wouldn't give them another opportunity to right their wrongs. No, he'd bring them back in, run them through some type of test to see just how deep their loyalty was, and then go from there. Na'tori never knew what those tests entailed or the punishment that followed if they failed; all she knew was that they never came back if they did.

With how deeply the corporation played a part in helping the government, she believed there were well-kept secrets that weren't meant to be shared, like the fact that there were humans with abilities and creatures of the night that assisted her brother in attempting to apprehend the Immortal beings known as Eternals. If the world ever knew the truth, chaos would surely ensue.

She tried once again to get answers. "Lukas? What's happening at the warehouse? Did another associate leave? Did one of the tests go wrong?"

"Stop asking questions and do as I've told you." He replied harshly and hung up without another word.

Several moments after he hung up, Na'tori simply stared at the screen of her phone as her mind fought over what she should do. For years, she'd told herself to get answers, to find out the truth behind her family's wealth and status, because she knew to the depths of her heart that she had been lied to for most of her life. Shit, she believed they were still lying to her. She knew something was happening within the company, but they weren't telling her what it was. Ever since the freak accident that had happened months ago, she was being left in the dark more and more.

That stopped now.

Without thinking too deeply about her actions, she left her condo, climbed into her car, and made her way towards the warehouse hidden amongst other buildings deep within the bowels of the center city of Van Scive. When she pulled up thirty minutes later, the warehouse appeared to be closed for the night, yet she could make out a few of the guards patrolling the outer area of the building. She parked on the side where the least amount of security and cameras sat before she turned her car off and sat behind the wheel for several long moments. She wasn't good at sneaking around, or at least she wasn't sure if she was because she'd never had to apply that tactic to her arsenal, but she needed to know the truth.

Na'tori carefully climbed from the front seat of her car, crouched down behind it, and quickly made her way to the access gate that would allow her admittance into the parking lot. When she input an access code, she used one of her brothers' numbers before slipping through the opening to run and hide behind a parked vehicle in the lot. Her heart raced in her chest as she scanned the lot and checked the camera's positioning to ensure she wasn't caught. The feeling of sweat beginning to perspire on her skin was evident by the wetness on her back and the moisture gathering within her bra. She was playing a dangerous game to get the answers she desired. She knew that, and she still pushed on. Moving carefully through the scattered vehicles, Na'tori made her way to the closest entryway, input her brother's access code once more, and slipped through the crack in the door before she was engulfed in utter darkness.

The hallway was vacant and dark, with barely any light coming in from the crack in the doorway several feet ahead of her. She could hear the drone of the HVAC system and the murmur of voices. The excitement of finally discovering something her brothers didn't want her to know ran through her and caused the hair on her arms to stand at attention beneath the fabric of her blouse. Her breath came out in short pants as she crept towards the door leading to the warehouse's main floor.

The warehouse was slightly similar to the one that had burned down months ago, except the lower levels that were only accessible by badge weren't yet complete, at least not to her knowledge. How her brothers kept finding these places and getting the funding to own something so covert left her wondering where the money came from. There was no way the business was completely legal, and if it was, then why had she never been able to interact with the subjects who had agreed to help them with the cure?

THREE

Alaric cursed himself for not being more vigilant. He'd allowed the mysterious woman to escape them and then had to practically plead with Silas to follow her scent to wherever she was going. It hadn't been easy. According to his partner, following someone in a vehicle was a lot harder than it looked or seemed, and it took over thirty minutes before they were standing in the shadows across from a luxury condo that screamed of wealth.

"Are you sure this is the place?" Alaric questioned as he scanned the streets, searching for anyone or anything that seemed out of the ordinary.

Silas gave him a bored look as he leaned casually against the brick of the building they stood in front of. "We trailed a woman to her home, and you have the nerve to ask me if we're at the right place?" He scoffed. "We're definitely at her place, but she's not here. I don't hear her or sense anyone inside."

Alaric leveled him with a stare. "Then she won't mind us having a look around while she's gone." He crossed the street before Silas could stop him and chuckled when a slight curse could be heard within the quiet of darkness.

It only took him a few seconds to get her front door unlocked without looking as if he didn't belong there before he and Silas snuck into the condo and closed the door softly behind them. Alaric couldn't see in the dark, but the floor-to-ceiling window in her living room allowed the moonlight to come in. It was easy to make out the quaint sitting area and coffee table that sat before an unlit fireplace and the beautiful kitchen that looked like every chef's wet dream. He moved to the bookcase beside the couch and began to scan the selection as Silas headed for what he assumed would be the bedroom and bathroom. As his eyes roved over the spine of each book and took in the many titles, his mind reached out to Silas.

"How do you think she knows about Rogues?"

It took Silas a moment before he responded. *"My guess is that she might have encountered them before and knows how to handle them based on her previous interactions. We don't yet know her ability, so she might also have that going for herself. Her mind was wrapped as tight as yours so she could be a telepath that read his mind and any Rogue she might have interacted with in the past."*

"Why do you think she ran when you came out, and what was that shit she released into the air?"

"It's possible she's never encountered my kind before and didn't know how to react, but she did seem unnaturally terrified when I approached. It could be the unknown that scared her. As for the gas, I believe it was meant to obstruct our view of her and her scent, but the latter didn't work in her favor. She has a unique scent that sets her apart from everything else. I can't place it, but I could locate her no matter how far she ran."

"Was she the intoxicating scent you caught inside the club?"

"Without a doubt. Now, what the hell are we looking for, and why did you have me follow her home?"

Alaric fell silent and turned to head for the bedroom to explain why he felt an inexplicable need to find out more but paused when the muzzle of a gun pressed firmly against his forehead, and he met the cold gaze of Ezekiel Titan. Several guards stood behind him with guns pointed toward him, yet he couldn't take his eyes off the man who looked nearly identical to Lukas. The only thing that made a difference was the bald head, the assortment of tattoos that decorated his skin, and the fact that he didn't carry any scars on his face like his brother did.

Ezekiel's voice was rough, as if it hadn't been unused for several days or weeks. "Are you here alone, or will my men find someone waiting in the shadows? We know you've teamed up with Romulus and his people." He tilted his head to the side to indicate his men should check around and smiled a sinister smile that caused Alaric's blood to boil in his veins.

With the gun digging further into his head —most likely leaving an indent within his skin— he dropped the shields around his mind and slammed every single ounce of thought and power into forcing Silas to do his bidding. *"Leave now before they find you, but follow us back to wherever they plan on taking me. This is our way into Titan. Do it now!"* He felt Silas struggling for several precious moments against his order before the compulsion sank its claws into his mind and forced his partner to flee and hide from sight. Only when he felt Silas's mind settle did he focus back on the men that stood before him.

"I'm alone." His voice was filled with more confidence than he felt because if this went poorly, this could possibly be his last few moments alive.

Ezekiel smirked. "You expect me to believe they left you without protection? I don't believe you for a second, but nice try, Alaric." He tapped the muzzle of the gun against his head and glared, "If I have to ask you again, I'll beat the information out of you. Is anyone waiting to attack me and my men?"

"Why don't you ask your men? I'm sure they'll each walk back in here and reveal that there's no one lying in wait for them because if there was, they wouldn't return, and it would just be you and I."

"You'd like that, wouldn't you?" Without taking his eyes from Alaric, he reached behind his back, pulled out a familiar gold collar, and held it between them. "My brother tells me you have the ability to pierce someone's mind. I'm told you can read it and coerce people to do your bidding, so let's not put that to the test tonight and have you put this on where it belongs, shall we?"

Alaric smirked and did as he was told. The second the collar was latched and locked around his throat, he felt his gift dwindle down to nothing. It caused a panic to rise inside of him that he hadn't felt in a while, but he forced himself not to react nor attempt to remove it. He knew he couldn't without an electronic key because it seemed this collar didn't have a keyhole. Anyone else might have fought against being powerless and simply attacked, but Alaric wanted answers, and to get those, he needed to subject himself to the whims of Titan. He had to get back into their building and find the person responsible for creating the poison that was running through his bloodstream.

Ezekiel cocked his head to the side and observed him. "You're being awfully complacent, Subject 2. Do you have some sort of plan up your sleeve?"

"Would you like me to have a plan, or can we simply get on with it?"

"Oh, we'll get on with it, alright." Ezekiel swung his arm back, slammed the butt of the gun into the side of Alaric's temple, and watched as he slumped to the floor unceremoniously.

ALARIC CAME AWAKE with a start when a burst of electricity shot through his body and caused him to tense up unexpectedly. His eyes flew open, and he scanned the room to take in the bright fluorescent lights and the fact that he was alone. The room wasn't familiar in any way. He grit his teeth and clenched his hands into fists as another current of electricity traveled through his body once more and he just knew it was coming from the collar around his throat. His body jerked atop the bare mattress he laid upon before he stilled.

A familiar voice spilled from the speakers within the small room. "It's a pleasure to have you back, Subject 2."

Alaric sat up slowly and noticed a piss bucket in the corner of the room, along with a camera that hung from the ceiling. The urge to relieve himself was there, but he ignored it and instead stared into the face of the monitoring device before he spoke. "I can't say the same."

Lukas's chuckle filled the room before silence descended. Several seconds later, the sound of a lock disengaging came from the door. It swung open to reveal Ezekiel with a shit-eating grin and Lukas Titan strapped into a motorized wheelchair with a blanket over his legs. They both resembled each other enough to know that they were siblings when you looked at them, but it was evident by the wicked look in Ezekiel's eyes who would be in charge of his interrogation for the day. If there was any type of torture involved, Ezekiel would definitely be the man to dish it out.

"How far did you think you would get before we caught up to you?" Lukas questioned as he rolled to a stop right in front of him. "And where are those bratty sisters of yours?"

Alaric made sure to keep the murderous rage he felt towards these bastards at an all-time low as he stared into the tired, pain-filled eyes of the man who had tortured his sisters for the hell of it for years. When he spoke, even his voice didn't let in on the genuine anger he was harboring.

"My sisters are none of your concern, and they never will be again. If your plan is to kill me, then you've already ensured that I won't live past the ripe age of thirty. So let's get on with it because anything you do to me will be ineffective in getting me to talk."

Ezeziel's expression transformed into a murderous glare. "What the hell is that supposed to mean?"

"Exactly what I said. If you can't piece two and two together then that seems like a you problem."

"You're infected with the virus," Lukas stated with a frown. He glanced at his brother and shook his head slightly before his eyes found Alaric's once more. A smile graced his lips when he spoke. "I suppose it matters not what type of testing I do on you now, does it?"

FOUR

S ilas bared his fangs in disgust and anger as the compulsion Alaric had forced into his brain finally abated and released him from the thrall. He stood within the shadows of a building located across the street from the warehouse he'd seen his partner being dragged into only an hour before. It was the perfect vantage point that allowed him to see the comings and goings of everyone who entered and left the building and any car that drove by. He clenched his hands into fists and moved as if he planned to head for the building and launch a full assault when his king and leader of the Eternals—Rome—appeared before him in a flash of dark writhing shadows that bled from the black wings that draped his back. Silas came to a halt and watched as Rome's wings disappeared.

Calm blue eyes stared back into Silas's heterochromia irises. "Where is Alaric?" Rome questioned. His eyes scanned the area around them and stopped when he spotted the warehouse. "So this is their new base of operations?" He inhaled sharply and frowned.

Silas tried to ignore the need to kneel before his king when a wave of power was released, but instead, he found himself kneeling and bowing deeply. Since the events a few months ago, Rome had developed a more potent array of abilities that the Gods had gifted him with after his wife and mate had been captured by Titan. His shadow wings, along with his immense increase in power, had made him a formidable warrior who tended to react when it came to the ones closest to him. Considering Alaric was his brother-in-law, his protective streak was rearing its head in aggression and causing his powers to fluctuate almost uncontrollably.

"Sir," Silas stated, his eyes still staring at the ground as tingles of awareness raced up and down his spine, "Alaric forced me to leave his side to ensure that we found this place, but you're bound to give us away if anyone inside feels the immense change in the air."

Rome glanced over his shoulder and frowned. "You're right, but why are you kneeling Si?"

"The amount of power you're giving off sort of forces me to." He stood swiftly and pointed toward the warehouse. "We need to get inside before they break him...or worse, kill him. If they do that, Alara will never forgive us for letting him hunt."

"We won't be heading inside."

The expression on Silas's face conveyed shock. He couldn't be serious. He meant to leave Alaric to their enemies, and then what? Would they be burying their friend in the ground if there was even going to be anything left of him to bury once Titan was done with him?

Silas stepped forward until a breath separated him from the man he respected most in this world, and he bared his fangs in anger. "He's one of us!" He snarled, "You mean to leave him to our enemies?"

Rome simply stared back, his eyes glowing faintly with his power as he regarded his friend with a simple nod before speaking. "That power you felt me unleash was my attempt at locating him beneath the layers of the ground where they have him locked up. I breached his mind, Si. They have a collar around his throat that leaves his mind vulnerable to me, and he's asked me to give him time to locate this doctor. He believes he can get out of Titan without our assistance, so I'm willing to give him that time." He paused and glanced over his shoulder to watch as the guards began to change shifts for the night. "I've given him three days to get the answers he needs, and if he doesn't, then I will be raining hell down upon Titan faster than they can draw their next breath."

"He's dying, Romulus. He shouldn't be doing these missions in the first place. Why haven't you changed him? I told you I've seen his death, and it's coming soon. We have to do something."

"You think I haven't offered him!?" Rome exclaimed and released an exasperated breath a second later before walking deeper into the shadows around them. He smacked his hand against the rough cement bricks and sighed heavily. "Alaric doesn't want this life, Si. He still has hope that he can get a cure to reverse the effects of the virus. It doesn't matter what I say. Even Alara can't get through to him. He won't do it."

"Then don't give him a fucking choice, damn it! Make him!"

Rome glanced over his shoulder to pierce him with a deadly stare that would have reduced most men to ash. "I won't rob him of his life. If he doesn't want to become an Eternal, I can't force him, nor can you. I'm shocked you would even say such a thing. You're usually more rational than this."

Silas pushed his hair back from his face and shrugged solemnly. "I've gotten to know him in recent months." He sighed heavily and turned back to stare at the warehouse that stood several feet away. "He's courageous, selfless, and he's taught me more patience and understanding in this thing we call life than I've felt in a long time. He's helped quiet my mind, and I've never seen anything like it. He's become like a best friend. I don't want to lose this new brother I've acquired."

"Then have faith in him because that vision you saw months ago might no longer be relevant."

"I don't think we can risk it."

Silence stretched between them, yet the sound of vehicles and people milling about the street indicated that there was movement and life all around them. The men behind the fence where Alaric was being kept were talking too low for a human to make out their words, but Rome and Silas could hear them clearly amongst the other noise.

"I hear the bastard just gave up and didn't even try to escape." One guard said with a chuckle as a cigarette dangled from his lips.

Another guard checked the safety on his gun and scoffed. "I bet you he's here spying for that fucker, Romulus. I hear he works for him now, selling all the secrets he has on Titan, and that's why Lukas has been hunting for them so fiercely." He glanced up and smirked, yellow teeth gleaming under the light they stood beneath. "I hear the king is railing the younger sister. I always wanted a piece of her ass. That lucky son of a bitch."

The whole lot of them laughed along with him, yet Rome wasn't laughing. Instead, his shadow wings reappeared, angry snarls were leaving through parted lips, and claws were ripping from his fingertips before Silas grabbed him by the shoulder and spoke softly into his ear.

"Get out of here before you level the damn building and trap our guy in there along with them."

For a moment, it looked as if Rome planned to still move forward and possibly kill everyone who worked within and around the building, but he collected himself, retracted his claws, fangs, and wings, and sighed heavily before he spoke. His voice was scratchy and filled with annoyance.

"I'll go hunting after I check on Alara. She isn't to know what happened with her brother, so I don't want you showing your face after tonight until he returns to us. I don't need my mate stressing even more than she already is, especially not with everything going on with that sister of hers."

"Damn, so more secrets. Ok, but won't she know something's up when he doesn't come in for a healing session? He goes at least twice, sometimes three times a week."

Rome ran a hand over his dreads and closed his eyes briefly, his mind milling over what the next few days would do to his warriors. It wasn't easy being the man everyone looked to for answers, and it was even worse when he had to keep things from the woman he loved to protect her from the things that would ultimately hurt her. They had done that since the moment they met, and it seemed he was still incapable of allowing her to be harmed, even by the truth.

"We won't lie to her. Alaric is on a mission, simple as that. She doesn't need the details of that mission." Rome finally replied. "Now, do you plan to stay here and simply watch the warehouse, or do you plan on hunting at all tonight?"

"I think I should stay in case they try to move him in the middle of the night."

"Suit yourself and call if you need me."

Rome disappeared in a cloud of black smoke, leaving Silas alone once more in the darkness of the alley. He leaned against the brick of a building, his eyes steadily leveled on the Titan warehouse as he slowly began to scan the minds of the soldiers that milled about. He wanted to get as much information from the people who worked for their enemy as possible because once it was time to attack, he wanted to be well and truly prepared for it, and he would leave no one standing in the end. The visions he kept getting of the future left his skin feeling tight, and his nerves shot, and he hadn't yet been brave enough to tell his brethren what he had been seeing. He definitely hadn't informed Rome. If he had, things might be moving differently, and everyone would be a lot more vigilant than they already were. He didn't need the rest of them freaking out, so he was secure in the idea of keeping the visions to himself. At least for now, because he intended to change them.

Normally, he would never interfere with fate, but lately, the things he saw so vividly in his dreams were leaving a sick feeling in the pit of his stomach that told him he needed to do something before it was too late. Just as soon as Alaric removed himself from his enemy's clutches, he would act.

CHAPTER
FIVE

N a'tori stepped through the lower level doors for the first time since Titan had moved to this new warehouse. Her brothers Ezekiel and Lukas were by her side, and her nerves were all over the place. It had been two days since she'd snuck into the warehouse and been unsuccessful in finding any info on why their movements had been so sketchy lately. She'd never found out why they hadn't allowed her onto the premises, but today, that all changed. Forty minutes to almost an hour ago, Lukas had called her to come in because he had something to show her, so here she was with her body sweating like a woman who just left the sauna, her eyes running over every surface and face she walked by. The fear of them showing her video footage of her sneaking into the warehouse ran in a loop in her head and caused her heart to pound within her chest. She needed to know why she was here.

"So, where are we heading? What are you planning to show me?" She questioned hesitantly as she ran sweaty palms against her gray slacks and kept pace with the rolling wheels of her brother's motorized wheelchair.

"You'll see soon enough," Lukas replied with his signature smirk.

That response didn't make her feel any better or calm her nerves by any means. Her brothers could be very vindictive and conniving when they wanted to be. Na'tori had been on the receiving end of their cruelty for many years now, and this situation screamed sketchy.

She tried again to get answers. "You sure you can't even give me a hint on what you're about to show me?"

"Ask one more question, and I'll reintroduce you to the collar," Ezekiel commented with a snarl as he stared at the side of her face with an icy glare.

She ducked her head obediently and kept pace beside Lukas. Of all of her brothers, Na'tori feared Ezekiel the most. He was sadistic and cruel for the fun of it. His actions were never justified, but no one ever corrected him. Not even Lukas could control him. In fact, he never tried because he was an intelligent man. He knew that standing in the way of his brother's anger would most likely put him on the receiving end of Ezekiel's cruelty. For years now, they all walked a thin line around him. It was a shock that he never tried to take the Titan reins from Lukas and instead enjoyed his position as an enforcer. Probably because he couldn't lead shit if directions and a map were right in front of him. Lukas was the brains, Ezekiel was the muscle, Evan was the glue that tried to keep them together, while Na'tori would always end up being the punching bag some-how. She would get the grunt work, although she had the higher intelligence.

Na'tori worked hard throughout her years at Titan. At a young age, she was pushed to excel in everything she did or suffer the consequences from their mother—Alma. Their mother is where Lukas and Ezekiel got their cruelty from. She had been the needle that drove them into their sadistic nature and fed the side of them that yearned for the pain of another. If not for her, they could have grown to have a normal life, but fate had not granted them that; fate hadn't given them a mother with a heart. Instead, they were birthed from a woman who only saw them as a means to an end. The year she was murdered was the year her brothers had turned their evil proclivities to a whole new level. That was the year life had changed for Na'tori as well.

She noted every hallway and door they passed, her eyes scanning the numbers beside the doors and the red activation pads that required a badge scan just to get inside. How had they accomplished this all within such a short period? Her eyes were still checking out the hallway around them when they suddenly stopped before a door that had two guards standing before it with large assault rifles hanging from their shoulders.

"Are guns really necessary?" Na'tori frowned at the show of force. "What could they possibly be protecting that needs a gun involved?"

"We're not protecting what's behind the door; we're protecting the staff and everyone involved in this company from the person inside," Lukas replied, heading for the scanner beside the door. He leaned forward and scanned his eye before a green glow popped up, and the door came open with a click.

Ezekiel grabbed her by the shoulder and applied pressure as he whispered into her ear, yet it was so low Lukas couldn't possibly overhear him. "You tell us what you see when you look at him. You hear me, little sis!? And don't get any ideas of feeling sympathy for that fuck, or I'll remind you why you keep a wide berth from me."

Na'tori could hear the restrained anger in his voice and nodded solemnly. Whoever was locked behind the door was of high importance, which meant they weren't a human or a Rogue, but now she knew he was male, and Ezekiel clearly had it out for him, but how didn't he know what this person could do? Was it a new Kindred, or had they finally apprehended an Eternal and were unsure of what abilities they could wield? Her curiosity, as well as a bit of excitement, was pulsing through her veins now.

To the outside world, they were a pharmaceutical company that supplied highly sought-after drugs that ran exclusively to the government and the wealthy who could afford them. To her knowledge, only the covert ops group that worked with them in finding and taking in Gifted humans and Eternals were aware of the paranormal world they encountered to develop the cures their genetics supplied. Na'tori was well on her way to discovering what made the Kindred possible, yet she was missing something. Being one of the head scientists specializing in genetics put her at the top of the food chain with her brothers. If not for her ability to spot the difference in another's aura and her sharp mind when splitting genes, she would have been discarded instantly. If Lukas hadn't killed her, Ezekiel would have done so long ago just for simply being born. The only person who would pause and think hard, only to ultimately choose to leave her be, would be Evan—her other brother.

"Are you paying attention, or do you plan to stand there all afternoon like an imbecile?" Lukas snapped, causing her to pull herself from her deep thoughts.

"I apologize," she replied softly before she followed him into the room, only to come to a shuddering halt as her eyes widened in shock.

This wasn't at all what she had been expecting. One of her brother's most significant enemies and the man she'd met two nights ago was tied down to an examination table with only a pair of boxers covering him. He wasn't moving, yet his muscles looked like they were straining against the metal as sweat poured from him. The gold collar around Alaric's neck stood out starkly against his skin, and Na'tori could see the rise and fall of his chest as he took great heaving breaths she could hear clear across the room. This didn't make any sense to her. She wasn't sure how he had ended up here or what they were doing with him. She knew he was a Kindred; it was in their file on him, but there were clear orders to capture him and send him to jail. It's why she had been questioning herself on whether to tell her brothers that she had met him on the streets and had done nothing to bring him in. He hadn't seemed like a threat to her, and he didn't know who she was, and yet, months ago, Alaric, his sisters, several other Kindred, and the Eternals were the cause of why the warehouse had burnt down, and why her brother had been injured. Now, her mind spun at the idea of all that documentation being a lie that her brothers had fed her. What had really happened that night?

Her words were barely a whisper when she spoke; that's how

shocked and disarmed she was by his presence here. "Why is he here, and what's wrong with him?"

Alaric stiffened at the sound of her voice, yet his eyes never strayed from the ceiling, and his entire body continued to twitch uncontrollably. Na'tori knew without a doubt that he had no control over the jerkiness that was taking place within his muscles, and it made her pay attention to him that much more. Something was seriously wrong with him. Something physical. Something she felt a need to figure out and find a solution to.

"That, my dear sister, is why you're here," Lukas replied as he rolled his chair right up to the head of the table and stared at the side of Alaric's unresponsive face. "I need him healthy again. Not this sick, unmoving mess. The only reason he's strapped to this table right now is because of the seizure he experienced last night. He was jerking so hard the doctors were afraid he would damage or kill himself, and I need his mind in tip-top shape. Can you do that for me?"

"I thought he was the enemy?"

"He is."

"Then why would I make him better?" Na'tori finally tore her eyes away from the man on the table and instead focused on Lukas. "I thought we were supposed to send him to a government-owned facility where he would be under lock and key. 1 thought he was an enemy to the United States government."

She would have felt compelled to even if he hadn't asked her to figure out what was wrong with him. Na'tori wasn't sure what it was, but something about the man strapped to the table made her want to dig for answers. He didn't act like the enemy. Instead, he acted like any other man she encountered outside of Titan. To her, he was unthreatening in the best way and handsome in all of the ways that mattered. She was attracted to him.

"When did you start asking questions instead of simply following orders?" Lukas glared at her as he spoke, his hand clenching around the knob on his chair that allowed him to move around freely. "Have I allowed you too much freedom in recent years? Do you no longer realize how things work around here, or do you simply need to be reintroduced to the way I run things?"

At his words, she tensed up but allowed her eyes to glance recklessly between the man on the table and the brothers, who looked like they were itching for a reason to punish her. She didn't want to risk that, but she also wanted answers. What was happening here, and why weren't they turning him in? She wasn't brave enough to ask those questions now that Lukas had pointed out his displeasure with her. She needed to play it safe.

"What do you need me to do?"

Ezekiel rounded the table until he stood near Alaric's head and glanced down into his eyes when he spoke. "What is his aura telling you? Can you tell if someone is dying?"

"Wait, he's dying?" She gasped and moved to the side of the examination table as genuine alarm filled her. "How? What's wrong with him?"

Lukas grabbed her by the arm and squeezed. The action pulled her attention away from the man on the table as her eyes closed briefly in pain. She winced, but she definitely didn't pull away. If she pulled away from him, there was no telling what her punishment would then be, so she stood there and allowed the tight grip on her arm to tighten even more before he spoke once more.

"That's what we need you for. Now quit with your bleeding heart and tell me what he looks like through those freaky ass senses of yours." He released her with a push yet never removed his murderous glare from her face as he awaited her response.

She met his gaze for several more moments before finally forcing herself to look at Alaric. It actually wasn't too much of a chore. She wanted to look at him. Na'tori needed to know why he was bad news and what his being here would mean for the company. She had to push thoughts of how attractive he was to the back of her mind as she looked him over and allowed her power to bleed through her gaze. Normally, this wouldn't be a thing, but for some reason, she couldn't see his aura by looking at him as she could with most people. For him, she had to dig deep into the core of her being until her eyes were a swirling mass of power as she scanned him

40

from head to toe. When her eyes returned to his face, he stared back at her with a glare and a snarl that curled his lips back from his teeth. If he had been a Rogue or Eternal, it wouldn't be teeth showing; it would be fangs.

"Finally, a fucking response," Ezekiel chuckled and moved until he stood on Na'tori's other side. "So what do you see, Tori? What is his aura telling you?"

What she saw couldn't be described in a way that they would understand, so she lied. She lied to protect herself and the man lying before her because staring into Alaric's eyes and seeing the colors that bled from his skin told her the truth. Her brother's were lying to her. If what she was seeing was accurate, then there was so much more going on at Titan than they told her, and she had done the ultimate evil.

"He's reading as a Kindred," she replied after pushing her abilities back until her eyes lost their unusually bright color. "I can't tell if he's dying. He looks fine to me."

Lukas nodded solemnly before turning to head for the door. "Run some blood work on him and tell me how we fix his little problem, and if you can do that for me, then we can see just how much else you'll get to know about the family business." He left the room before she could respond.

Ezekiel stayed where he was, his gaze fixated on Alaric as he spoke. "You can go with our dear brother. I have a few more questions to ask my old friend here."

Na'tori witnessed the evil look in her brother's gaze and knew to the marrow of her bones that if she left him alone with him, then Alaric might not survive whatever punishment her brother would mete out. She had to save him from whatever torture he planned to inflict on him.

"I thought Lukas wanted me to start now with his tests, or was I wrong?" She questioned as she observed Ezekiel carefully.

He clenched his hands into fists and gave her that infamous glare of his. She tried not to flinch beneath his gaze and held her ground, daring him to tell her to leave again. He wouldn't, not if he didn't want to hear Lukas's mouth on the matter. If there was one thing she knew Ezekiel hated, it was earning a lecture from their eldest brother because sometimes that talk never ended once he got talking. She watched him lean forward and whisper something into Alaric's ear before he stood and headed for the door.

He paused to glance over his shoulder. "Fix him, little sis, or need I say more?"

He walked out, leaving her shaking slightly as memories battered her mind of just how twisted his mind worked. Na'tori leaned heavily against the table as she wiped the sweat on her forehead, then jerked when a cold, clammy hand gripped her by her other wrist and held on tightly. Her eyes flew down to see Alaric's hand clutching her; the tendons in his arm were tight, and she felt the tremors that coursed through his body and into hers.

"You have to let me go, or they'll come right back in here." She whispered, hoping the hearing devices in the room couldn't pick up her voice.

She vaguely remembered seeing a camera when she'd entered the room, but she wouldn't dare look around to locate it in case they were watching them now. She tried to peer into Alaric's eyes and silently pleaded with him to release her, but he wasn't even looking at her face. He was transfixed on the wrist he held as his thumb rubbed soothing circles into the softness of her skin. She tugged a little harder before his eyes flew to her face and fixed her with a frown. His misty gray eyes flecked with green swirled with an emotion she was afraid to name.

"You look nothing like them." He commented before slowly releasing the hold he had on her. "They want you to fix me. Why you?" His stare was full of suspicion. "What other secrets are you keeping?"

Na'tori lowered her voice even more, compassion filling her eyes that had begun to brim with tears. "I think I'm the reason why you're dying. I created the virus I think is in your blood."

CHAPTER
SIX

Alaric rubbed at his wrists and stared at that damn piss bucket in the corner as he sat rigidly on the corner of the bed he'd been provided. Three hours had come and gone since Na'tori had left him. After taking several vials of blood and checking his vitals, he had been dosed with a tranquilizer by one of Lukas's goons in order to release him from his bonds before they removed the table in place for a bed. Apparently, he was too much of a wildcard to be trusted, yet he hadn't given them a reason to doubt his next moves. He definitely planned to get out of there, but not without the woman who had just admitted to creating the virus that was slowly killing him as well as harming the people he cared for.

He growled in frustration when his muscles continued to jump uncontrollably beneath his skin. Agitation filled him. He wanted to lash out and punch something but knew that would only expel energy he couldn't risk losing at the moment. It had never been this bad before. Usually, Alara would be right there, ready to heal him the moment he began to feel weakness within his body because if she wasn't, then next, his mind would start to turn on him as he lost his ability to control his powers—even in sleep. It was worse when

45

he slept, according to Silas and Rome. When he slept, his abilities were more challenging for even them to contain between them. It's why he and Silas had been told to move into a home deep within the woods of Van Scive, away from civilization. At least there, Alaric wouldn't be at risk of hurting anyone, yet sometimes even Silas wasn't safe from his abilities.

Even now, with the collar weighing heavily around his throat, he thought it was entirely possible for his ability to go haywire the second he closed his eyes and slept. His powers had been strong even before the virus. Still, now that his body had been practically riddled with it, his mental telepathy and ability to persuade, change, and erase thoughts from one's mind had reached a level that even shocked Rome. His mind wasn't dying like his body was. The virus was infecting his mind in a way that made him that much more lethal than usual. Only a week ago, he'd spoken with Silas privately, basically begging him to finish him before he ever had the opportunity to hurt anyone, especially the people he loved most in this world. He would never forgive himself if he hurt someone not deserving of his particular brand of pain.

The lights shut off completely, placing him in utter darkness, and he knew that tonight had to be his last night here, or the Guardians would swarm this hellhole until they located him. If he wasn't out of her by tomorrow night, the building and everyone inside would be eviscerated, especially if Silas was leading the charge, and he couldn't have that. He needed to leave here with Na'tori in tow, or he wouldn't leave this building alive.

A wave of exhaustion hit him unexpectedly, and he knew it had everything to do with the virus. If he didn't make it to his sister within the next seventy-two hours, Alaric had a feeling it would be too late to do anything even remotely close to saving his life. He was laying back and falling into a sleep he honestly didn't want, yet there was no way of stopping the feeling of fatigue from slamming into him like a freight train missing its breaks. The second his eyes closed, Alaric experienced a sense of weightlessness that surprised him before his eyes were shooting open in shock. What he saw now raised his blood pressure and sent his heart rate careening out of control before he slammed his eyes closed once more.

What sort of wicked sorcery was this?

Had he finally lost his mind?

Alaric forced his eyes to open once more and could do nothing but stare. Small hands glided over porcelain pale skin dotted with sun-kissed freckles that he had familiarized himself with within his mind. He knew this skin. Recognized the dainty hands that reached up to apply another dollop of body wash onto a loofah before they brought the soap to a lather and began to cleanse the body those hands belonged to. He couldn't stop his heart from pounding or still his eyes as they attempted to catch every bit of her that he could see. He wasn't seeing her from his point of view, but instead, he saw her through her eyes. Small, rounded breasts with pink-tipped nipples, a narrowed waist, and slim, fit legs with dainty feet painted in white stared back at him. That sweet heaven between her thighs was barely hidden behind thin platinum blonde pubic hair that matched the waterfall of hair on her head.

"Fuck me, you're breathtaking," He groaned.

Na'tori froze. Her chest rose and fell rapidly before her eyes shot up to glance around the small bathroom. When she spoke, she spoke aloud compared to the words he'd whispered into her mind unknowingly. "Who is there?"

His words were a purr against her spine when he spoke. *"Sorry to disappoint princess, but I'm in your head and seeing from your eyes even though this shouldn't be remotely possible. I suppose my self-consciousness couldn't help but seek you out. I'm just as shocked as you are."*

"How about you get the hell out of my head!" She screeched as she covered her breasts and pussy with her hand and arm before slamming her eyes shut. *"How did you get access to my mind anyway? I've been working on my mental barriers since the first time I felt someone trying to read me."*

At first, Alaric didn't respond, although guilt began to pull at him. He shouldn't have stared so unabashedly, especially without her knowing, but he'd been just as shell-shocked as she was. He'd never done this before. He couldn't deny that he liked it, and a part of him wondered just what else he was capable of experiencing through her eyes. He tried to read just a single thought of hers and met that diamond wall he'd encountered before, yet he felt a tether between her mind and his.

He broke his silence with a question. "Can we talk, and I promise not to watch you?"

"No, that's not logical," she snapped, "I need to know how you're doing this. How are you in my head when you're wearing the power-dampening collar?"

He chuckled softly. *"At least here we can talk privately without your brother or anyone else hearing our discussion. Do you have listening devices in your room? I'm guessing you're still within the building if I can communicate with you so easily."* Alaric paused as a twinge of pain shot through him, yet he wasn't sure where it was coming from. *"Finish your shower, princess, and I'll be back soon."* He moved to follow that tether back to his own mind and body but paused when hesitant words passed through her lips and froze him to his core.

"Will you actually come back?"

Alaric decided to give her the truth. Na'tori didn't act like her brothers. He saw empathy and pain in her gaze when he looked into her eyes. He saw a woman who cared about the pain she inflicted on people, even unknowingly, and he felt that if he pressed just the right buttons and told her the unadulterated truth, he could have an alliance behind enemy lines. She could be someone he could lean on for information, among other things, when it came to Titan. So he went with his gut.

"I'll be back because we both need answers, and I plan on being as transparent as possible with you. If you want honesty, I can give that to you." Another lash of pain went through his entire body once more, but he pushed through it to finish his statement. *"I want something in return, though, princess. No lies. Can you promise me that?"*

She was silent for so long that he thought she didn't plan to respond before her voice whispered through his mind. Her eyes slowly opened, allowing him to see the shower walls. *"I'll give you the only truth I know. Just remember that I can't tell you what I don't know."*

"Then I'll be back soon."

Another shock of pain sprang through him, and he followed that pain back into his body and jerked up with a barely restrained snarl as currents of electricity powered through him. His muscles strained, his body jerked, and he bit into his bottom lip to attempt to quell the ongoing pain even when the current ceased. His eyes zeroed in on Ezekiel's smiling expression as the bastard leaned against the door that could grant him his freedom. His expression was giddy, and he knew that only spelled trouble for him. It looked like he would be in for another round of torture if the duffel bag sitting at that bastard's feet was any indication.

"What the fuck do you want now, Zeke!?" He glared and forced his stiff body to move until he sat on the bed's edge.

"I figured I could get my pound of flesh from you since you're the reason my brother is now wheelchair-bound. If not for your deceit, we would be further in our research and closer to what we've been trying to accomplish all this time." Ezekiel's expression could only be described as feral, his eyes alight with an untamed look that most would shy away from.

Alaric couldn't keep the look of disgust off of his face as he met his stare. "You think I give a shit about you and your family? Your family enslaved mine since before I was born. I will see your world burn before I ever allow you to get an inch of what you want in this lifetime or the next. I'll see you in hell first."

"And yet you're here...exactly where I want you." He smirked and pressed the button of the small device in his hand.

Alaric didn't even try to tense as electricity volts ran through him again. This time he had no control over the bladder he hadn't realized was full, and piss filled his boxers only to run down his legs as he twitched uncontrollably. The moment Ezekiel stopped pressing that Godforsaken button, he slumped onto the floor and groaned painfully. He could deal with torture. Alaric had grown incredibly accustomed to it after all of the years of working for Titan and going through the tests to prove his loyalty, so this was nothing to him, but he wanted to get it over with. A pressing need to find his way back to where he'd been only moments ago with Na'tori is what kept his mind busy. Whether that place had been her mind, his, or something in between, Alaric had known it would be a place he viewed as a safe haven. He wasn't sure what about this woman drew him in, but she did. And the fact that she did it so effortlessly is what surprised him even more.

Ezekiel's voice came from right beside him. "I wonder what or who is on your mind, Subject 2. I don't remember you being so distracted before."

"I don't remember ever interacting with you to deserve such attention from a bastard such as yourself, but if you must know, I'm thinking of all of the ways I plan to kill you, your brother's and all that you care for."

Alaric opened eyes he hadn't realized he'd closed to find Ezekiel staring at him quizzically as he held a sharpened Bowie knife and a pair of pliers. He didn't even want to touch on why the hell he had them. He knew only bad things would come next but was prepared for them. Pain was nothing when you could simply shut off the receptors in your brain that processed those feelings.

Ezekiel smirked. "I see you've left sweet Na'tori from your threats. Should I worry about my sister's innocence and naivety, or maybe I should bring her in here to witness you beg for your life? Or maybe I should let you watch as I torture that lying little bitch."

The words registered in Alaric's mind and triggered a visceral and unnatural response that drove him to act. He was launching up from the floor and snapping his hand forward to hit the flat of the blade. The momentum sent the tip of the knife sinking into Ezekiel's deltoid muscle before a scream tore from his lungs to pierce the air. Alaric snatched the pliers from his loose hold, gripped him by the throat, and threw him back into a wall even as his body screamed at him to take several seats, but anger was driving him. Anger at what Ezekiel had implied filled him as he choked the bastard without a lick of mercy bleeding through. The pliers were shoved between Ezekiel's wailing mouth and pinching the sensitive tissue of his tongue before he could utter another sound.

An eerie calm filled Alaric as he stared into green eyes filled with unshed tears. Soft sounds that sounded exceptionally close to sobs tickled his ear as he spoke with a calm he didn't feel and applied pressure to the windpipe and pliers within his grip.

"I could kill you here and now, Zeke, but we'll call this a teaching moment. Threaten her again, and you'll watch me rip your tongue from your mouth just to shove it down your sick fucking throat. We'll see if she'd rather watch your torture and death." He held him for several seconds more before he shoved away and dropped his weapons to retake a seat on the bed. "Now run along and get me new boxers and a bed before I change my mind and end you now."

CHAPTER
SEVEN

N a'tori paced the length of the small bedroom her brothers had provided for her, or more accurately put… forced her to be in. When she'd attempted to leave the facility, one of the guards stopped her and directed her to Lukas's office. She needed to stay for her safety. At least, that was the claim he had made to her, along with how he worried deeply for her since Alaric had appeared after being a ghost for months. She knew that to be a lie. They had never cared before. This was a power play, yet for once, she didn't care. For once, she wanted to stay exactly where she was because now she had a reason to.

Forty minutes ago, the most intimate moment of her life had occurred within her shower walls. Hearing Alaric's voice in her head and learning that he could see what she could had sent her heart flying in her chest and a feeling of heat rushing through her. It definitely hadn't been because of the temperature of the water. No, her body had lit up like a firecracker on the Fourth of July at the sound of his earthy, deep baritone. She was attracted to him for sure, and Na'tori wondered how deep her attraction went since she hadn't actually been as offended as she'd let on when he'd entered her mind. She recalled what he had seen of her and blushed, but that wasn't the only emotion running through her. Worry, genuine, unadulterated worry, was whipping through her because Alaric's voice and presence within her mind had not returned. She was several seconds from leaving her room to go see what had happened when the sound of an alarm started filtering in from the hallway. A second later, an announcement was made throughout the facility about a code red within the lower levels.

She was moving for the door without thinking. She knew without a doubt that it was Alaric. Whatever a code red meant didn't matter. All she knew was that Alaric was involved, and whatever was happening spelled trouble for him if he was truly involved. She didn't want or need anything happening to the man who had the potential to help her understand the life her family had dragged her into.

Na'tori took the elevator down to the lower levels and practically pulled the doors open with her bare hands when it alerted her that she'd reached her destination before she sprinted down the hallway to the room where they were keeping him. She slowed when she approached what could only be described as a cell and let her jaw drop in shock at what she saw. Alaric was pinned against the wall by a guard with his hands zip-tied behind his back. His bottom lip was split, and the beginning bruises that could only be brought on by fists were starting to darken along his chest, back, and abdomen. Her brother Ezekiel was standing in the corner of the room, holding a bleeding shoulder as he glared daggers at Alaric.

"What the hell is going on?" She questioned with concern as she stepped across the threshold and stood only a few feet away from Alaric and the guard who had him pinned.

Alaric's head whipped towards her, his gaze boring into her own as a wickedly sexy grin replaced his glower. He trailed his eyes up and down her body, and she witnessed the look of interest that entered his expression before he quickly cleared it and returned to his glaring match with her brother.

"Tori, go back to your room where we fucking put you. I won't tell you again." Ezekiel stated as he pressed his hand harder into his wound before he spoke to another guard she hadn't realized had walked up behind her. "Escort my sister back to her room and then get me the damn doctor to check this shit out before I put a bullet in this bastard's skull."

Harsh hands gripped her by the arm, causing a yelp to burst from her lips as she was dragged backward.

Alaric's voice pierced the air around them, causing every hair on her arm to stand to attention with how menacing and cold it was compared to the tone he'd used with her earlier. "Release her or die!" His eyes were on the guard standing behind her, filled with a fire and malevolence that caused her to step back.

She didn't know him at all, really, but the level of anger that was morphing on his face was scary and alarming. It was like a switch had clicked in his brain the moment she was touched, and yet the guard still held her arm tightly; in fact, his grip tightened and caused her to wince in pain as a throbbing began to take place in her arm. The room dropped several degrees in temperature, and everyone seemed to stop breathing when a feeling of something twisted and wrong filled the space. Na'tori couldn't begin explaining what she was feeling or what took place right before her.

Simultaneously, everyone but her and Alaric crumpled to the floor unconscious before he moved to stand before her. The alarms started blaring again, yet she wasn't sure if they had ever stopped. She knew the cameras within the room and hallway had witnessed what was taking place, and guards would be heading for them at any minute now. She didn't know what to say or how to process what was happening because it shouldn't have been possible. He had done something to them even with the power dampener locked around his throat. Her mind raced with ideas and ways to figure it out, yet his eyes distracted her and made her focus only on him before he spoke low enough to where there was no possible way the cameras could pick up their conversation.

"Princess, I need you to look scared because I'm getting out of here with or without your help, but with it, I can give you what you need. Answers, but first show fear, release me from my bonds and then fall to the floor as if you are unconscious. When I get the hell out of here, I'll find you, and we'll talk."

Na'tori whispered just as softly back to him. "How did you do that? You're collared. The power dampener should be working."

He moved closer until his lips brushed against her ear and his chest pressed against hers. When his head lowered into the crook of her neck, she felt her eyes slide closed as a sexual awareness bloomed in her gut from the contact he was initiating. "Breath," his lips caressed the skin of her throat, "they'll be here soon, so will you release my wrists, or shall I fight my way free with only my mind? I can sense them coming, and I don't want you hurt. Decide now."

It wasn't a hard decision for her to make. Na'tori fixed her face to appear terrified, retreated a step until she felt the guard behind her limp on the floor, and turned to search his body for a pair of scissors as well as the universal key that would unlock the collar. She quickly removed the offending items while attempting to hide the giddy feeling that had now taken up residence within her. She couldn't believe she was doing this and going against all she had ever known in life for a man she didn't know, yet trusted. She could have been making the wrong decision, but when she glanced into his eyes, she knew she was making the right move.

Alaric smirked and reached up to push back the loose hair around her face. "They'll be here in five, so I need you to fall and make it look good, but first, I want to send your brother a message, princess."

She wasn't sure what to expect, but him grabbing her by the back of the neck and yanking her forward to crush his lips against hers wasn't it. She melted into the kiss and moaned into his mouth when his thumb caressed the side of her throat, and his other arm took her waist in hand and pulled her until his dick brushed against her navel. Even through her clothing, she felt his hardness through his boxers, but she wanted to feel more. Her heart began to gallop in her chest as she moved to touch him, but then he was pulling away and speaking loud enough to where the speakers would hear him.

"Forget this interaction and fall asleep. You will forget ever meeting me, and when anyone asks, you know nothing about the last three nights. You were ill. Now fall asleep."

Na'tori didn't think about how much this might hurt before she softened her entire body and forced her knees to bend as her eyes fell closed and began descending to the ground. Strong arms caught her and eased her to the floor before she heard him take off down the hall. She lay utterly still and tried to keep her breathing even and calm for whenever the company guards showed up, yet she struggled. She wanted to open her eyes and watch his departure because she still couldn't get the thought and feel of his lips and touch off her skin. Her blood was pounding in her ears, and the coolness of the ground was settling into her overheated skin. It was a struggle to not move the longer she waited for someone to come, but it was becoming easy to ignore the more she thought about the events of the last few days and the man who had slammed an essential wrecking ball into her life.

Ezekiel would be pissed when he woke up and discovered Alaric gone, and she knew Lukas would stop at nothing to get him back. Na'tori knew she would see him soon, though, and she couldn't wait. She had so many questions she needed answers to, and she had even more assumptions about her life. Everything she had done to help Titan in their research had been a lie. She knew that for a fact now after receiving the results of Alaric's blood tests. He was indeed dying. Dying from the cure she thought she had created when, in fact, it was a virus that was replacing his good cells with something twisted and corrupt. She needed to figure out how to stop it, even if that meant going against her family.

CHAPTER
EIGHT

His head was pounding, and he knew his nose was bleeding, yet he pushed open the door that would lead him outside and stepped onto the asphalt to see that the sun was just beginning its slow descent from the sky. He wiped at the blood dripping onto his lip and, in a last-ditch effort to get the hell out of dodge and back to his people, Alaric sifted through the minds of everyone within the building until he located the man in charge of the cameras and doors. He didn't want to do this but needed to protect himself and keep the people he cared for.

"Open the outer gate and erase the camera and video footage of the last three nights. Ensure every trace of me is gone from this building. When you're done, I want you to take out your gun and kill yourself."

He watched as the gate slowly began to open and headed for it as the alarm droned on behind him. By the time reinforcements would show up he would hopefully be long gone. He passed through the gate, his eyes searching from left to right for anyone who looked as if they worked for Titan before crossing the street to step into the alleyway, where he leaned heavily against the brick wall of the building. His breathing was choppy and uneven as he gripped his side where his old wound used to be. Sometimes, when the virus progressed too quickly, the phantom pain of where he'd been shot nearly a year ago would flare up and ache. He rubbed his hand against his side and leaned his head back against the wall. He needed to keep moving, but he also needed a moment.

His mind was still racing with the knowledge he'd gained and what he had just done within the walls of Titan. Something was happening to his abilities. They were growing and expanding in ways he didn't understand, and some were even beginning to make him nervous. It was becoming too easy to compel people around him to do whatever he asked without question, and the feeling of euphoria that filled him after the fact was what caused his nervousness. He rubbed his throat and frowned. He shouldn't have been able to use his power while wearing the collar, but he'd done it multiple times without even realizing it at first.

He began coughing roughly, his heart pounding in his chest as his vision blurred when he felt a gust of wind at his side. He didn't bother to open his eyes, but he knew it was Silas even before the man spoke.

"My friend, you look like shit. What the hell did they do to you?" His arms wrapped around his waist, pulling him in to support his weight. "Can you handle me running, or should I call Rome?"

Alaric coughed and spat out the blood that filled his mouth. "Fuck," he groaned, "call the bastard, I need Alara."

Seconds passed before shadows filled the alleyway, and Rome stepped from them. His eyes scanned him from head to toe before he reached out to grip him and Silas by the shoulder. Weightlessness rushed through him before the heat from a burning fireplace brushed against him. His knees shook, and Alaric found himself being helped into a chair.

"What the hell happened!?" His sister's voice cracked through the air like a whip just as soft hands landed on his temples, and her healing energy began to flow into his body.

He opened his eyes and met the teary-eyed stare of Alara's gray-blue ones. He reached up to wipe them away and smiled softly, "I'm okay, angel. I made it back to you in time. Don't cry for me."

"Let Romulus change you," she whispered, "please."

"There's a cure, Alara. I know there is, and I'll get it before I even think of taking his way out." He jerked his chin toward Rome, where he stood beside Silas; his expression was like a thundercloud in a rainstorm.

"And if you die?" A new voice spoke from behind him, but he knew who it was before she rounded the corner to stand beside Alara.

Alondra was the spitting image of Alara from her height to her eyes, hair, face, and body. When they stood next to each other, it was hard to make out who was who unless you knew them. Alara had a sweeter disposition, while Alondra despised everyone but her sister. For a time, he hadn't known whether she cared for anyone but herself, especially not after last year's events when she'd assisted Titan in capturing Alara and Rome. It had taken almost a year for the guardians to trust her and even longer for Alaric. She was his sister, sure, but she had done an unforgivable act that only through the strength of Alara did he concede.

Alaric couldn't keep the smirk off his face when he spoke. He knew his words were a stab at her. "I thought you could care less if I lived or died, Alo." Another healing wave pulsed through him from Alara's hands and caused a soft groan to part his lips.

When she dropped her arms and stumbled back a step, Rome was immediately there to catch his mate and press his lips into the crook of her throat as he wrapped his arms around her body. With Alara's ability to siphon, it was clear to see that Rome was supplying her with energy after she'd put so much into healing whatever the virus had done to Alaric. It had become their ritual whenever she healed anyone—even herself. Everyone knew that Rome could never stand by and watch as fatigue washed over her because sometimes she passed out if she used too much of her ability trying to heal someone.

Alondra looked Alaric up and down before she spoke; all the while, her fingers nervously tugged at the hem of her shirt. "Just because we can barely stand each other doesn't mean I wish you dead."

"Could have fooled me." He replied dryly and came to his feet to tower over her.

"As entertaining as your bickering is, I think we need to get to the main topic here." Silas interrupted, "What did you learn at Titan?

"Where's everyone else?" He ignored the question and glanced around the living room, realizing no one except his sisters, Rome and Silas, were present. Everyone else must have been out already hunting down Rogues for the night.

Rome had taken a seat in the armchair directly across from where he stood while Alara lay curled in his lap. He whispered something into her ear, and if Alaric had been an Eternal, he knew he would have clearly made out his words. It bothered him only slightly because he knew the conversation had to do with him nine times out of ten. That's all they discussed lately because he knew they were worried for him. Silas stood near the fireplace with a scowl on his face that made the scar over his right eye look positively harsh, while Alondra took a step forward and screwed her face up into a frown.

"Your mission had to do with Titan?" She questioned and shook her head slightly, "You promised Alara no crazy missions and nothing that would severely endanger your life, and then you show up here nearly dead. What did you do, Alaric!?"

He stared into Alondra's murderous gaze but ignored her and looked toward Rome and Alara to find them staring back. The view was no better. Tears were leaking from his sister's gaze, giving him pause. He felt guilt for the first time since allowing Ezekiel to take him behind the walls of Titan, yet when he thought of Na'tori and her soft eyes and lips, his resolve hardened.

"I needed answers." He replied, never breaking his stare from Alara's, "I met someone willing to help me get those answers, and she happens to be the one that created this damn virus in the first place. I know she can cure me."

Silas stepped forward, his expression morphing from displeasure into shock. "You did? Well, where are they? Wait, did you say she? A woman created the virus?"

Alaric attempted to keep the smile off his face so they wouldn't see his desire for the woman who had punched a hole through the wall of his hate for everything related to Titan. He didn't know her but felt a pull towards her that couldn't be explained. He knew he wanted her and would go to any length to get her, like heading back to her condo and waiting for her to show up. The question was... would she show?

"Lukas's sister," he finally spoke after letting his mind race with thoughts of Na'tori and what he would do once he saw her again. "The person that created the virus is their sister."

Alondra's face blanched of color, and she left the room without a word. He wanted to follow after her and see what the hell was up, yet Rome's voice stopped him.

"Are you telling me that the creator behind the virus is the younger sister? I've seen pictures of her; she looks like she wouldn't hurt a fly."

"She thwarted us with a gas that nearly made it impossible to track her to her home, so I don't think she's as innocent as she looks." Silas interrupted.

Alaric gave him a sharp look. That wasn't information he'd wanted to get out there. Them stalking her to her home was a no-no. At the time, they hadn't known who she was or that she worked for Titan, so following her home could have been seen as a huge red flag, but by the look on Rome's face, he didn't see that. So what was he seeing? Alaric didn't need anyone viewing her as less than what she now was to him.

An asset...or maybe more.

"She's not a threat to us." He broke the silent communication that transpired between Rome and Silas. "I plan to meet up with her in a few days to figure out a game plan and learn how much she knows about the company and what that could mean for us."

Alara spoke up from her position in the chair. "You're not going back out there. You almost didn't get back to me in time. Let someone else go after her."

He shook his head vehemently. "I can't do that, angel. I have to be the one she sees. She won't trust anyone else." It wasn't just about that. He didn't think he could deal with anyone else handling her. He needed to be the only one. His stomach clenched in revulsion at the thought of another navigating her through their world.

"I don't fucking care!" She screamed as a fresh wave of tears poured from her eyes, and her hands balled into fists as if she wanted to thrash him. "Are you aware that your brain was bleeding Alaric? I couldn't heal it all. Your ability did something to the part of your brain where your thoughts are held. That means that the next time you use your abilities to whatever capacity that strained them, you might not be walking away again because you'll be fucking dead. Is that what you want?"

She was furious. It didn't take a genius to figure that out, yet all his mind could seem to process was that his brain had been bleeding. That would explain the inexplicable pain he'd experienced right after forcing the minds of everyone within the Titan building to fall into a deep slumber if they had intended to capture or stop him. Taking control of their minds as he had shouldn't have been possible, and he wasn't sure if telling them what he could do now would be in his best interest. They already looked at him hesitantly because he couldn't control his abilities while he slept. Alaric didn't want to give them another reason to look at him sideways. He hoped that his expression showed that he wouldn't be moved by her tears enough to stay home and not go out to get the answers he needed. Alaric knew without a doubt that Na'tori would slam the door in a Guardian's face if they tried to go to her for answers, and then she would disappear. He couldn't risk that.

Rome frowned as he took a step closer. Alaric could feel him attempting to probe his mind, and he quickly slammed down his shields with more force than necessary. Rome's voice was cold when he spoke. "What are you hiding? What happened while you were behind those walls?"

"I did what needed to be done to get out. I read a mind that showed me Titan has been creating Rogues left and right to gain the upper hand in this war, and they're working on a new drug to help combat against us. I planned to get more answers when I met with my source." He shoved his hands into the pants he'd borrowed from a guard that had looked to be his size.

Alara stepped forward and shoved her hands into his chest. "You're not going back out there." She snapped.

"And who plans to stop me?"

He didn't plan on being a dick, especially not to his family, but he meant it when he said no one else would be going after Na'tori. He needed to be the one coming after her and discovering all of her tightly kept secrets, but that's not all he wanted. Alaric wanted to see her blush again. He wanted to feel her lips pressed against his once more and see if her face always gained the rosy pink color she'd expressed after he'd stolen a taste of her mouth.

"Romulus," Alara pleaded to her mate and husband, "tell me you'll stop this before he gets himself killed."

Rome met his wife's stare for several moments before his intense blue gaze landed on Alaric and held. He met his stare with just as much fire and sent a thought towards the king of Eternals.

"I'm the one dying here. If this is how I go out, so be it, but I'm getting my answers with or without your say-so. I'd prefer to have your blessing, but I won't bat an eye if you don't give it to me. Just know that if you try to keep me here against my will, possibly locked up like before, I will die in my attempt to get away."

"Something happened with you and this Na'tori woman, didn't it?"

"She's mine, Romulus."

"Noted." Rome nodded his understanding and reached for his wife before he spoke. "Little flower, I can't keep your brother here. If he wants to go, we have to trust him enough to let him explore this discovery. He knows how to get the answers he's been searching for, so let him. Trust him."

Alara cried and jerked from Rome's arms to wrap hers around Alaric. He curled his arms around her more diminutive form and sighed heavily. Since he was still shirtless, he felt her tears fall onto his chest as she cried for what seemed like hours but was really only minutes, yet each teardrop sent a spear of pain to his heart. He didn't want to hurt her, but he knew he couldn't stand on the sidelines as his time slowly ran out. No matter how often she healed him, Alaric could feel his time coming soon, and he'd be damned if he went out without giving a good fight.

"Will you be going alone?" She finally whispered through her broken tears.

Silas spoke up before he could get a word in. "I'll be with him and call Rome at the earliest sign of trouble."

Alaric glared at him and shook his head softly. There would be no convincing him that he could do this alone. There was a resolve in his gaze that ensured he would not be moved by whatever words Alaric spoke, so he didn't even try. He simply held Alara closer and closed his eyes in an attempt to collect his thoughts and plan out his next move.

Getting to Na'tori wouldn't be easy. Titan would have her guarded after the spectacle he'd put on for her brothers. He hadn't done it just to piss them off, no, he'd done it so he could get a taste of her lips, but now that Alaric had forced someone to erase all footage, they would never see what had transpired between them, but he knew there was still a chance of them guarding her because of his escape. He remembered her lips being the softest thing to ever touch his own. She had made his mind race with how smooth the rest of her might possibly feel beneath his talented tongue. He hadn't been disappointed, and Na'tori had been just as eager to taste him as he had been to sample her. He wanted more of her in every sense of the word, but first, he had to get to the bottom of why Alondra had disappeared as soon as her name had come up.

Something was going on there. She knew something. Something important enough to make her zip her lips tighter than a vacuum-sealed container before striding from the room. As soon as Alaric was done consoling Alara, he would head for Alondra's room for a long-needed chat. He was getting his answers tonight whether she liked it or not. He would do it even if he had to dive into her mind to learn what she knew about Na'tori.

CHAPTER
NINE

Alondra bit at her nails nervously as she paced the length of her bedroom. The name Na'tori triggered memories in her mind that made her heart sputter. She knew her. She knew her better than she knew her own siblings, and that scared her. If Na'tori was around, then all of Alondra's secrets could possibly come to light, and that wasn't something she was willing to risk. It had taken her nearly a year to earn the trust of the Guardians after the web of betrayal she had spun. Helping Titan apprehend Rome and her sister had landed her on their shit list, but she'd done it for a good reason; at least, that's what she had to keep telling herself in order for the guilt not to eat her alive. Telling herself wasn't helping; worse still, she couldn't hold back the memories of the day she'd first met Na'tori Titan from crashing against the shields in her mind like waves to the shore.

ALONDRA, Age: Twenty-six

Alondra paced the expanse of the room known as the infirmary within the Titan facility. It was large enough to hold an elephant with four medical beds, several cabinets filled with god only knew what, and several machines she didn't know the names of. She'd been in here plenty of times to learn not to touch anything or risk Dr. Salazar's wrath. He didn't like his things moved or even breathed on, for that matter. Not here or within the lab where he did most of his work, but she hadn't been to the lab since she was a teen. The infirmary was more like a home to her than her own bedroom because of what she did in this room for the soldiers and strange beings brought here.

She pressed on the left side of her temple as her pounding headache became known. Her entire body was dripping sweat, panting breaths were leaving her lungs to pass through dry, chapped lips, and she couldn't stop the twitching that was taking place throughout her nerves. Every sound she heard was like nails scraping across a chalkboard, yet there was nothing she could do against it but bear the noise. If anything, she wanted to scream obscenities that would impact or resonate deeply within the universe to make her feel somewhat better about her current situation. She knew what this was. It had been a warning to her at an early age that they had an untested drug that could help her, but they had no clue what it would do to her. She'd taken the chance as soon as she was old enough to know what the doctor had been trying to tell her back then.

Now, she was going through withdrawal.

The drugs had been given to her by Dr. Salazar, and now, when she needed them most, he was nowhere to be found. She wanted to raze the earth beneath her feet and cry simultaneously. The pain was slamming into her from every side but primarily within her chest. Her heart felt like it was beating for two people, not just herself. She could feel every thump like it was her last and anticipated the moment she would lose her fight with the land of the living. She'd been fighting it all her life. Now, it would make no difference.

She turned from the door just as it opened and spun back around to see a woman—or more like a girl—walk through, nose pressed into the notebook she held within her hands. Platinum blonde hair was pulled into a tight bun, and mumbled words flew from her lips a mile a minute. Was she talking to herself? Alondra frowned, cleared her throat, and watched as the woman's head jerked up. Unusually opalescent eyes stared back at her in shock before the woman took several hesitant steps back.

"No one is supposed to be in here," she whispered as she glanced over her shoulder nervously.

"I wouldn't be in here if I didn't have an access badge," Alondra replied

dryly as she held up the badge in question and took a step forward to look her up and down quizzically. "Who the hell are you, and where is Dr. Salazar?"

"I'm Tori...or Na'tori, Dr. Salazar's apprentice. I've been shadowing him for months, and I've never seen you before." The fear was gone from her gaze, and now only interest shone back at her. "What do you do here? Are you a patient? I can see that you're gifted. What can you do? Oh my god, this is the first time one of you has been awake enough to chat."

Alondra took a step back and reached for the hidden blade within her jeans pocket when Na'tori moved forward with a massive smile on her face that unnerved her. Why the hell was this chick so happy?

"If you keep staring at me like I'm some science experiment and circling me like a vulture, I'm liable to stab you in the eye, no matter how pretty they may be. So cut it out and tell me where the doc is." Alondra snarled as her annoyance heightened, and her skin began to itch and twitch violently.

Na'troi paused and watched her carefully. "You're in withdrawal. What has he given you? Maybe I can find it in your file." She headed for one of the monitors and began to log in, smiling from ear to ear like she'd just won some prize.

"Is it that obvious? The withdrawal?"

"Of course. Symptoms include shakes and headaches. I'm sure the itchy feeling is running through your veins since you keep twitching. It's small but noticeable." She glanced over her shoulder and frowned. "Wait," Na'tori paused and turned as her face screwed up into a frown, "you shouldn't be withdrawing from any type of drug we have. The drugs we create should be assisting you, not harming you or making you dependent on them. What have you been given? A pill? An injection? Maybe blood transfusions? Oh god, I hope he didn't give you something that would cause any neurological problems. Or maybe he gave you something that hasn't been FDA-approved. Shit, I hope not! What's your subject number?"

Alondra stared at her as if she sported three heads. Was this chick crazy, or was she missing something? No one sounded this happy, especially no one she knew within Titan. Not that she had met many people within the company.

"Subject number?" Na'tori questioned again, "I need it to access your file." She smiled sweetly and waited with a patience Alondra didn't feel.

"Three, I'm subject three."

Na'tori's fingers hovered over the keyboard for a second before she started typing, and a file with Alondra's name and face popped up. Alondra stepped forward to see just what was in her file since no one had ever shown her before and frowned when she noticed a locked folder within the document.

"What does that mean?" She pointed as she came to stand right beside the mystery woman with the even more mysterious eyes. "It's locked?"

"Looks like it. And before you ask, I don't know why it's locked to begin with, and I don't have access, but it's okay because I don't need it. Your medication file is right here, so I'll just skim it and see what we can do to help you."

Alondra stepped back and moved around the infirmary. She didn't need to see her file to know precisely what drugs would be there or what tests she'd undergone to get where she was now. She'd moved up in the company faster than most. At least that's what Lukas had been telling her for the last few years, so she didn't need the withdrawal symptoms to be a setback that would keep her from doing more and advancing farther.

She was running her gaze over several bottles of ibuprofen as well as other drugs within a glass cabinet when Na'tori spoke.

"Okay, so I see the issue." She chuckled softly and typed furiously on the computer, "Your lists of drugs popped up, but they don't make any sense to me, so how about I just whip something up for you. I'll focus on the imperfection in your heart and make an antibody that should help you. How does that sound?"

"You're going to help me just like that? I don't need to do any favors for you?"

Na'tori's expression went sour. "Is that what the doctor has you do to receive your meds? He makes you do things?"

Alondra didn't bother responding. The answer was evident in her expression; she wasn't hiding anything, but she also wouldn't voice what the doctor made her do in their free time. She wasn't even sure if the facility knew what the good doctor was up to on the side, but she damn sure wasn't going to be the one to rat him out. They stared back at each other, both never looking away, yet Alondra couldn't stop the small tremors from wracking her body. She began her pacing again as she spoke.

"So, how long will it take you to make this new antibody?"

"Maybe an hour, and I'll give you injection needles. I can get started now if you'd like, or would you rather wait for Dr. Salazar? I'm told he won't be back for another day or so…something about a family emergency."

Alondra tried to keep her excitement at bay as she looked to this woman who was willing to help her without needing anything in return. It wasn't common to *come across someone willing to do for her within the company without scratching their back first, so this was new, uneven territory, but she was ready to finally make a friend.*

She extended her hand with a small smile she wasn't used to giving. "I'm known as subject 3 here, but my name's Alondra."

Na'tori smiled brightly once more and gripped her hand to give her an enthusiastic shake.

A knock on her bedroom door yanked her from her memory. Her head whipped towards the door before it cracked open slightly, and Alaric stepped over the threshold. The expression on his face was positively murderous.

"When was that memory? When did you meet her?" He slammed the door behind him and stalked forward. "I see you're still sticking to your deceitful ways because you know more than you've been saying."

Alondra's first urge was to reach out and slap the ever-loving shit out of him the second he came close enough to do so, but the reasonable, more understanding side of her said that doing so wouldn't be within her best interest. She kept her hands to herself but let her words fly recklessly. "How dare you stand there and question me about my choices and what information I provide when you're the reason I'm in this situation in the first place? You worked for Titan, too. You fucking tortured me, Alaric! You tortured me for hours because you couldn't simply peel back the layers of my mind. If you had wanted to learn anything you could have in those few precious moments that I was too weak to keep you out, but now that time is lost, my walls are stronger now. So, when I feel like providing you with answers, I will, but until then, get the hell out of my room and stay the fuck away from me!"

He balled his hands into fists at his sides and glared. "I did what I needed to do to get you out, Alondra, but this isn't about what I did; this is about your secrets. You were more involved in Titan than you let on. You know Na'tori intimately; you've met her before, so tell me how that is. Tell me, at what point in your life within those walls did you have the opportunity to be on a first-name basis with our enemy!?"

"I suppose around the same time, you were climbing the ladder and getting in good with the boss!" She put air quotes around the word boss and turned her back to stare out the window, "Now please leave, and don't bother me with this again."

"I need to know what you know, Alondra. This could help me."

"I don't care to help you. Now get out."

Alaric was silent for so long she figured he'd left, but instead, she found herself tensing when a puff of air rushed across the shell of her ear, and his presence grazed her back. His voice was a menacing snarl. "I'll be getting my answers, Alondra. Maybe not tonight, but soon, because you may not care to help me, but Alara does, and I know how much you want to look good in her eyes. All I need is patience. Sleep well, little sis, and remember that I tried to do this the easy way."

He left before she could respond, and she was thankful for it. Alaric was overbearing in a way that she wasn't sure how to combat against, but he was also correct. She held secrets deep enough to fracture the bonds she was slowly building with the people she'd hurt. Alondra wasn't sure if telling those secrets would make anything better or put her in a hole too deep to climb out of.

CHAPTER

TEN

N a'tori slammed her front door closed on the guard that stood sentry outside her home and groaned in frustration as she headed for her bedroom. Four days of lockdown because of Alaric's escape had made it impossible to leave the Titan warehouse. Was Alaric even still waiting for those answers? Would she see him, or had he given up because she'd been MIA? She glanced around her bedroom, saw the mess of clean laundry piled on her bed and her shoes scattered around the floor, and sighed heavily. She started cleaning as her mind replayed the last four days.

Pretending to wake up on the cold floor where Alaric had left her had been a test in her acting skills, but the real test began when her brothers badgered her with questions. For days, the questions came; all the while, she'd worked on the drug she was sure could help Alaric combat the virus running through his veins. There was no way to really know if it would work without testing it on someone, but that wasn't something she could easily do. How would she explain to her brothers what it was for? If they knew it was a possible cure for the virus she'd created for them, then they might actually kill her. She needed Alaric because it was likely that what she had created would only work with his physiology.

"Shit!" She exclaimed as she shoved her last pair of shoes into their desired spot within her closet. She did it with more force than necessary and stormed from her closet to shower when the sight of Alaric crossing the threshold and entering her bedroom greeted her.

His gaze ran over her body in a heated caress before he glanced around the bedroom and quickly brought his gaze back to her. A smirk touched his lips briefly when he spoke. "Are you always so upset with your shoes? Or is this just a one-time thing?"

She smiled weakly as nervousness rippled through her, and her stomach swarmed with butterflies. "Um… one-time thing." She slid her bottom lip between her teeth and bit down before she loosened her lips to speak again. "How did you get in here? I know my brother has guards right outside."

His black curly hair was pulled into a severe bun at the top of his head, but it didn't make him look any less appealing to her. A black henley covered his muscular chest and arms while form-fitting jeans molded to his lower half, along with a pair of shit-kicker boots. The intricate tattoo that peeked from beneath his sleeve on his left wrist made her pause and stare. How had she never paid attention to it before? She'd seen him shirtless; she knew he had tattoos, but now her mind wondered just what exactly had he gotten etched onto his body.

"He does, and they were easy to get by. A little trick of the mind and I slipped inside with no one the wiser. The better question is," he stepped right up to her until his chest was inches away from hers and his scent wrapped around her, "Why do you keep looking at me like you're trying to see beneath my clothing, princess?"

A blush filled her cheeks, and she glanced away when she whispered her following words. "Your tattoos. I never paid much attention to them before, and now I'm wondering what they are."

Alaric gently took hold of her chin and made her meet his stare. His smile was alarming and warm, making her body sway into his until his heat seeped beneath her skin. "Would you like a closer look?"

Her heart took off with a gallop as her eyes began to lower toward his chest, and his raspy chuckle made every feminine part of her tingle in awareness. Her chest rose and fell rapidly with every inhale and exhale she took as she watched in quiet fascination. Alaric dropped his hands, gripped the bottom hem of his shirt, and slowly lifted to expose his bronzed skin. He stood shirtless before her, that wicked grin of his still in place as he dropped it to the ground and spread his arms as if to say, 'Look, your fill.' And so she did.

Na'tori started from his right wrist, where she had first seen the dark marks of tattoo lines, only to realize that they were vines from a flower that looked like they were digging into his skin. They climbed up his arm and wrapped around his shoulder until you reached his chest, where a burning rose sat. Her eyes instantly flew to the tattoo of a dagger on his left rib cage with words written in another language on the blade, but she wasn't sure what the words were.

She caressed them and watched as his muscles flexed beneath her touch. "What does it say?"

"Freedom through bloodshed. It's written in Japanese," He replied, gripping her hand to press it into his skin when she tried to pull away, "keep touching me; it calms my mind."

Her blush spread to her chest as her eyes continued to roam over his body and take in the scars that littered his skin. They stood out due to the realistic tattoo work that covered each scar as if they had just occurred. She ran her hands over each one and watched as the muscles within his abs clenched before he gripped her roaming hands and stilled them on his lower stomach where the edge of his jeans sat. Na'tori glanced up to find his eyes watching her. Lust peered back at her, and her core clenched as her panties went damp with need.

"I thought this was calming you," she whispered.

He stepped into her and kept walking until he had her back pressed against the nearest wall before he leaned forward to caress the shell of her ear with his lips as he spoke. "You're calming my mind, princess, but you're making the rest of me incredibly aware and very much in need of something more."

"I don't know what you mean."

He chuckled darkly as he pushed her hands to cover the bulge that had grown behind the zipper of his jeans before nipping the lobe of her ear. "Don't you?"

She moaned softly as the sensation of his teeth and the feel of his cock within her palm registered in her mind. "What are we doing?" She groaned breathlessly when his lips traveled to her throat and nipped lightly at her pulse point.

It was Alaric's turn to moan when her hand tightened a fraction. "I'm doing what I should have done the moment I saw you in that club."

He released her and gripped the back of her head and hip before crushing his lips to her own. Na'tori couldn't explain what happened next. She melted into him like he was exactly what she needed to continue breathing, yet found herself incapable of taking in air as he devoured her lips like they were his last meal on earth. She moaned into his mouth, her hands pulling at the button and zipper on his jeans in an effort to reach his skin, yet the second she had them undone, Alaric pulled away. He turned his back to her; uneven breaths filled the space between them as his hands balled into fists in an attempt to keep his hands to himself. She also tried to catch her breath, trembling with the need to touch him. An overwhelming desire drove her. Whatever this was, she wasn't used to it, but she wanted more. She wanted Alaric with every fiber of her being. Na'tori didn't care what it would cost her because this was the first time in her life that she had ever felt so alive. She reached out and gripped his bicep, and he tensed beneath her hold as he looked over his shoulder to pin her with a look she wasn't sure how to decipher.

"If we don't stop now, I'll have you spread out on a surface faster than you can comprehend, and I'll have every part of me buried in your pussy. Is that what you want, princess?" He watched her, eyes never leaving her own as he fought against his need to take her lips back beneath his own.

He was giving her an out, trying to ensure that this was what she wanted. Na'tori hardly knew him or the situation between him and her brothers, but one thing she did know was the desire tearing through her. This level of attraction had never happened to her before. Not enough to make her want to throw caution to the wind and mount him on the floor or the bed directly behind him, but for him, she was ready to risk it all.

"I want this." She finally responded and waited to see what he would do with that information.

"Then show me." Alaric jerked his chin towards the bed and stepped back, "Take off your clothes, climb onto the bed, and lay on your back."

Na'tori watched him warily, unsure if she'd heard him accurately. He simply watched her expectantly, and she knew he was serious. He crossed his arms over his chest, causing his muscles to become more prominent as he leaned casually against the dresser. A soft smile graced his lips, drawing her attention to his five o'clock shadow and the small scars that peppered his skin.

"So you just want me to strip down and climb onto the bed?" She frowned, "Is this a control thing?"

Alaric tilted his head to the side, brushed his thumb against his bottom lip, and closed his eyes with a soft sigh before he spoke words she never thought she'd hear. "You have all the control." His eyes opened and pinned her with a breathtaking look. "You say stop, and we stop. I want you to do this because you want me just as badly as I want you. What I desire from you would scare you if I made the first move, so I put distance between us, and now I'm setting the stage. Do you want my lips, tongue, fingers, and cock buried in your pretty pussy, or would you like to stick to figuring this out? I won't force you, princess, but I'll demand your pleasure in all ways if we do move forward."

He never moved from his position against the dresser, but each word was a cord tugging her towards him. Na'tori gripped the edge of her shirt and quickly lifted it over her head before she lost her nerve. It fluttered to the floor as she watched his gaze deepen with desire before he dropped his hand to his cock and gripped it through the fabric. A bright red bra cupped her 34b breasts as she reached for the loose-fitting pants she'd donned just that morning and pulled them down until they pooled around her feet.

"All of it," he groaned, "please."

Her heart raced once more, but she was convinced it had never stopped pounding in her chest. This was a dangerous game they were playing. They should have been discussing Titan, but her desire to feel him was too great, and she was sure his desire was just as high as hers. For once, she wanted something for herself. She wanted Alaric. Na'tori reached behind her back to unclip her bra and dragged the fabric down over tight, peaked nipples. The sensation sent sparks to her core before she also dropped it to the floor. Alaric fisted his cock through his jeans and shifted uncomfortably as she dropped her panties and moved carefully for the bed. The moment her back met the cool sheets, he chucked his jeans but left his briefs in place. Her eyes never strayed from the massive erection confined within as he approached the bed.

"Eyes up, princess," he ordered.

Her eyes drifted to his face reluctantly and held.

"Beautiful," He reached the bed and grabbed her by the legs to drag her to the edge before he knelt between her parted thighs. His eyes zeroed in on her pussy, and his hands tightened around her legs before he met her gaze again. "Last chance, Na'tori, you tell me yes, and I plan to wreck your entire world, or tell me no, and we'll get dressed right now."

"I want this," she replied, "but you should know… I'm a virgin." She didn't think his expression could become any more feral than it already was, but that was a lie.

He grinned like the devil himself. "I'll take care of this pretty pussy. Trust me."

Before she could take her next breath or fix her lips to say anything else, his head disappeared between her thighs, and his tongue slid through the lips of her labia. Her moan was breathy and uncontrolled as Na'tori reached down to grab him by his hair. Her fist wrapped into the soft strands as his lips and tongue worked her over. Her body arched upwards as her moans grew in strength before he reached up and slid two fingers into her mouth and held her chin in place, instantly turning those moans into soft groans.

"Sssh," he whispered against her clit, "We don't need anyone hearing you, princess. Can you stay quiet for me?"

She moaned softly and nodded before his fingers left her mouth to trail down her chest to grip one of her breasts within his palm. Her hips shifted with every controlled lick he delivered to her clit. The ringing began in her ears, and she felt delirious as her pleasure continued to climb with each rock of her hips. She could hear the slurping sounds aided by the wetness that dripped from her core and leaked towards the crack of her ass. Just when Na'tori thought the sensation couldn't get any more pleasurable, she felt one of his thick fingers sliding between the lips of her pussy and into her center. His hand left her breasts to slap it over her mouth just as a scream tore from her lips.

"Fuck," he snarled, "that's right, baby, cum on my fingers. Keep cuming. Give it all to me." He fucked her with his fingers, but not deep enough to break the barrier she knew was there. "Give me more Na'tori."

Her cry of pleasure was muffled by his hand when his fingers curled within her to rub against her g-spot as he sucked at her clit. Her eyes rolled back as another orgasm slammed into her, and a gush of moisture left her involuntarily. That was way more than a simple orgasm if the liquid running down onto the sheets was any indication, but she couldn't take in enough air to care.

CHAPTER
ELEVEN

Alaric didn't know how to describe the sensation rushing through him. All he knew was that the taste of Na'tori's pussy was something he wanted to eat for the rest of his life. His hands shook as he eased her grip from his head and sat back. His breathing was labored as he removed his shaft from his briefs and gripped the base to still the orgasm that wanted to lurch forward. His eyes were laser-focused on the woman moaning softly atop the bed. Her legs were still spread, shaking slightly and giving him an unobstructed view of her pink center. The sight made his balls jump up as the scent of her pussy wrapped around him and choked him off from logical thought. She was the tightest he'd ever felt around his finger, and he knew if his dick entered her now, he would hurt her because he wouldn't know how to ease her into his line of fucking, but his dick was trying to convince him otherwise. It was telling him he could be gentle.

"God," she whimpered, "is that how it always feels?" She glanced down between her thighs, her eyes a swirling mass of color.

His cock continued to drip precum, but the urge to orgasm had left, so he stroked his shaft and caressed her trembling leg in a soothing gesture before he thought to reply. "Only with me."

He planned to be a selfish bastard. Now that he'd tasted her, he wasn't letting her go. She'd awoken a hunger in him that he'd never felt before, and he wanted more, but he couldn't lie and say that fear didn't have a hold on him. It did. He wanted to take and take until all that was left was a whimpering mess that could barely put two words together, and that might scare her. His needs were greater than most. He was a demanding bastard even on the best of days, but on any other, he would fuck her until she could barely breathe. She was a virgin. Untried and new to sex. He couldn't introduce her to his brand of pleasure, at least not yet, but maybe he could ease her into it.

He tucked his dick back into his briefs, although it was a tight fit, and came to his feet to stare down into her face. "We should talk."

Her face twisted into a look of confusion as she sat up slowly. "What do you mean?" Her eyes drifted to his cock and held, "Aren't you supposed to cum too?"

He dragged a hand over his face and regretted it immediately when the smell of her cum still sat wrapped around his finger. He pulled it into his mouth and sucked. His groan was more of a growl as he locked his eyes on the heaven that was her cunt. He spoke words he didn't want to say but knew they were the right words for the moment. "I'll show you how to take care of it later."

Her expression dropped as she dragged her comforter to her chest to shield herself from him. He wanted to snatch the fabric from her hands and look his fill, but he stepped back instead and forced himself to turn and approach his discarded jeans before he pulled them over his legs and forced the zipper and button into place. Only when he heard her run into her closet to get dressed as well did Alaric turn back around. She emerged wearing an over-sized sweater with baggy sweatpants that hid every inch of skin from his gaze. He forced himself not to react, picked up his shirt, and pulled it over his head.

He broke the silence that had grown between them. "What happened after I left?"

For a moment, she looked as if she had no intention of replying before she sighed heavily and went to sit on the edge of her bed—

far enough away from the wet spot they'd created. "They made me stay on site and questioned me for days. They wanted to know how you'd gotten around the failsafe within the collar and how you could incapacitate everyone. There was no video footage of what you'd done, and the guard responsible for monitoring the system committed suicide. Did you make him do that?"

He nodded, no ounce of guilt within his expression. "It was that or erase the footage myself, and that would have taken longer than I had time for. Did they hurt you?"

"No…" she paused, deciding if she wanted to divulge any more information.

"What is it? What happened?" He moved until he stood before her and watched her face, hoping to get a clue of what she could be holding back.

"They wanted to, but I convinced them not to."

Alaric frowned. "How? What did you promise them because they wouldn't just walk away from an opportunity to get answers out of you?"

"I promised I could find you and bring you back."

The words should have angered him, but instead, he was relieved. They hadn't hurt her, and for some inexplicable reason, that had been his primary concern. So what if they wanted him back. By the look in her eyes, she had no intention of serving him up on a silver platter. He supposed he should have been thankful for that, but instead, it begged the question of whether she would have to go back beyond the walls where he would have no way of reaching her unless he gave himself up again. Alaric would never go behind those walls again, especially if he wanted to keep breathing; he knew without a doubt that they would surely kill him the next time he was within their grasp. Now that they knew how easy it was to escape them, they would take preventative measures to ensure he never got out again.

"You're not upset?" She reached for him and gripped his hand lightly, "I promise I have no intention of getting you back to them. I don't work for them anymore. I want to right the wrongs I helped them do. Starting with you."

"What do you mean?"

Na'tori released his hand and left the bedroom. He wanted to follow her into the living room but knew that the shades were open, so any guards patrolling the perimeter would see him if he walked by a window. The bedroom was safer. It didn't even take her a minute before she was walking back into the bedroom carrying a case no bigger than her forearm. She approached him almost cautiously as she unzipped the case and presented 6 small vials and a syringe filled with a blue substance.

"What is this?" He questioned and watched as she removed the syringe from the case.

"I know I said this before, and you might not remember, which is probably why you don't hate me right now, but I'm the one who created the virus that is killing you. I lied to my brothers about seeing how sick you really were. I knew you were dying even before your blood results came back. Your aura is weak, Alaric; you're definitely dying and fast." She held the syringe between them and smiled weakly, "I think this will help you for the time being until I can find a better solution for you."

"I remember." He stared at the syringe and then glanced into her eyes. "Why do you think whatever this is will help?"

"The virus was created to kill off unusual genomes. I learned that it affects everyone exposed to it in different ways. Still, I've only seen the virus administered to three individuals, and each person has reacted differently, so I'm not entirely sure what this antidote will do to you because it's never been tested. When I ran a series of tests on the blood I took from you, I made sure to inject this substance into your blood cells. The results are promising, but I can't tell you with one hundred percent certainty that you'll be healed."

Alaric removed the syringe from her hand and stared at the liquid inside. A million questions were running through his mind, but what he knew for sure was that he was taking it regardless of the ramifications. If this could help him, he would risk it, and although he knew next to nothing about the woman before him, one thing was certain; he trusted her. He uncapped the syringe, rolled up the sleeve of his shirt, and plunged the needle directly into his vein to make sure it swam through his bloodstream. When he glanced up, he found Na'tori staring at him in shock.

"What?" He chuckled, "Was I not supposed to take it?"

She shook her head and smiled softly. "I was expecting you to test a little bit of it at a time. We don't know what it will do to you, Alaric. You could have adverse reactions." She ran her hands over his arms and observed him carefully.

His eyes followed her hands as a burning sensation began to spread through him like wildfire. His skin was itching, and his heart started to pound in his chest, but all he could focus on was the top of Na'tori's head. Everywhere her hands touched his body, his mind conjured images of her naked flesh pressed against his own. His cock was lengthening within his jeans when her hands froze, and her beautiful eyes flew up to meet his. He gripped her by the back of her neck and pulled her body flush against his own.

"I'm burning up," he growled and kissed her forehead, "is this supposed to happen?"

Her blunt nails dug into his sides. "I told you this is an untried drug. Tell me what else you're feeling because your aura is pulsing, and your eyes look brighter. I need to know the symptoms so I can help you."

"I feel..." he licked his bottom lip and smirked, "I feel like my skin is crawling. My eyes are pulsing, and my heart is pounding in my chest, but another matter entirely would be the erection pressed against my damn thigh."

Her cheeks pinkened in embarrassment before she pressed her face into his chest and chuckled. "I don't think that's a reaction I've ever heard of. Does this mean we can...you know...continue where we left off?"

Alaric desperately wanted to agree with her and feast on her until the sun rose and fell from the sky, but he knew that if he did, nothing would ever get done, and they needed to figure this out. The Eternals required answers, and the only reason they'd allowed him to come alone was because he said he could get those answers. The guardians questioning her would have granted them nothing. His gut actually churned at the idea of using her to gain anything to fight against Titan. He even hated the idea of having her create a drug that might help eradicate the virus within his system. He wasn't sure what it was about this particular woman that urged him to get closer, protect her, and make himself a permanent fixture in her life. All he knew was that when he looked into her beautiful face, the dark urges his abilities tried to push him to do would fade away, and he was left with only thoughts of her.

Alaric reached up to thread his fingers into her hair at the back of her head and tugged gently until her eyes met his again. "As badly as I'd like to lay you out and eat you until all I taste is you throughout this lifetime, I can't. We both want answers from each other." He released her hair only to grip her chin and run his thumb over her lush bottom lip, "I need to know what you know about Titan and the ins and outs of that operation, and whatever you want, I will do my very best to see that you get it."

Na'tori's soft hands slid under the fabric of his shirt to rest on his abdominal muscles as her eyes swirled and pulsed. He didn't know her abilities or what she had been doing for Titan all this time, but now he needed to learn. Whatever knowledge she held within her mind could have the potential to put them several steps ahead with Titan pressed under the heel of their boots, but would she indeed betray her family? Could she help him and the Eternals get their answers and possibly save whatever Kindred Titan had under lock and key within their facilities? There was no doubt in his mind that there were men, women, and children trapped behind steel bars with collars cutting them off from abilities that could help them get away.

Those dark urges he'd only just started to feel in recent weeks flared up and almost swallowed his mind whole with ideas of sliding into the minds of his enemies to simply end their miserable lives. He slammed his eyes shut, tightened his hands a fraction around the woman before him, and groaned as his body continued to pulse and throb with a need and tightness that made him question just what the hell that blue liquid had done to him.

"What's wrong? What's happening now?" Na'tori's voice was concerned as her hands reached up to cup his cheeks.

A throbbing pain began behind his eyes as his head began to pound, but at the feel of her hands touching his skin, he found comfort in it. Alaric never wanted it to end, yet he knew something was seriously wrong when a crippling pain tore through his mind. He groaned painfully, knocked her hands away from him, and knelt on the ground to clutch at his head.

"Fuck," he snarled harshly and attempted to lower his mental shields to reach out to Rome or Silas, but it was impossible.

The pain was becoming an unbearable agony that trumped the years of torture he'd endured while working for Titan. He wanted to scream. He knew Silas wasn't too far and would hear his shout for help, yet when he opened his mouth, no sound came out.

"What do I do?" Na'tori dropped beside him and reached out to touch him but decided against it when he held out a hand to keep her away.

There was no telling how he would react to her touch when he could hardly decipher the pain that was tearing through his mind and spreading throughout his body. It felt like his mind was splitting wide open, yet the barriers around it stayed in place, and the darkness that swirled inside began to pulse and thrive through every memory, thought, and feeling he possessed. His life played on a loop. Everything he'd ever done in his life stared back at him and taunted him with the life he could have had if he hadn't been a captive to Titan.

"Silas," he whispered brokenly, "get Silas princess."

Tears trailed down Na'tori's face as she spoke through her tears. "How? What do I do?"

He was going to pass out. There was no doubt in Alaric's mind that he would lose consciousness soon, and that was the worst thing he could do at a time like this, but the pain was climbing to levels he wasn't sure how to combat against. Every muscle within his body tightened as a silent scream parted his lips, and blackness filled his vision. He fought against the urge to pass out but couldn't stop himself from slumping to the floor on his side. Alaric's eyes were closed up tight, and still, it felt as if the light was tearing through his retinas and into his brain. Na'tori's hands finally touched him, her hands pressing firmly onto his shoulder to roll him onto his back as she cried louder. Any minute now, one of her guards would make their way inside if she didn't stop with the noise, but he couldn't use his voice to tell her to stop.

"Alaric," Na'tori whispered brokenly, "How do I reach him?"

He tried once more to open his mind and telepathically communicate with Silas or Rome and instead was swallowed whole by the darkness that had bubbled over within his mind.

CHAPTER
TWELVE

Alaric went limp beneath her hands, and Na'tori froze. His chest rose and fell several times before stopping entirely. The breath in her lungs stalled, her eyes flew wide, and terror filled her. She only froze for several seconds before instinct and the need to save his life took over. She started CPR and threw her whole body into the act, but internally, she was panicking. Her tears were falling faster, unadulterated fear clung to her like a cloak as sobs choked her, and her mind raced with what to do. Alaric had told her to find someone named Silas. Her best guess was that Silas was the Eternal he had been with in the alley the night they'd met. She didn't know where to start to find him, but she knew she couldn't stop what she was doing now. She needed to save Alaric's life, and Na'tori couldn't help but think this was all her fault.

The drug he'd administered had to be the reason he was now dead. There was no other explanation her erratic thoughts could come up with that would make sense. Only after administering it did the symptoms start. She'd done this to him.

"ALARIC!" She screamed, uncaring if the guards found them now.

Her heart was pounding in her chest as heaving sobs left her.

95

She could barely see through her tears, but he wasn't responding. He was so still and lifeless. Frustration bit at her. Was she too weak to even give him CPR? She'd never had to do this before. She'd saved a life once or twice before, but that was by scientific means. Her drugs were her saving grace. This...this was foreign territory, and she was epically failing.

"What the fuck is going on?" One of her guards exclaimed from his position at her bedroom door. "How the fuck did he get in here?"

Na'tori chanced a look over her shoulder, took in his murderous stare and the hand he had on his gun, and feared that he would stop her. She opened her mouth to make up some type of excuse for why her brother's enemy was currently lying dead on her bedroom floor, but he never got the chance. A tall form suddenly appeared behind him and quickly snapped his neck without a pause. She had a full view of the Eternal she'd seen before, when her guard slumped to the ground. His heterochromia eyes began to glow as he bared long fangs and moved too fast for her eyes to catch. She was face to face with a male who looked about ready to tear her throat out, and all she could do was continue her compressions as tears continued to trail down her cheeks.

"What have you done?" Silas snarled.

Another Eternal appeared within the room only inches from their position. Dreads hung to his waist, chocolate skin and clear blue eyes stared back at her, and Na'tori knew without a shadow of a doubt that this man was the king of his people. This was Romulus. She had seen his face enough times within the charts Titan kept that she'd know him anywhere. In fact, his file was the only one she had ever witnessed out of the group of immortal beings. Rome glanced down at Alaric's unmoving form, and a look of agony crossed his features.

"Help him," Na'tori pleaded, her arms finally fatigued from overexerting her movements, "please help him."

Rome and Silas shared a look between them that she didn't understand. Silas reached out to steady her hands against Alaric's chest before he simultaneously took hold of Rome's outstretched hand. It happened quickly. One moment, she was in her bedroom giving Alaric chest compressions, and within the blink of an eye, she was standing behind a cell door with no one in sight.

Na'tori looked around the space frantically while her heart beat in her throat, and pesky tears ran down her face. Where had they taken Alaric? She needed to know if he was okay. Had they saved him? She couldn't wrap her mind around the fact that he was possibly dead, and it was her fault. Her energy withered away at the thought. She turned away from the door, approached the small cot against the wall, and climbed under the thin sheet they'd provided her. Her emotions were all over the place, yet her mind still raced with thoughts of what had happened and what she could do now that she was here. What would the Eternals do with her now that she was the one caged?

It seemed like an hour came and went before the sound of someone clearing their throat filled the silent space. Na'tori sat up swiftly and turned to find Alondra on the other side of the bars, her face the same as she'd last seen, except for the dark circles resting below her eyes. Other than that slight difference, she had the same resting bitch face that she'd encountered on numerous occasions, but Na'tori also remembered what it looked like when she smiled and let joy light her features. She knew the softer side of Alondra that she refused to let others see.

"What are you doing here?" She came to her feet and approached the bars as Alondra simply stared back at her with a look of indifference and anger.

Alondra glanced over her shoulder towards the staircase she hadn't noticed before and gripped the bars when she faced forward again. "I need to know that you won't tell them how we know one another," she stated, "they can't know about my...problems."

"Alo...how are you here? Are you with the Eternals as well?"

"Are you listening to me?" She snapped in a hushed voice, "You tell them nothing about how we know one another, okay? Nothing."

Na'tori absently nodded as she approached the bars of the cell. She didn't know entirely what she was agreeing to, but she would agree to anything right now if it would get her answers because her life seemed to consist of unanswered questions. She couldn't keep residing in the shadows, knowing nothing. "Tell me how you came to be here, or I won't promise you anything. I thought we were friends, Alo. Friends enough to talk to each other about whatever the hell is happening right now."

Alondra stared back at her in shock. "Friends don't leave each other behind!"

"I was reassigned." Na'tori responded softly, her voice filled with guilt, "I didn't have a choice, and if I had asked to stay on my current assignment, Lukas would have questioned me, and I would have been putting us at risk. Besides, Dr. Salazar no longer needed my input on everything I'd helped him achieve. I know now that I was lied to and made to believe that the company was doing good deeds. I agreed to help Alaric, and now I think I killed him." She gripped the cell bars, desperation leaking into her expression and voice, "Do you know if he's okay? Do you know him? I have to believe they brought him here, and they could do more than I ever could to help him."

"What do you mean you think you killed him?"

"Well, isn't this a beautiful sight to see," Amirishka smirked as she strode down the staircase, a blade forever twirling between her agile fingers, "I'm sure everyone else hardly noticed you weren't present for your brother, but I noticed, you two can't stand one another, and now I know why. What else are you hiding from us, Alondra? Didn't you learn anything when you were locked up for months? Betraying us again isn't for the wise."

Na'tori's gaze shifted and locked onto the newcomer. Her breath left her in a rush as she took her in. She was downright gorgeous with large iridescent eyes that reflected a different color with each tilt of her head, and her hair was dyed midnight black with hot pink highlights littered throughout. She was a small thing at five foot five, a body most women would envy with a coke bottle shape, large ample breasts, and a full ass that had Na'tori glancing back to look at her own.

"You're the one female Guardian, aren't you?" Na'tori questioned. Fascination filled her. She didn't know much about the female Guardian, but she knew she was the only one of her kind—at least as far as Titan knew.

"And you're the bitch sister that created the Virus that's hurting my people, correct?" She snarled and flashed fangs, but she never stopped twirling the blade. "Seems like the both of you have unsavory traits."

The energy within the room shifted and dropped several degrees. Na'tori glanced between the two women when Alondra glared ruthlessly at the Guardian. She wasn't sure who to keep her eyes on when the tension continued to rise. She didn't take any offense to what had been stated. It was true. She'd helped her family in the dismantling of a group of individuals that she was slowly learning weren't a threat to the government at all. In fact, she was starting to believe they were the good ones in this war, and she'd been fighting for the wrong team this whole time.

Na'tori broke that tense silence, hoping to diffuse the situation before anything could even begin. "I never knew the truth about Titan, and I still don't know the full story, but now I know enough to know that I was helping, but not in the way I'd hoped. My view is different now. I just want to help."

Alondra spun back around, her expression conveying that she wasn't convinced. "You just told me you killed Alaric. You told me it was your fault my brother was dead. What did you mean by that?"

"He isn't dead," Amirishka stated as her glare drilled into the back of Alondra's head. "If you'd bothered to go into his bedroom, you would know that Rome's already taken the necessary measures to ensure he lives. Now it's only a matter of Alaric fighting to regain consciousness."

Relief filled Na'tori, but even more questions spiraled through her mind. He had stopped breathing, his heart had stalled, and he had died. She knew he'd died. She hadn't imagined that so what were they talking about. Had they restarted his heart? She needed to know.

"Are you telling me he's alive? How?"

CHAPTER
THIRTEEN

The stillness that surrounded Alaric was the most peace he'd felt in months. There was no pain, only a feeling of weightlessness and quiet. He wanted to stay right where he was for as long as he could, yet something tickled at the back of his mind. Answers. He was supposed to be getting answers from someone. Someone with beautiful opalescent eyes and perfect bow-shaped lips. Someone who made him feel like he was on top of the world and then some, yet he hardly knew her.

Na'tori.

He attempted to open his eyes or move, for that matter and found that he couldn't. Sound was also nonexistent, and he wondered how he hadn't realized that before. Why the hell weren't his senses working? He struggled uselessly until a melodic voice broke through the deafening silence, and the scent of roses and sex accompanied it.

"Will all of you struggle so pitifully when locked in a trance, or is it just the weaker ones that fear the stillness and silence? Is the human race truly so broken in mind that they can't discern when their neural pathways have transcended to a new level of understanding?"

"Who the fuck are you, and why can't I move or open my eyes?"

A male chuckle resonated through his bones and sent a chill down Alaric's spine when that voice spoke next. "Ballsy...I like him! Maybe we should let him free to see what he does."

"Of course, you would like that, Ares; you're always looking for a fight," Hera replied, "As for you, Alaric, brother of Alara and Alondra. I am Hera, Queen Goddess to Zeus. You would do well to respect that and watch your tone. The nuisance that spoke is my firstborn Ares, God of war."

Alaric froze. Was this really happening? He tried to open his eyes once more and gained no ground. He desperately wanted to move when he felt the presence of someone crowding him from behind. At least he could clench his hands into fists, but that would do him no good if anything happened to him. He couldn't fight a God or Goddess without suffering significant consequences, right? He frowned at the thought his mind took before another thought entered. Was he dead?

A new voice interrupted his thoughts. "You aren't dead, but you could be if you'd like. I am Hypnos, God of sleep, but I partake in other things as well, particularly the mind."

Alaric hesitated for only a moment. "If I'm not dead, then explain this to me. What do you mean I can be if I'd like. Elaborate."

Another feminine voice spilled through the room and made Alaric wonder just how many of these Gods and Goddesses were surrounding and filling his mind. "You need no further elaboration." She snapped, and he could feel her anger flowing through him like a cresting wave, "I am Athena, the counterpart to my brother Ares, but I come with reason and wisdom and not just a mind for battle. We need you to wake up, Alaric, and remove yourself from the darkness that is your mind. You have work to do for us. Your fight is not over."

"You'll bore him to death with words, sister; he seems like a fighter," Ares chuckled, "I say let him fight me to get back to the land of the living. I'm feeling a bit rusty."

"Enough!" Hera snapped. "Fight the demons in your mind, or you won't be returning to your body or the woman that is meant to calm your spirit and make you whole once more. The longer you stay within this limbo with us, the less likely you will return to our Guardians."

Alaric was tempted to curse her and everything she stood for, but the mention of a woman explicitly meant for him gave him pause. "Are you telling me what I think you're telling me? I'll be an Eternal when I wake?"

"I told you he was a lot smarter than he looked." Hypnos chuckled, "And as *for returning as a Guardian, that's exactly what will happen if you can beat back the demons within your mind long enough to return to your body."*

"Will I still be dying? Will I have a mate? Is this the woman you speak of?"

"We can't answer that for you," Hera replied.

He could sense the smirk on her lips and grit his teeth in anger. "Can't or Won't?"

"Won't."

He waited for more than a simple won't, yet no one else spoke. He had more questions; he wanted to know more about the life he would have if he did go back, this time as an Eternal, but he was slightly on the fence about it. If that woman wasn't Na'tori, he didn't think he'd want to live forever.

"Tell me I get Na'tori as my mate, or to hell with what you need from me." Alaric snapped.

Ares burst out with a full belly laugh that hurt Alaric's ear drums. "Aw, you've gone and done it now, my friend. Tell me we can loosen the bonds of his mental body and make him fight now."

"Do it," He challenged, "But if I win, I get Na'tori as my mate and answers to any questions I have. And I mean you answer everything. No lies, or you can let me meet Hades, and we'll share a glass of bourbon in hell."

That eerie silence greeted him again, and at first, he thought he'd pushed too much, asked for more than he should, and crossed barriers that would surely earn him a ferry ride to hell. The silence stretched, and he thought for sure that they were done with him until the feeling of being trapped evaporated, and he was capable of finally moving. His limbs felt loose when he took a hesitant step forward, and although he was still blind, he felt as if he was walking through dense fog or whatever resembled that.

His mind still swirled with darkness, yet he embraced it. They were going to allow him to fight the God of war. He could feel each of them watching him. Athena was to his right, an air of power and cunning surrounding her, while Hypnos stood at his back with waves of tranquility pouring from him. He could tell instinctively that Hera stood to his left when waves of rage and anger burned into his side, making him want to turn and face her. That left Ares standing at his front. He gave off arrogance and humor as if Alaric facing him was nothing but a simple gust of wind. God, the arrogance of the bastard made Alaric's teeth clench as his mind spun with ways of taking him down a few pegs.

"*Your anger is refreshing, human,*" Ares taunted, "*Now show me what you're made of.*"

Still with his sight lost to him, Alaric sensed the posture the God held, arms spread wide as if he meant to embrace him in a hug instead of what this really was...a fight. He launched forward, hoping to connect his fist to the face of the God but met air instead and felt a jab to his ribs that sucked the oxygen from his lungs and left him wheezing and bent over at the waist. The sound of Ares chuckling grated on his nerves while sighs of boredom came from the rest. The moment he stood, his head was knocked back when a fist that felt like steel slammed into his face and sent him sprawling to the floor as the taste of blood filled his mouth.

"*Stop playing with him and finish it, Ares!*" Hera remarked with displeasure.

Alaric rolled to his side, coughed roughly, and spat out blood, uncaring of where it landed or who it could land on. He wasn't sure how this mental plane worked, but he damn sure didn't think it was possible to experience this level of pain. He would have no more of it. This was a mental arena, a place where he was most comfortable. He refused to let this God—a being he hardly believed in —be the reason he threw in the towel and simply followed their word. He wanted answers, and he damn sure wanted Na'tori when he woke up from what-ever the hell this was.

His anger festered and grew as he felt the pain from Ares's blows. He went to his knees, the frustration of not being able to see aiding him in his annoyance and need for violence. He was moving to come to his feet and attack once more when an awareness tingled through him, and he knew without a doubt that another fist was flying towards his face. He blocked it and lashed out with a fist. When he connected with flesh, he tried not to smile but lost that battle and grinned triumphantly just before his feet were knocked out from under him, and he found himself flat on his back once more. He gasped for air again and felt some-thing flare through him.

Would his powers work here? Would they work against this God? He wasn't sure, but he had to try. He reached for his ability, found it pulsing and thriving within that darkness he usually tried to avoid, and took hold of it. It wrapped around him, filled him, and tempted him to do dark, dirty deeds to the four beings around him.

"*What the hell is that?*" Ares questioned.

"That shouldn't be possible!" Hera exclaimed.

Alaric didn't know what they were questioning, but he felt his gift pouring from him and flowing towards the bastard Ares like a missile seeking vengeance. He felt it wrap around the God before burying deep within his mind without much difficulty. His first instinct was to search his mind for a weakness, but all he found was that the male needed praise. Without worshippers, he weakened. His abilities gorged and fed on Ares's weakness without pause. Ares screamed.

Hera's voice broke through the darkness of his mind. "Hypnos, what is happening? How is he doing this?"

"I'm not sure." Hypnos replied, "Athena, we must stop this before he takes things too far."

Alaric tightened his hold on the God's mind and strangled. A smile stretched across his face as Ares screamed louder before the invisible hold that had held him in a thrall trapped his body and mind once more.

"Cease your struggles now!" Hera demanded. "You have three questions, Alaric; ask them wisely."

He paused and listened to the God of battle and bloodlust as he groaned softly in pain. He knew he had won the fight, especially if Hera was allowing him to ask his questions. He didn't remember agreeing to only three, but he would take what he could get at this point. Alaric wanted to be done with this and return to his family and Na'tori. He calmed his body and mind, forced the darkness that curled around him back once more, and shuddered at the sensation that the feeling left behind. He'd analyze the situation later, but for now, he settled on finally getting some much-needed answers.

Athena spoke softly, "Ask your questions."

"We should just let him die," Ares's pain-filled voice commented.

Alaric chuckled, "Your fists may feel like bricks, but you're clearly weak in the mind. I can't believe you need human praise to garner strength. I've shown you what true strength is, don't be a simpering bitch. It doesn't look good on you."

"Don't antagonize him," Hypnos chuckled, "you've already bruised his overinflated ego. Just ask your three questions, and let us be done with this."

He wasted no time in his questioning, especially when he felt Hera move closer, almost in a crowding manner. "Is Na'tori my mate?"

"Yes," she replied dryly, "next question."

"No elaboration?"

"Is this your next question?"

He could hear the smirk within her voice and shook his head in annoyance. "No, it isn't. Why does my life matter in this war with Titan?"

"Because with three comes victory." That was Athena, who spoke, her voice much softer than that of the vengeful queen goddess.

It was clear that their answers would remain elusive and cryptic, similar to the visions Silas would have. Alaric thought long and hard about what he needed to know before he spoke again.

"Will the virus still flow within me when I return as an Eternal?"

"Flow?" Ares chuckled darkly, "No, but you'll wish it did."

Before he could ask what the hell he meant, all noises ceased to exist, and the feeling of being pulled down a long corridor filled him. Only Hera's voice remained.

"Enjoy your new life, warrior."

Darkness and silence greeted him when the presence of the Gods left him, and he was left alone with his thoughts. The Gods played with words, and he knew their answers had been evasive on purpose. He knew one thing: he was returning to Na'tori, and she would be his.

Alaric couldn't help but smile as sound, scent, and awareness spread through him, and his eyes finally flew open to take in the bedroom he remembered intimately. He was home. The seductive scent of honey and elderberry flowers curled around his senses and sent him launching from the bed as he went to hunt down where it was coming from.

CHAPTER
FOURTEEN

H era felt Hypnos approach her from behind before he came to stand at her side. They both watched the world below from their position in the clouds where no mortal could see them. Their realm was separate from the humans, yet the Gods and Goddesses sometimes felt as if they were walking right beside them. Hypnos's calming presence didn't stop the fire in her blood that Alaric had caused with his disrespect, but the idea of what she had done made her smile with glee.

"What have you done, Hera?" Hypnos questioned with an exasperated sigh, "I felt something before Alaric's mind slipped away from us. What was it?"

"That insolent male needs to be taught a lesson in respect, so I'll teach him patience."

"Explain."

"Just know that mating for him will not come easy, and his new senses may be blocked for a while. I would like to see if he can live up to the potential the three sisters of fate have seen in his future. He shall learn patience, or his fate will be worse than even death itself."

Hypnos shook his head in annoyance. "You know better than to interfere with fate, Hera."

"Then my husband shall strike me dead if he isn't satisfied with the plan I've laid out for his little toys below." She turned to face the man beside her and glared, "Without the war I caused within our home, the Eternals would never have come to live. They would be nothing without our blood, yet fate has plans for them. Plans that neither you nor I or anyone else in our world can unthread, but I will continue to attempt to do so. My little tweak within Alaric's life shall make no difference if he follows the right path. If he doesn't, then that shall fall upon his shoulders. I want darkness to consume him because, with it, Zeus will learn that we should have killed them off when we learned of our mistake."

Hera stormed off, robes whipping behind her in a fury as she headed far away from his judgemental stare. In her mind, she had done the right thing. She had plans for the Guardians Zeus had promised protection to. Plans that if he knew of them then she might indeed die by his bolt, but she would do anything to derail what fate had in store for them.

Alaric would know pain before he knew happiness. For his disrespect, he would obsess and burn with a desire that could never entirely be satisfied until he found what he was looking for within the parts of himself he refused to acknowledge or tread through. Her smile stretched across her face because she knew without a doubt that Alaric would fail, and with his failure, she would get what she desired most.

Zeus's favor.

CHAPTER
FIFTEEN

Na'tori looked around the living room at the Guardians, who stood alert and prepared for anything. She had been within Rome's home for a week, but this was the first time she had been allowed to come out from the cells below. On her first night here, one of the Guardians had dropped off a suitcase of her things that had clearly come from her condo. It looked as if she would be staying a lot longer than anticipated. She was sure that the only reason she had been guided upstairs to sit amongst the immortal group of warriors was so that she would spill information she knew. No one had attempted to hurt her. In fact, no one had even spoken to her since her first night there, besides Alondra and Amirishka, but that didn't make her less terrified of the men and women around her.

Their auras pulsed and throbbed within the air around them. Rome's white aura was brighter, giving off an almost supernova charge that made her tear her eyes away. The woman sitting next to him on the couch across the way from her was the spitting image of Alondra in every way, yet she could tell it wasn't Alondra by the broad smile that graced her lips. Her violet aura mingled with Rome's. It looked as if it flowed around and through him. It was a sight to see and one she would remember for the rest of her life. Na'tori had never seen multiple auras mesh before, but now that she had, it had become one of her favorite sights.

Next to her, Alondra sat with her ever-present resting bitch face as her slightly lighter violet aura swirled around her. She knew why Alondra's coloring was lighter, which made the next person on the couch that much more interesting. His eyes were blood red like a Rogue's, and his hair was white like snow. This had to be Erick, the Eternal she knew the least about. He watched her, his white-hued aura not pulsing or throbbing like everyone else's. It was simply suspended in time.

"Do you plan on staring at everyone so intently or just Erick? I assure you, I'm better looking than his ugly mug." The voice that spoke was deep and smooth.

Akio stood on the other side of the room, eyes as black as midnight, watching her closely while a slight smirk lifted his lip. She knew who he was based on the small conversations she had overheard through the vents. If an argument arose, it was always between Akio and the feral-looking Immortal Maverick, who she could feel staring daggers into the side of her face from his position near the kitchen. She refused to even glance his way because the hate that bled through his gaze was clear enough for her to feel without looking. Based on the slight snarls emanating from his chest and the fact that the female Guardian—Amirishka—kept elbowing him in the ribs, she was sure his anger was directed at her.

"Ignore the idiot, and let's get our answers," Cairo, the always impeccably dressed warrior, spoke up from his position in front of the floor-to-ceiling window. "You're a Kindred, but we know that already, so tell us what your ability is and why Alaric says you're willing to help us in this war against your family."

Her eyes flew back to Rome and stayed. If anyone deserved her full attention, it was him. He would be her judge, jury, and executioner since Alaric was still MIA as far as she knew. No one would tell her what had happened to him or if he was truly dead or alive. Na'tori knew that if she was going to get through this questioning, then she had to be honest and open because she needed answers, too. Had Amirishka told the truth and Alaric was truly okay?

"If I provide answers to your questions, will I get answers as well?" She questioned, even as her hands shook within her lap, "Alaric promised me answers."

Maverick snarled in annoyance. "He had no right to promise you a thing."

"Easy, Mav," Rome responded sternly before his eyes returned to her and settled, "Give us your honesty, and I'll answer whatever questions you have. Are we agreed?"

She nodded, sure this male wouldn't lie to her for any reason. "What would you like to know?"

"To Alaric, who are you? As far as we know, you just met him, but he's willing to risk the wrath of my Guardians and me. Why?"

"We just met." She glanced down at her hands and paused momentarily as an emotion she couldn't decipher just yet ran through her, "Maybe it was by chance, or maybe there was something in the works. I can't say I believe in fate, but by some type of miracle, I ran into a man who was dying from the virus I unknowingly created. Alaric is dying...or I guess dead now because I thought I was helping him when I gave him what I thought was a cure for what was killing him." Tears leaked from her eyes as a sob tore from her chest, "I killed him, didn't I? He's dead, and that's why you won't let me see him."

Na'tori was too afraid to look up and see the sure expression on their faces that Alaric was indeed dead, so she kept her teary gaze locked on her hands as Rome spoke.

"So whatever you gave him wasn't meant to harm him? This wasn't your intention?"

Her head shot up in surprise. "Of course not! My intention was to right my wrong. I don't know everything about the company my family built, but I know enough now that I don't want to play a part in anything they have going on. If anything, I want to dismantle the foundation of what they built and reduce it to ash."

"Can you create a cure to fight against the virus you created?" Erick questioned.

"Yes...but I need to see what went wrong with Alaric." Her mind raced with ideas and how she could have screwed up so badly. "What he took should have helped him...unless the virus had spread exponentially before the time of injection. His blood cell count from when I made the injections, to begin with, must have changed and thrown off the ratio. That's the only thing that would make sense."

Alara sat up straighter and frowned when she spoke. "Did my brother agree to inject himself, or did you take matters into your own hands?"

"I would never force something on someone; in fact, I told him he shouldn't have injected the entire vial into his veins, but he did everything too fast. I had no chance to warn him against it."

"So you've never experimented on anyone before while working with your family?"

"I was told that everyone within the walls of Titan was a willing participant." She looked each person in the eye before settling back on Rome. "I know now that my family lied to me. I will do whatever I can to help you bring them down."

Rome glanced towards his mate to stare into her eyes. To Na'tori, they looked to be communicating in their own way without ever speaking a word, but she also knew they might have been speaking telepathically. Rome's power was vast. She didn't know much about the woman at his side, but if she was his partner, it wouldn't surprise Na'tori to know that she was powerful in her own right. Alondra was a potent healer; it was why she had been such a hot commodity for her brothers, but there were things her brothers didn't even know about the woman. Things she would never voice.

Amirishka stepped forward and snagged her attention effortlessly. When she spoke, her voice was husky and mixed with a sexual undertone that made her voice compelling. She'd noticed it before, but now it was stronger. "Would you return to the lion's den and be a double agent for us? Would you learn everything you could and report back to us?"

Na'tori's eyes widened in shock. That had been the last thing she'd been expecting. Going back into the lion's den? It didn't sound like a smart plan. If her brothers ever learned what she was doing, she was dead. That was a given. She stood swiftly and paced the bit of space in front of her, her mind running through all the possible scenarios that would come of this if she did what Amirishka was asking. No one voiced concerns, not even Rome, so they must have all been okay with this. Had they already talked and agreed that she would be their double agent? She didn't think this was something she could do. She opened her mouth to voice that she didn't think she could do what they were asking of her when a gust of air hit her back along with the press of a muscular body as an equally muscular arm circled her waist and held her captive.

"Shit!" Akio exclaimed as each warrior stood up and locked intense gazes on the person at her back.

A nose skimmed her throat as the arm around her waist tightened a fraction more, and the feeling of an enormous erection pressed against her lower back. Her nails dug into the skin of the man's forearm just as the scent of him registered in her mind. He smelled like winter. It was a fresh scent that caused her nipples to peak and her core to dampen in embarrassment, but joy also filled her. Without needing to look, she knew without a doubt in her mind that Alaric stood behind her, but that didn't explain why everyone else in the room looked worried. Everyone watched them with shocked expressions as his wet tongue slid along the base of her throat and caused a soft mewl of need to leave through her barely parted lips.

"A-a-Alaric?" Na'tori whispered as embarrassment flooded her veins. "What are you doing?" She couldn't believe he'd just licked her as if there wasn't a room full of people watching them just as intently as she watched them.

"Shouldn't we be breaking this up?" Maverick frowned. "He looks hungry to me."

"Yet he hasn't attempted anything." As he took a hesitant step forward, Rome stated, "I haven't been able to pierce his mental shields to gauge his feelings. His shields are stronger now."

A feral snarl came from the male at her back. The sound caused every hair on her body to stand at attention as awareness spread through her. Fear and desire made her pulse leap beneath the pressure of something sharp scraping against her jugular. She'd never been bitten by a set of fangs before, but she was sure that's what she was feeling, and the last time she checked, Alaric didn't have any.

"We need to stop whatever this is." Silas frowned, "Something isn't right, Romulus."

Na'tori felt Alaric shift behind her; his hand had somehow worked its way beneath her shirt to caress his thumb against the softness of her skin. She wasn't sure what was happening with him, but the fact that he was alive and moving around made her giddy with excitement, even as everyone else remained tense. They thought something was wrong, yet she knew everything would be alright now. She hadn't killed him.

Rome spoke calmly, yet she could see the apparent concern written in his gaze. "Erick, do what you need to do."

One moment, she was being embraced by Alaric as everyone stood around them with fearful expressions, and the next moment, she was blinking; his hold was gone, and Alaric, Silas, Erick, and Rome were no longer in the room with them. She didn't have to look around to know that Alaric had been pulled from the room. She couldn't feel him, yet she could hear a bellow of rage coming from the lower levels where she had been locked up before and knew without a doubt that it was him. She moved for the hallway that would lead her to him but had to pause when a massive chest filled her vision, and Maverick's growly voice spoke to her.

"We can't let you down there until we figure out how he's feeling. Rome doesn't want you getting hurt because Alaric can't control himself."

"Control himself for what purpose? He wasn't doing anything wrong. Can somebody tell me what just happened and why I didn't see anyone move and yet four people are missing." She replied with more fire behind her words than she'd intended, but she couldn't help it. Na'tori was pissed. Nothing made sense, and the one person she knew would be on her side was being kept from her.

"He's not the same Alaric from before. I'm sure Rome will explain everything to you later, or maybe even my brother will."

Alara commented. "For right now, there's nothing you or anyone else in this room could do to help Alaric through this transition in his life. Maybe we should spend this time getting to know you more to put everyone at ease with you being here. My husband is still focused on everything going on up here, even if he's dealing with the problems below."

"Yeah, maybe you can finally tell us your ability." Cairo interceded.

She met his stare even as Maverick towered over her with his fuck you attitude. "Explain to me what just happened, and I will."

"Erick can manipulate time. He paused it for the time needed to get Alaric, Rome, and Silas out of the room and down to the cells below." Cairo approached them and pushed Maverick to stand elsewhere as his turquoise and dark purple gaze observed her. "Now you…what ability do you have?"

Na'tori wasn't intimidated by him in the slightest because he didn't give off his friend's aggression, but that didn't stop her from being wary of the male. She hesitantly stepped back and glanced over to see Maverick and Amirishka whispering to each other while Alondra and Alara watched them intently.

"Auras," she finally replied as she focused back on the male before her, "I see the waves that ripple around a person, and they tell me whether they are human, Kindred, Rogue, or an Eternal."

He cocked his head to the side and smiled. "And what does my aura say?"

His aura pulsed like Rome's, white and blinding yet softer in nature and closer to his body as if something contained it. The white energy curled around him like a second skin. There was no mistaking him as anything but an Eternal that was very put together and balanced. Maybe even too controlled.

"You like control. You're definitely an Eternal but more self-contained than the others. Your aura doesn't flare. It flattens to you as if you're controlling its very presence."

"Hmmm," he stepped back and inclined his head as if to say thank you before he spoke again, "And when you look in the mirror, what do you see of your own aura?"

"All Kindred have a violet aura around them. Mine is brighter than most, though."

Alara grabbed her attention when she stepped forward with a frown that screamed confusion. "If you're a Kindred but Lukas, Ezekiel, and Evan are your brothers, does that mean they are Kindred as well?"

She shook her head vehemently. "No! If they had abilities, this war you guys seem to be in would be going much differently. My mom cheated on their father with someone unknown, and I came out of that union. I'm still unsure who my father is, but he has to carry the Kindred gene. He may have recessive genes and no powers to speak of."

"That would suck." Alondra chuckled.

Alara gave her sister a sharp look and shook her head. "It isn't funny, Alo," she looked toward Maverick and Amirishka and frowned, "The meeting is over, so I suggest you two head out while there's still darkness out."

"Rome would kill us if we left you alone with her." Maverick snarled.

"Do you think I can't handle my own? That you and Ami haven't trained me well enough to knock someone on their ass? OR the fact that Romulus is right downstairs." She snapped back.

Na'tori didn't think seeing a male as large and imposing as Maverick blush was possible, but she was seeing it firsthand. He looked apologetic for several moments before nodding and leaving the room quickly, with Amirishka following closely behind him. Cairo stayed until Alara gave him a stern look as well, but when he left, he did it with a smile.

"Before you ask, they're more afraid of my mate than me. Now, are you hungry? I planned on making some baked chicken with greens and potatoes, and I know you haven't eaten anything since early this morning. Nevertheless, let's talk while I cook." Alara walked away, Alondra followed behind her, and Na'tori glanced towards the door leading downstairs before she followed them.

CHAPTER
SIXTEEN

Alaric paced the length of the cell Rome and those other assholes had thrown him in and barely contained the snarl that vibrated within his chest. He could smell and hear everything more intensely now, and the feel of sharp fangs poking into his bottom lip assured him that he was indeed an Eternal now. His body was stronger, and so was his mind. He realized his ability was fighting against him when the urge to crush the minds around him slammed through him, and he barely held that dark, twisted need back.

"Alaric!" Rome snapped as he slammed his palm against the bar of the cell and allowed his skin to pinken slightly before he pulled back with a glare. "We're trying to fucking help you, but we need you to tell us what you're feeling so we can do that. Silas nor I can read you, so fucking speak, dammit, and drink the blood we've left you."

Alaric ran into the bars and growled in agony when his hands gripped the silver and burn marks appeared on his flesh almost instantly. He pulled away but kept his eyes trained on the men before him. His flesh didn't begin to heal like it should, but he didn't care. They'd snatched him away from Na'tori. He'd been so fucking close to sinking his fangs into what he knew would be a heavenly source of blood when they'd stopped him. Now, he wanted their blood on his hands. He wanted their pain, yet something held him back. It could be his conscience, but Alaric knew it was more than that. Alara would forever hate him if he injured her mate, so Rome was off-limits, but the other two…Silas and Erick were fair game.

Silas sighed heavily. "Dammit, just drink the damn blood, would you?"

"You fucking drink it!" Alaric snarled, grabbed a bag of blood that sat on the cot within the cell, and launched it towards them.

It splattered on impact, sending blood everywhere as the aroma of copper filled the air. His gums pulsed, and a twinge of pain rocked his gut as hunger beat against him. The need to feed was foreign and uncomfortable, but it fueled the rage that was already pulsing through him, so he acted without regret and said fuck the consequences. He focused on Silas and Erick and dove into their minds with little effort.

Silas's shields were more challenging to break, but when they broke, there was a wealth of knowledge he hadn't been anticipating. Silas was a lot smarter than people gave him credit for, and seeing the future allowed him to see things that had not yet begun. Alaric viewed a moment like that now. It was something hazy, almost as if it had yet to happen. Silas appeared to be sitting alone, yet he was speaking aloud or telling someone how fate had fucked them all, and someone would die. He attempted to dive deeper into Silas's mind, or more specifically that memory when the man himself spoke.

"Alaric, what the fuck are you doing? You need to get out of my head! You aren't meant to see these things!"

"It's okay. I've seen enough as it is."

Alaric pulled from Silas's mind, but not before forcing him to fall asleep. Rome's curse could be heard, yet he ignored it and pierced Erick's mind only to find that it was laid bare, and everything looked as if it were moving in slow motion. Is this how he saw life? Did his ability to manipulate time also bleed into his thoughts and memories? Alaric smirked at the idea and decided to speed things up a bit to help him out before he pulled from his mind as well. He kept Erick awake, though, and smiled when he stared back at him in utter shock.

"What have you done?" Erick whispered almost brokenly as he placed his palm against his head.

"Just helped you out a bit."

Erick stormed off without another word as Rome crouched beside Silas to push healing waves into his body. Alaric stepped back until the cot hit his legs. Then, he took a seat and simply waited. Rome didn't need to speak for Alaric to know that he was pissed. He could feel the wrath that radiated from his body. It was potent and barely contained, especially when his cool blue gaze landed on him, and his fangs peeked out from behind his lips.

"Get a handle on that anger, or I'll forget you're my mate's brother." Rome ordered just as Silas jerked awake beneath his hand, "Now drink that fucking blood before I shove it down your damn throat, you ungrateful piece of shit."

He was tempted to ignore him, but the hunger pains persisted, and an ache began to resonate through his bones, signaling that something was very wrong. Alaric picked up another blood bag and stared at the red liquid. His stomach cramped violently before lifting it to his lips and punching his fangs through the plastic. The first drop hit his tongue, causing him to groan in pleasure as he sucked it down in seconds. His entire body tingled when he dropped his fifth bag onto the cell floor, and his mind finally settled enough to piece together the last thirty minutes. His mind searched for Erick's mental signature, attempted to right the wrong he'd committed, and found him inaccessible.

"Fuck," he murmured and came to his feet slowly.

"Fuck is right, my friend," Silas glared as he climbed to his feet, "what the hell did you do to Erick?"

"I sped up his memories and thoughts." He replied as guilt tore through him.

"Explain," Rome stated calmly, yet blue fire raged within his eyes, and black shadows swirled around him.

Alaric stepped up to the blood-coated bars and sighed heavily.

"His mind was slow. It was moving at a snail's pace, so I manipulated his thoughts to speed up."

"And what did you hope to gain? You don't even know the first thing about Erick to subject him to that." Rome snarled as his wings snapped out. The force of them and the telekinetic energy he released sent objects crashing to the ground around them as his anger mounted with every word he spoke. "His ability to manipulate time causes his mind to process things differently than us. You could very well have just signed him up for a mental roller coaster of a lifetime. This could break him, Alaric, so I suggest you fix it!"

"I can't. I already tried."

A pulse of energy slammed into Alaric's chest and sent him crashing into the wall before he was held there by an invisible force. He wasn't choking, but he might as well have been when he realized he couldn't catch his breath and a few of his ribs might have been broken. He groaned in pain yet didn't struggle to be let down or seek retribution for being thrown into the wall. He stayed still and simply waited. He wouldn't anger him more because, for once, he wasn't sure Rome would care if he walked away from this alive.

"Romulus," Silas cautioned, "I'm sure he didn't actually mean to leave a lasting mark on Erick's mind. Maybe he thought it would be an easy fix, and that's why he chose to do that."

"Of course, you want to stick up for him." Rome snarled, "You have no idea what he's done, Si. You have no idea how hard Erick might now struggle with using his abilities! You understand nothing!"

Silas held his hands up in a placating gesture and took several steps back when Rome's wingspan spread wider, and his fingertips began to sprout claws. His energy swelled within the room, seeming to suck the life out of the very air around them. Alaric attempted to speak and explain himself yet found it a struggle when he realized he was still incapable of catching his breath. Every inhale and exhale sent a shooting pain through his lungs, and all he could do was groan even when the taste of blood settled on his tongue. He watched Silas open his mouth to speak again, yet paused when Alara and Na'tori descended the steps together.

"Put my brother down this instant, Romulus, or so help me, God, you'll be cut off from all access to me!" Alara snapped as she stormed for her mate. "And open the damn cell so I can heal him."

Rome released an exasperated sigh, dropped his hold on Alaric, and composed himself in a matter of moments, but Alaric could see the desire within his gaze to keep going. If his sister hadn't walked in, there was no telling what would have transpired without her interruption. Rome could have very well killed him. And he would have deserved it.

"He's an Eternal now. He can heal himself." Rome grumbled as he unlocked the door to the cell and shook his head in annoyance.

Alaric could barely keep his feet beneath him as he made his way to the cot to sit down and breathe through the pain. One thing he made sure to do was keep his eyes on the woman that he'd returned for. Na'tori looked out of place among the people he considered family, yet she refused to stand on the sidelines and keep her distance. She was right on Alara's heels as she entered the cell, her platinum blonde hair tied tightly into a bun atop her head, and her opalescent gaze watched him wearily when she stood only a few inches away from him. He felt it the moment Alara began to knit and heal the damage that had been done to his body, but he was incapable of focusing on that. No. His senses and every part of his being were centered on the woman who smelled of honey and elderberry flowers.

He grew uncomfortable as his cock lengthened in his jeans and his fangs sharpened within his mouth, yet he had no control over the reaction. The temptation to snatch her right off her feet to impale her on his dick as he sank his fangs into her throat was so alarming that he jerked away from Alara's healing touch to cross the cell and put distance between him and the woman that was begin-ning to live permanently within his mind. That darkness within his mind that always urged him to use his gifts to do bad pressed heavily against his mind as thoughts of ravishing her drowned his thoughts, and all he wanted to do was take her beneath him in the worst way. His mind flashed back to the time his face was buried between her thighs; the remembrance of her taste caused his fangs to sharpen further as his hands balled into fists, and he was sure his eyes were now glowing.

"What's wrong?" Alara questioned with a frown, "I haven't finished healing you yet; your ribs still need healing."

She moved to approach him once more, but Rome grabbed her arm and pulled her back. "Wait, little flower, let him adjust." He blocked her with his body and watched Alaric calmly; the anger he'd had only moments ago was now replaced with concern. "Gather yourself and tell me what you're feeling."

Alaric's eyes were laser-focused on Na'tori when he spoke, "I died. I know I died because the Gods told me when I saw them in whatever plane they exist in, that I could come back but I would be changed. I knew what that meant, but I gave them stipulations because they wanted me back here. They wanted me to fight in this war for whatever purpose suits them."

"You argued with them and gave them demands?" Silas asked incredulously. "I'm surprised you're even here right now."

"Agreed," Rome chuckled. "So what happened? What did you ask for?"

"I wanted a mate, but it could only be Na'tori. If not her, then they could go to hell."

Na'tori's eyes widened in shock. "You asked for me?" She whispered, "But we barely know one another." She shook her head adamantly, "Alaric, I'm the reason you died. I caused all of this. I can't be the reason you chose to live."

"I don't give a shit." Alaric snapped. He wanted to drag her into his arms and keep her there, but he needed to get these strong urges that were running through him under control before he did anything to jeopardize whatever they were to each other. "I have forever, which means I can take years, maybe even centuries, getting to know the woman I know I want to make mine. I can't tell you why I feel the way I do. I don't know what draws me to you so utterly and completely, but I want to figure it out. I want to see what this could be. I wanted it enough to fight that bastard Ares to get what I desired."

"You fought Ares and walked away?" Silas chuckled, "No

fucking way you fought a God and lived to tell the damn tale. No fucking way."

Alaric finally pulled his eyes away from his woman to focus on his best friend. "I was promised that if I fought him and won, I would get three questions and the woman I desired, so I made sure to fucking win Si. I wasn't coming back here otherwise, and you know I never wanted this life. I never wanted to live forever." He met Na'tori's gaze again and finally felt the tension leave his body. "I never wanted forever until that night on the dance floor."

He held out his hand, hoping she would come to him, and wasn't disappointed when she crossed the room and took it. She smiled softly as he pulled her into his body and inhaled harshly. He groaned in pleasure and almost closed his eyes to bask in the sensation of having her pressed against him, but his gaze caught on Rome's questioning stare, so he kept himself from burying his nose into her hair to take in more of her scent and straightened.

"What is it?" He questioned, making sure to show his annoyance in his tone.

Rome shook his head slightly and turned his gaze on Na'tori. "You don't know what mating an Eternal is, do you?"

Alaric snarled and pulled her behind his back. "We aren't there yet, dammit. Didn't you just hear what I said? We have time to learn from each other. She has time to learn everything she would need to know and if she wants this."

"You think I don't know the urges that are driving you? I can see in your eyes how much she's affecting you just by being near you, Alaric. You won't be able to help yourself. You'll want to fuck her and bite her at every opportunity. What if she disagrees? You're newly turned! You don't have years of teaching yourself to push back certain urges you'll have. Do you not remember what you did to Erick only moments ago because of your anger or whatever the hell that was?" He stepped forward and glared, "Don't do this, brother. Think about what I'm telling you and let it digest. You remember how I was with your sister. You may not know the nitty gritty, but you knew enough to know I wasn't acting rationally at times. Everyone did."

129

"What is he talking about?" Na'tori frowned. Her small hands gripped his arm and sent a spike of desire running through him.

Fuck. Rome was right. Even though his need had leveled out, he still felt a pull. It wasn't just sexual; there was something more, something hard and demanding that tugged at his entire being, but he forced himself to ignore it.

"So what would you suggest, Romulus?" Alaric slowly released his fists until his hands hung loosely at his sides, but that darkness in his mind rammed against the barrier he'd slid into place.

Rome glanced at Alara and sighed heavily. "Many won't agree with what I'm about to say, yet it needs to be said." His gaze sharpened on Alaric, "Maybe it would be best if you stayed below within a cell at least until you get a handle on your amplified emotions and Na'tori comes around to everything that goes on in our world."

Alaric was already shaking his head in denial when Na'tori's blunt nails dug into his arm, dragging his attention away from his pain-in-the-ass brother-in-law. He glanced into her eyes and frowned at what he saw there. His mind reached out for hers in an effort to read her and know why she looked fearful but encountered her diamond walls instead. His voice was soft when he addressed her. "What is it, princess?"

"I think maybe you should do it…" She fiddled with her fingers and refused to meet his eyes, "just for now." She whispered.

He looked to Rome and nodded solemnly. Something was making her hesitant, and if his being behind bars would ease her through whatever this was between them, he would do it. Besides, Rome was right. The desire to take her was strong, and he was barely holding it back, along with the overwhelming flood of sensations that were filling him. Alaric didn't just need to do this for her; he also needed to do it for himself. He kissed the top of Na'tori's head and mentally prepared himself for the road ahead, but he also needed to get his body on board. That's where the real challenge would lie if he couldn't push the dark thoughts back.

CHAPTER
SEVENTEEN

N a'tori sat across the island table from Alara as she cooked breakfast at the stove, yet her eyes stared at the man standing several feet away. The sun shone through the window, illuminating his form as he stood at the sink with crossed arms and ankles. The rest of the warriors were already asleep due to the sun's appearance in the sky, yet Rome was moving freely about.

She tapped her fingers against the countertop as she spoke. "How are you awake, yet the other Guardians were forced to fall asleep? I know the sun affects your kind, but you seem unbothered; why is that?"

Alara chuckled, and Rome smiled softly at his mate before his blue eyes found Na'tori. His voice was softer now than it had been hours ago. "I'm the King of my species for a reason. Not because I'm the eldest of my kind but because I was gifted by the Gods at a time in my life when I nearly lost the other half of my soul. They granted me the ability to walk among the sun's rays again after blessing me with gifts so I'm not weakened by that big ball in the sky. Age does help an Eternal in some ways to deal with exposure, but

133

most are compelled to sleep almost instantly. Alaric, for instance, will be especially susceptible because he is newly made."

"Can you explain how that's possible? I was told that you're the reason he's alive. You did something to make him as he is."

He nodded and seemed to think his answer over for several moments before he spoke. "Telling you these things ensures that you will be incapable of leaving my group if I do. Regardless of the path you and Alaric take, I won't allow you the freedom you could have with the knowledge I could provide you with. Are you okay with that?"

Na'tori played with the idea in her mind. If her and Alaric's paths didn't align, she would still have a place among the Eternals, but would she want that? Would she want to see him day in and day out and not have him? She couldn't answer that. Alaric was right about one thing, though. There was a pull between them, something urging her to be closer, know him deeper than maybe he even knew himself. The draw to know his every fear and desire, the draw to know his body as intimately as she knew her own, and the draw to find herself entangled in him. All of that was there, but it scared her. The feelings he brought out of her were intense, and she didn't know how to decipher it or what any of it meant. She did know she didn't want to go back with her family. She wouldn't be sucked back into the darkness and despair that they'd draped around her throat for the entirety of her life. Was this her chance to be free of them?

"If I decide I don't want the answers and I just want to be free of everything, including your people, could you do that for me? Would you help me stay off the radar from Titan?"

Rome chuckled. "If that's truly what you wanted, I could, but why would I?"

Alara grabbed a nearby dish towel and tossed it at him. "Don't act like you wouldn't help her. Since she got here, I've been telling you that she didn't know anything about her family's actions. She was an accessory to crimes she wasn't even aware of. You'll help her or else."

He grabbed her from behind by her throat and smirked before his face dipped into the crook of her neck to speak. "If you threaten me one more time, little flower, I'll spank your beautiful ass until you're begging me for release. We have company, so unless you want her to see you spread out and split open by my dick on this island, I suggest you watch your tone." He kissed her cheek softly and stepped back before reclaiming his spot in front of the sink, "Now finish making breakfast, love. You know I love to watch you cook."

She watched as a deep blush covered Alara's face before she quickly went back to cooking and busying herself. Na'tori felt like an interloper as the sexual chemistry between them snapped and sparked throughout the room, yet when Rome's eyes settled on her once more, she saw that he was hoping Alara would test it. She blushed furiously and looked away.

"I apologize, Na'tori, although my mate is correct, I would help you if that's truly what you wanted." He stated.

She nodded in understanding and weighed her options, but it didn't take her long to decide. Learning what she could about the Eternals would put her in a place to get close to the men and women who held a wealth of DNA within them that she wanted more knowledge on. The scientific part of her couldn't deny that she wanted answers, but there was also the side of her that simply wanted to know the man who had fought death for her.

She found the courage to look him in the eyes again as she spoke. "I want to know more, and you can just call me Tori."

"Alright, Tori, I'll give you a little history lesson then, but first answer me this," he circled the island until he stood beside her, and his eyes gave off an eerie glow as his aura pulsed around him almost angrily. "Why can you keep me out of your head, and if I asked you to lower your mental shields, would you?"

"When I was younger, I felt the malevolence that surrounded what you call Rogues, and I did my best to protect myself. I never really knew what they could do, and then I ran into a Kindred who could read my mind, and she taught me how to protect myself from those who would try to use my thoughts against me. I also learned that it's a lot harder for a Rogue to compel you if your mental shields can keep them out." She replied as she steadily tapped her fingers against the counter. "To answer your other question...I don't know how to lower them even if I wanted to. I've kept them up for so long that I struggle to peel the layers back."

Rome seemed to accept her answer and stepped back before he sat in the chair beside her. "What happened to the Kindred that taught you? Where did she end up?"

"I'm not sure."

"You are unsure, or you don't want to say?"

"Both," she whispered brokenly as she dropped her gaze. "The things I did for my family make me feel ashamed because I didn't know their true evil, and now that I do, I replay the things I did for them, all for the sake of family, and it makes me sick. I don't know where she ended up because the last time I saw her, she was in a coma." Tears gathered in her eyes and poured over to coat her cheeks.

"Tori, I need you to look at me and tell me how."

"Romulus," Alara chided, "can't you see that this is hard for her?"

"You're too soft, little flower. You know that I need answers just as she does. She wants to know the history of my people, and we had plans to enlighten her on what she has to look forward to if she truly plans to deal with your brother. She needs to be ready for this world. We can't wear kid gloves here."

Na'tori wiped furiously at the flow of tears because he was right. Her brothers wouldn't fight fairly in this war. They would use every dirty trick within their arsenal. An arsenal that she had helped them to build. She needed to be stronger to deal with this and ready to talk about the complicated topics that would put her in a bad light no matter how brightly that light shined. She swallowed to rid herself of the tight, burning sensation in her throat before revealing one of her dark truths.

"I never knew her name; my family always labeled them as subjects, so she was known as subject 6. I don't know if that made her their sixth test subject or what, but she was by far the sweetest person I'd ever run into. Her aura told me she was gifted. She was a Kindred with the ability of telepathy and empathy. The empath part took my mother a long time to figure out, but when she did, she used that against her. I don't know how she did, but when it came time for my mother to test out the drug I'd created, subject six volunteered...or at least that's what my mother told me. She was under anesthesia when she came to me. I never had a chance to talk to her; I just believed what my mother was telling me, so I gave her the drug. She never woke up again, but her vitals remained steady. After that, I never saw her again."

Rome frowned, "So, at what point did she have the ability to speak to you to teach you how to shield your mind, and why did she never tell you her name?"

"She was awake for her blood draws, so we spoke every chance we got. All the cameras and gadgets weren't necessary then, so my family never knew until Dr. Salazar walked in one evening and found us laughing together as if we were friends. They enforced monitoring systems and told me not to engage, but by then, she had already taught me what I needed to know." Na'tori's sigh was full of pain and anguish, "I can't tell you why she never told me her name, and I never thought to ask. She was my first subject."

Alara dropped the pot she was holding, oatmeal scattered across the kitchen floor, and sent Rome teleporting to her side.

"What is it, little flower? Are you hurt?" He looked her over carefully before guiding her to sit at the island.

She shook her head as she peered into his eyes, a look of anguish filling her expression as she clung to him. Na'tori wasn't sure how to react. She wasn't even sure what to say, but Rome seemed to know. His eyes bore into Alara's, and she just knew they were speaking telepathically. So, she waited, although her mind spun with scenarios and possibilities.

It had to be something she'd said, but what?

Rome sighed heavily, kissed his mate's head, and moved to clean up the mess on the floor as he spoke steadily and calmly. "Did you know that my wife and her siblings were victims of Titan since their birth?"

Na'tori shook her head. "No, of course not. I thought they worked for the company willingly."

"If that had been the case, our lives would be operating much differently than they are right now." He threw the noodles into the trash and mopped the floor earnestly as he spoke. "They were known as subjects one, two, and three, so discussing the woman who fell into a coma from your doing is a bit of an emotional roller-coaster for her. You'll have to forgive her; she's just not used to hearing these stories about others who have been victimized by your family."

"It's okay, I understand. Did you want to know anything else, or maybe now we could discuss Alaric and how his being an Eternal is even possible?"

She wasn't trying to simply dismiss the conversation, but she had answered his questions, and now she needed some answers of her own. It wasn't just the scientific curiosity that made her want to know; the discovery of Eternals being capable of producing more of themselves drove her. The very thing that would build her brother's empire was the very thing that had made Alaric. She wanted the knowledge so that she could keep it forever hidden from her family if possible. She couldn't allow them to know.

Rome returned the swifter to where it belonged before he moved to stand beside his wife. He placed a gentle hand on the back of Alara's throat and rubbed soothing circles into her skin as he spoke. "Are you aware that only one pair of chromosomes separates a Kindred from a human?"

She nodded slowly, wondering where this was going. For years, she had known that a Kindred had one pair of chromosomes that made a difference in their DNA enough to separate them from a human. Even a doctor wouldn't notice the slight difference if they drew blood and ran it through every test known to man. That singular cell was buried so deeply within a Kindred's genome that even she had missed it, at least until she'd stopped looking at things from a scientific standpoint. She'd stepped back, used her ability to look into the microscope where a slide of her blood had sat, and saw the small trace amounts of a violet aura peering back at her. She'd identified it through new eyes but had never been able to separate it.

"Kindred carry one percent of DNA that gives them abilities.

That's the one thing that makes them unique among humans." Rome stated calmly, "An Eternal, on the other hand, is different. I can't tell you about our genetic makeup because I never wanted to know, but our blood has healing properties. Enough properties that if given to a Kindred, we can essentially turn them into a Guardian, but it is forbidden. In fact, it wasn't until recently that my people even knew it was possible, but circumstances with Alaric changed things."

Na'tori's mind raced. She wanted to dissect the information given to her and then do the research herself. Could she separate the cells that created their makeup and locate what made that possible? Was it a blood transfer that gave them that edge? She had so many questions rattling her brain that it took her a moment to notice that Rome was speaking again.

"It sounds callous, but if not for the fact that I was given specific instructions by my superiors to save him, then he would have died, and my people never would have known just what their blood is capable of doing."

"You have superiors?" She frowned as she watched him, trying to piece together what that meant when Alaric's statement from earlier tugged at the back of her mind. "Wait, do you mean the Gods? That wasn't just a figment of speech earlier when Alaric said he fought Ares, God of war? Did you really mean the Gods assisted you before? I thought they were myths and legends."

"To most people, they are, but to us, they are our rulers. To us, they carry the gauntlet that sets us on the paths we must take to ensure the survival of not just humans but of our own species as well. They are our creators."

"Eternals are Gods!?"

Alara chuckled lightly, her emotions finally bottled away from earlier as she smiled softly, yet the smile never touched her eyes when she spoke. "They aren't Gods, but they carry trace amounts of their DNA within them, giving them immortality. Rome's as close to one as they could possibly get."

"But you're still a Kindred," Na'tori looked her up and down as she analyzed her deeper, "Won't you die while he continues to stay young? You don't have his longevity, do you, or am I missing something?"

Alara blushed furiously as Rome sifted his fingers through her hair and kissed her forehead with a chuckle. "I'll let you explain this part, little flower. Tell her what she needs to look forward to if she goes through with things with your brother."

"Can you make a new pot of oatmeal to go with the bacon and eggs?"

"Of course."

Once again, Na'tori felt like she was seeing an intimate moment meant for only them when Rome nodded and dragged his mate into his arms to kiss her. It wasn't a chaste kiss. It was a kiss meant to sear someone to their very soul and make their toes curl if the slip of tongue between them was any indication. Na'tori cleared her throat when Rome gripped Alara by the throat, and dark shadows began to slowly circle them in an embrace. She watched him reluctantly draw away after giving her a hard stare. His eyes brightened and illuminated his annoyance at being interrupted, but he moved away and began to make the oatmeal even as his eyes stayed on his mate.

"Ok," Alara tugged at the hem of her sweater as she spoke. "I'll remain a Kindred, and as long as Rome gives me a few drops of his blood every few months, then I will remain young and healthy beside him."

"Everything is in the blood," Na'tori whispered back. "But what does that have to do with Alaric and me? I won't be exchanging blood with him."

"You might think differently if you take up his offer to mate. I can't tell you I know my brother in and out, but I know enough to realize that he's a very serious man when it comes to getting the things he desires. He got me out of Titan. Without him, I would still be trapped within those walls, experiencing God only knows what, but he wouldn't have that. He wanted to save Alondra and me, and so he did. When it comes to you, I think he'll pursue you unless you tell him otherwise, and if you do agree to mate with him, an exchange of blood needs to happen while you're...um, intimate."

It was Na'tori's turn to blush. Sex wasn't anything she'd ever discussed with anyone before, so doing it now, especially with the sister of the man who had recently gone down on her, made her face heat with embarrassment. It wasn't that she didn't know the mechanics of sex. She knew them quite well due to her extensive research in her early twenties, but discussing them outside of a scientific standpoint made her nervous. Everyone she knew had some experience, and all she had to go off of was the feelings Alaric had elicited from her. She wanted to learn more, but was his sister the best person to discuss this with?

"S-so," she tucked her hair behind her ear, trying to keep the nervous stutter from entering her voice again. "By intimate, do you mean sex? We have to have sex and exchange blood for me to age at his pace?"

"No, you have to have sex, and he'll mark you with a bite to solidify the mating. The exchange of blood comes after that. Even Rome and I were unsure of how everything was supposed to go, but we learned quickly when I started to feel the urge to take in his blood as well. At first, I was disgusted at the thought because it's blood, you know, but our mating triggered something in me that had me questioning if I should, so one day, we took that next step and noticed how healthy I was beginning to look after a few days.

"So if there's no bite, what happens?"

Rome jumped back into the conversation just as the oatmeal finished cooking on the stove and served each of them a bowl with a small plate of fruit, bacon, and eggs. "Without the bite, there will be no mating, but if you are, in fact, his "one," he will feel the urge to mark you every waking day until it happens. It's a biological need for us to mark what we consider to be ours."

"And if I refuse?"

He shrugged. "Alara and I are the first mated couple to exist, so there's no telling if you'll even be able to deny the need that will go through the both of you. Not just him."

"Okay, I understand. Could I do some research to further discover what this mating phenomenon does and causes between couples? And would it be okay if I used you as the foundational basis of discovery?" Na'tori questioned.

She wasn't sure if they would agree, but she couldn't help but ask. The wealth of knowledge within their bodies could help her and Alaric navigate this biological need if she knew what buttons to push. Rome and Alara studied each other before Rome nodded.

"It's possible that your research could help my people if or when their mates come along. I can already tell Alaric may have a tougher time than I did because of his newborn status, so I need to know if anyone else will react negatively. This is something you could do?"

"I can do my absolute best, and thank you for trusting me with this information. I won't disappoint you." Na'tori made sure to look into Rome's eyes when she spoke to convey that she meant every word she said.

He smirked. "I know you won't, Tori."

She wasn't sure if the look in his eyes was a veiled threat, but she didn't let it bother her. She now knew things that could help her assist the men and women she was now siding with. Whatever she needed to do to help them fight against her family, she would do it. Na'tori shoveled food into her mouth as her thoughts ran through the conversation. She began to plot her first move in helping the Eternals and the Kindred to better their race, but in the back of her mind, she thought of Alaric. She wanted to check on him but knew he would sleep until the sunset. That gave her time to discern how she would approach their relationship because even though she hardly knew the man, she understood that they were something. The pull towards him was strong; she wouldn't deny it, but what did that leave her with? Would he let her lead, or would he take the reins and bend her to his needs and will?

CHAPTER
EIGHTEEN

Alaric at Age Sixteen

Two chuckled as he read over the message he'd received from Lukas. It looked like he wanted to get into some more trouble later today, and Two was down for that. Lukas was like the older brother he needed. No other teens or kids lived within the building, and Lukas was the closest one to his age at thirty-one and the only one who seemed to want to be around him. The rest of the men and women saw him as a freak of nature.

Lately, things had been quiet within the facility, and Lukas's mother—Alma—hadn't been hard on him to interrogate the strange fang-like beings known as Rogues that they employed, but she'd asked him to meet her in lab three. That's where he was headed now, but he wanted to be anywhere else. He had worked for Titan since the age of thirteen but had been with them since birth. He scratched the skin beneath the collar around his throat and entered the lab to find it empty and sterile. It was unusual, surprising even because someone was always in the labs. To see them empty meant something was possibly wrong. He gripped the gold band around his throat and groaned in annoyance. He wished he didn't have to wear the damn thing, but Alma had told him his abilities made the others nervous, and how he used them to expel information made them even more scared to be around him. The collar was for protection. He wasn't sure if he fully *believed that statement, but he never went against it when they reactivated the device after he played his part.*

He sent a quick text to Alma and Dr. Salazar and notified them that he was in the lab before making his way over to the doctor's desk, where he sat down and kicked his feet up. The weight and force of his large feet hitting the wood sent the stapler and a few other items scattering to the floor. Fuck. He sighed heavily and moved to pick up everything. If the good doctor walked in now and saw his shit all over the floor, he'd be forced to clean the lab from top to bottom and donate blood on top of it. If he hadn't been around the man for years, he would have thought Dr. Salazar was a Rogue as well, given how he took blood from him nearly every week.

He was under the desk, picking up the last bit of paper off the ground, when the edge of a letter caught his eye. It was wedged between a part of the wood desk as if placed there and not something that had simply fallen. It took some doing before he pulled it out. Three names were scrawled across the letter: Alaric, Alondra & Alara. Who the hell were they? He opened the letter and pulled out a thick parchment paper before reading.

DEAR CHILDREN,

It is our hope that you find this letter before your lives are completely overrun by the restrictions and regulations that Titan instills in its people. From the moment of your birth, you three were taken away from us and given numbers as names. You were only seen as Subjects 1,2 & 3, and each of you had a specific purpose within the company if you were to show that you were gifted like your mother and I. We prayed that the day would never come and that you all would remain powerless, but our prayers were never answered. We knew it even before your birth; we just prayed we were wrong, but Alara's abilities presented themselves six months after birth, and from there, it was a domino effect that triggered the rest of you. When that happened, we knew you three would be some of the most powerful beings to walk the earth.

Don't let the company control, contort, and diminish your worth. We know they'll separate you three as soon as possible, but for now, you're as thick as thieves. Alaric, son, I need you to protect your sisters when you're able. I know you'll be the telepathic child with the most significant possibility of greatness. Your mental fortitude will be the strongest to ever exist; I just know it, and your mother felt it as she carried you. With that gift, I need you to get you and your sisters away from this darkness. I need you to save them from the hell that could be their lives if you stay. Alara, your abilities are similar to your mother's. They will drain you and have you questioning if you're more of a danger to people than a help. Don't question yourself. Trust your instincts and fight for the things you love. Your heart will never steer you wrong. And finally, Alondra... our fighter, the baby that caused your mother all the pain in the world when she felt your struggles in the womb. You also have a part of your mother's gifts: the ability to heal. Use it. Heal those around you and heal yourself. Hold your siblings together when you each learn the truth and be the bridge that binds. Love endlessly and know that you are loved. All of you are so deeply loved, and we're sorry we couldn't do more to protect you.

P.S. Use this sign-on information to access the files you need to learn that this letter is authentic.

Email: ESalazar@titan.com

Password:Zxyw1234_ES

This letter is our plea to do what we couldn't. Save yourselves and find your joy.

Love, Mom & Dad

Two glared at the paper in his hands and scratched once more at the skin beneath the gold collar around his throat before he quickly used the login information to access whatever files this letter was referring to. He wiped at the stupid tears running down his cheeks, glanced towards the door to ensure he was still alone, and waited as the system booted itself up before he accessed a file labeled Triplets.

It took him nearly ten minutes to read through the entire thing because he had to read it twice to ensure he saw the words scattered before him. He knew Alma or Dr. Salazar could walk through those lab doors at any moment and punish him for what he was doing. Shit, he was lucky to even have a cellphone, so he knew being on the company computer would probably land him in solitary confinement or something much worse, but he couldn't bring himself to care.

Alaric.

His name was Alaric, not Two, and everyone within Titan had been lying to him for years, even Lukas, the only person he had ever really trusted. Anger festered and grew as he logged out of the system and rid himself of the letter that implicated him and everything he now had to care for. He would do what his parents had asked of him and save his sisters, but first, he had to find them. He would find them and save them, or he would die trying.

ALARIC JERKED awake to a stand with a snarl rumbling in his chest as his fangs dropped and his heart galloped away within his chest from the dream he'd torn himself away from. He nearly picked up the cot within his cell to throw it against the bars but paused instead when Na'tori's scent tickled his nose and sent his eyes scanning the dark room in search of her. He watched her tiptoe towards him before the bright overhead light flickered on and caused her to pause in the center of the room. A belly shirt and a pair of sleep shorts covered her body. Her hair had been pulled up on top of her head into a tight ponytail that made his hands itch to grab it, and he was once again stunned by her beauty.

He knew his eyes were still glowing and swirling with power when she simply stood there watching him reverently. Her eyes fell to his bare chest before skimming down to the black sweatpants that obscenely clung to him. There was no hiding the massive erection he sported. Since waking as an Eternal, it had been nearly impossible for him to not feel the thing in his pants as if it were another heartbeat. He remained hard constantly, and her standing there in basically nothing wasn't helping matters. Alaric could make out the hard tips of her breasts, and with his heightened senses, he could smell her need. A rumble started in his chest as he walked up to the bars and tilted his head in a predatory manner. He wanted her.

"I don't know what I felt, but I knew something was wrong," she whispered as she glanced over her shoulder to look back the way she'd come. "Everyone else went out for the night except for your sisters. It's ok that I came down here, right?"

"Come closer." His voice was deep, more animal than man.

"I think I should keep my distance." She rubbed at her arms as if she was cold and frowned. "Rome told me that you would be testy for some time and that I should never get too close to you, especially when your eyes are glowing as they are now."

He growled low and began to pace the length of his cell. "So why are you down here?"

"I told you because I felt something. Are you okay?"

"I'll be even better if you come over here."

"Tell me what you were dreaming about first."

He came to a standstill before approaching the bars once more. He dropped his voice to a seductive purr as he cupped the erection straining within the fabric of his sweats. "You want to bargain with me, princess?" He watched her bite into her bottom lip with a nod and smirked. "Okay, love, I'll tell you my dream, and you'll give me something I want. Deal?"

"Deal."

He tightened his hold on his dick and told himself to calm the hell down, but staring at Na'tori made that hard to do. She was breathtakingly beautiful. She watched him expectantly, just waiting for him to tell her what he'd been dreaming, yet he took his time drinking her in with his eyes as he plotted on what he wanted from her. He was tempted to ask her for her throat to sample a taste of her blood, but he knew that was a line they couldn't cross yet. Now that he was watching her facial expression, he knew exactly what he wanted from her.

"When I was about sixteen years old, I found a letter from my parents meant for my sisters and me. I was dreaming of the moment I learned of Titan and just what they were capable of."

Her eyes widened in shock as she approached the bars and wrapped her small hands around them. "You've fought against Titan since then?"

"Of course I have. As soon as I learned that they separated me from my sisters and caused the death of our parents, I needed to get Alondra and Alara as far away from that place as possible. I'm pissed it took me so long, but I needed your brother to trust me enough to never doubt me when his world started burning all around him."

"My family killed your parents?"

Alaric watched as tears built in her eyes at his admission, but he couldn't focus on that and tell her so because the darkness he thought he'd locked behind a mental vault shoved and slid its way into his mind, and he was moving before he could register what he was doing. His hands slid between the silver bars and yanked her forward until her body was pressed against the steel. Her eyes widened in fear when he wrapped a fist around her ponytail and throat. His hold was delicate as he ran his thumb over her bottom lip, but his gaze wasn't. The bit of his flesh that had touched the silver stung for only a moment before his healing properties worked overtime to heal him. He knew he would be unsuccessful. Rome had already told him it would take him a few months to a year to get used to the healing cells and generate enough of them to heal himself without problems.

"Alaric," she moaned breathlessly when he trailed his hand down her chest and tugged on the tight peak of her nipple, "what are you doing?"

"We made a deal, princess, and I know what I want." He tugged, rolled the bud between his fingers, and smiled when she squirmed. "I want you on your knees with those pretty lips wrapped around my dick. Can you do that, or must I request something else?"

Desire flared in her eyes, but he also saw insecurity as well and knew exactly why when she spoke. "I don't want to disappoint you."

"You could never disappoint me, love. I've been imagining you on your knees for me since the moment I met you, so trust me when I say I'm more afraid of losing control than of you doing anything wrong."

"Ok." She responded with a soft moan when his hand slid

between her breasts, and he rubbed his thumb against her lips once more.

Alaric tightened his hand around her ponytail and pulled gently until her neck craned back and her eyes found his. "Are you wearing panties?"

She shook her head, and he couldn't help but smile and flash fangs. God, the plans he had for her body would probably send her running screaming from him, but he had to risk it. He knew she was inexperienced, and there was no way in hell he'd be able to fuck her from inside a cell, but there were other ways to please her, even if that meant having her please herself.

"Slide your shorts off and get on your knees, princess, and I'll tell you what you need to do."

She shook her head and tugged against the tight hold he had on her hair, but he held her steady and pulled her face flush against the bars before he captured her lips in a punishing kiss. His fangs nipped her lip on the drawback; although not hard enough to break the skin, he was tempted to steal just a sip of her blood. She moaned into his mouth but made no attempt to pull away. Instead, she dragged her shorts down her hips until her lower half was bare to him. He groaned at the thought of seeing her pussy again but was denied when she did as he asked and slowly knelt on the floor at his feet. Na'tori's hands reached through the bars to tug at the waistband of his sweats, and he let her.

His throbbing member sprang free from its confinement when she slid his pants down to his ankles and moaned at the sight. His balls drew up to his body when the scent of her wetness strengthened, and her smaller hand wrapped around the base of his cock. He hissed in pleasure and begged to the heavens that he would last longer than a minute. He needed this to fucking last. Na'tori dropped her hand at the sound of his hiss and yelped when he clenched his fist in her hair and jerked her head up to look him in the eye. He was being rough; he knew it, yet he couldn't stop. He bared his fangs at her and snarled, and Alaric could swear on his life that her scent got even more potent. Was she turned on by his aggression? Did she want him to be rougher, or was he hurting her?

"Am I hurting you?" He softened his hold and removed the band from her hair to rub at her scalp as she shook her head and turned enough to kiss the inside of his wrist.

The action caused his skin to slightly graze the silver bars. He didn't react when the metal singed him, but he did jerk when Na'tori gripped his dick in a tight hold that had him choking on his breath as she spoke.

"Stop worrying about hurting me because we both know you won't, now tell me what to do."

Her breath blew against his leaking tip with each word she spoke. His muscles tightened in anticipation, and he knew without a doubt that her lips wrapped around him would sever him from reality. She would be his undoing, not because of the act itself but because of the woman currently on her knees staring back at him like he hung the moon and stars.

Alaric tangled all ten of his fingers into her long tresses and stepped as close to the silver bars as he could without touching the offending metal. His dick speared through the bars and gave her all tip and just enough shaft to please them both. It had to be, or he'd be begging Rome to free him from this damn cell just to get a proper blowjob.

"Princess," he whispered almost painfully, "wrap your lips around me and do what comes naturally. It's okay to graze me with your teeth; just be gentle. You won't mess this up, baby, I promise you."

Na'tori smiled up at him seconds before her lips wrapped around the crown of his dick and swallowed. A spurt of precum coated her tongue, and his entire body tensed at the onslaught of sensations that were her mouth. They moaned in unison as her tongue swirled around him and her cheeks hollowed out. His hands tightened in her hair, and an animalistic snarl echoed in the room as she sucked as much of him as she could reach through the bars.

"Fuck," he groaned when her nails dug into his leg and her teeth grazed his shaft. "Reach between your legs and play with your pussy baby. I need to hear you." He ordered.

She obliged almost immediately and moaned around him. The

vibrations caused his legs to stiffen as the sound of her fingers running through the folds of her cunt reached his ears, and her other hand cupped his balls. Her hands were explorative, her mouth was sloppy, and the sounds that filled the space around them made Alaric nearly feral. He wanted to close his eyes and simply bask in the sensations and sounds, but his eyes were locked on hers, and he refused to look away. When her eyes fluttered closed, he forced her motions to still and growled low as he carefully tugged her head back.

"You keep your eyes locked on me as you finish me off, princess, or I'll keep you from coming. I want to see the moment my seed marks your throat. You won't rob me of that. Are we understood?"

"Yes." Na'tori conceded.

Tears gathered in her eyes from how tightly he gripped her hair, but that didn't stop him from bringing her lips back to his dick to watch her take up where she'd left off. There was nothing pretty about the action. Spit flowed around the edges of her lips, soft tears trailed down her face, and the urge to fuck her throat until she could hardly breathe was creeping in on the back of his mind, and he knew the only thing stopping him was the bars that separated them. She sucked him enthusiastically as her fingers twirled, dipped, and pet her pussy until she was near orgasm.

"Grab my balls and give them a pull, princess," He whispered as tingles continued to run up and down his spine almost non-stop.

She moaned, her teeth grazed the underside of his dick, and her hand wrapped around his balls before tightening fractionally and pulling lightly. His orgasm was instant. His cum poured into and down her throat in a matter of seconds and triggered a climax from her that was so strong that she screamed around his dick and closed her damn eyes when a gush of wetness could be heard over the ringing in his ear.

Na'tori slipped her lips off of him and smiled sweetly as he caressed her scalp and rubbed the sweat off his brow. "Was that as good for you as it was for me?" She asked with such a look of inno-cence that one would think she hadn't just had a dick down her throat.

Alaric opened his mouth to speak but instead jerked his head towards the stairwell to find Silas staring back at him with a look of shock. He was going to kill the bastard. He had no choice but to now that his best friend had witnessed a side of Na'tori that no one else should have been able to see.

CHAPTER
NINETEEN

E zekiel used the tip of a blade to clean out the gunk beneath his nails as he sat across from his brother Lukas. His brother was pissed because they still hadn't located Na'tori. Personally, he could give two fucks about the bitch. She was a thorn in his side. Sure, she was brilliant and the only reason they even had a fighting chance against the freaks of nature known as the Eternals, but she had a bleeding heart. He wanted to cut it out of her. He smiled at the thought, then frowned when Lukas cleared his throat to gain his attention. He was another person he wanted to kill but couldn't until he learned every one of his secrets.

"What has you grinning, brother? Care to share?" Lukas questioned.

Ezekiel looked him over. He couldn't keep the look of disgust off of his face if he tried, but he really didn't care either. Any time he looked at his older brother, he wanted to end his life. Lukas was weak. Even before he had lost the ability to walk, he had been weak, but now it was worse. Looking at him, he saw a man desperately trying to save face. The same brother that used to pick on him, the same brother that tortured him for hours on end, and the same brother that had turned him into the monster he was today now needed him for nearly everything.

Ezekiel shook his head in denial. It was best he didn't let him know how close to killing him he was. He had to keep reminding himself that he needed him. More specifically, he needed his brother's secrets.

Lukas frowned. "You hardly ever smile, so what is it? What has you so happy?"

He lied easily. "I'm thinking about how beautiful it'll be when I get my hands on whoever took our sister. Just thinking of their torture."

It looked as if Lukas wasn't convinced before he shook his head and returned to whatever work he was doing on his computer. His fingers flew over the keys as he spoke. "There's no definitive proof that the Eternals killed our guards and snatched Na'tori, but nothing else would make sense. We have enemies, but none are bold enough to do this. Only Romulus would stoop so low and kidnap a woman. We need to find her before she gives them anything."

Ezekiel laughed loudly and without care. "She broke the second she was taken. You know our sister Lukas. She can fight and handle herself appropriately, but torture will break her. She's soft and too empathic towards any and everyone. Why do you think I stay far away from the bitch? She tries too damn hard to fit in and be a part of things. If the Eternals offer her love, she'll take it with both hands and never look back. There's no loyalty in her bones, and you know it."

"You don't know Tori like I do. She wouldn't turn on me. She'd sure as hell turn on you without batting an eye, but Evan and I are safe in that regard. Which brings me to my next question…Where is Evan? I know that you know."

Lukas turned his stare back onto him, but he remained unfazed. Most wouldn't meet Lukas's stare because he was known to see the truth staring back at him no matter who it was, and yet Alaric had tricked him for however many years that he had plotted on the company, and now Ezekiel was doing the same thing. He wanted to work for Titan; he believed in its mission to learn the truth about how Eternals were made because he wanted it for himself. If nothing else, Ezekiel wanted power just like his brother did, but the difference between them was that he would do anything to get that power; Lukas wouldn't.

He couldn't tell him this truth either. Evan was no longer with them. In fact, his body was dissolving inside of an oil drum several blocks over beneath several layers of concrete. Evan had gotten too curious; he'd watched him too closely and learned just what Ezekiel had been up to. His brat brother had wanted to run to Lukas and tell him all of his dirty deeds and what he had been doing behind their backs, and he couldn't let that happen. Killing him hadn't been the plan, but he hadn't backed down, and so…death seemed to be the only answer.

"Zeke, I asked you a question," Lukas snapped. "Where the hell is Evan?"

He smiled and stood before leaving the office without another word. He wouldn't be answering him now or ever. Ok, maybe not ever… perhaps when he planned to kill this brother as well. Then and only then would he tell him what he had done to their baby brother. Yeah, he chuckled to himself. Definitely, when he killed him, too, he would tell all of his dirty secrets, but first, he needed access to whatever Lukas was hiding from him. He knew there was something big and he wanted answers. He would get his answers. Soon.

CHAPTER
TWENTY

everal Months Prior

Na'tori shook with fear and uncertainty as the alarms continued to blare and ring throughout the facility. She wasn't even supposed to be in Van Scive; she should have been on a flight headed back to Ezekiel and Evan, yet here she was with two of her guards as she raced through the hidden tunnels in search of Lukas. She knew he was down here somewhere, and although she had promised him she knew nothing about the lower levels, she had lied. She'd known all along that there were rooms below. She just never knew what was inside of them, but these tunnels...she'd had access to them for months because she'd wanted to learn his secrets. She'd gotten none, except that her brothers were very secretive men.

"Tori, we shouldn't be down here!" Austin—her favorite guard—grumbled irritably. "We told Lukas we were taking you home. I don't even know why he wanted you out here to begin with. Three hours spent doing jack shit."

"I had to test a new drug, but it doesn't matter. I know something's wrong. I can feel it. And if I'm right and we don't help him if he's in trouble, then it's your ass as well as mine, so stop fucking complaining and come on. I think I might know where he is." She snapped back.

She passed doors left and right, knowing they were empty because she'd checked them the last time she was there. The only room that looked like it had been prepared for a guest was four more doors down. She'd promised herself today would be the day she got answers, but then the alarms had to start ringing on her way out the door, and her need to find out the truth sparked her into heading where she shouldn't.

As soon as she reached the hidden door, she ran her fingers along the wall and pushed. It opened slowly to show a room with a comfortable-looking cot, chains, and what looked to be a makeshift bathroom area. She gasped in shock when she spotted Lukas slumped over onto the floor with a sword embedded in his back and his guard Blakley being held up by a sword through his chest.

Na'tori moved quickly and pulled two slim vials from her pocket. "Austin, help me with Lukas and Jerry get Blakely down. Give him this!" She handed a vial to her guard, Jerry, and knelt beside Lukas as she spoke. "Pour the vial down Blakely's throat, and let's get the hell out of here before whoever did this gets back, and whatever you do, don't remove the blade."

She tipped the vial's contents down Lukas's throat and looked at Austin before they grabbed him on both sides and lifted him. He was a heavy bastard, but she was determined to save her brother and get them the hell out of there, so she fought against her shaking muscles and headed back towards the way they came, with Jerry following closely behind with an unconscious Blakely. They needed medical attention fast, but what she'd given them should hold them off until then. She had to believe that because she couldn't lose her brother.

On her way out the hidden door, she pulled another glass vial out and dropped it on the ground near the door before making sure it closed behind them. That should mask the scent of them if this had been done by the enemies her brother spoke of often. She wouldn't allow them to be hunted by someone who could do this to a man who only wanted to better the world. Na'tori knew her brother wasn't all good, but he did his best, and she'd be damned if she allowed anyone to wipe him from this earth.

"I'm getting you out of here," she whispered into her brother's ear as she struggled to support his weight.

He groaned weakly, and she knew she still had a chance to save him. Whether he could walk again was another matter entirely, but she would be there for him through it all.

. . .

Na'tori came awake with a start; her hand flew back to touch the birthmark that was always covered with makeup on the back of her neck, and she felt the urge to throw up as her mind tossed and turned at the memory. What had happened that day? She needed to know because now that she knew the Eternals and how they operated, she knew there was no way in hell that her brother had told her the truth. She wasn't sure who she needed to ask to get those answers, but she needed to start learning things now, especially if they were planning to make moves on Titan. Na'tori needed to know her enemy.

She climbed from the bed and looked around Alaric's bedroom. It's where she'd been staying since Rome had allowed her to leave the basement cell, and she'd gotten pretty comfortable over the last few days. Her face flushed with desire when she recalled three nights ago how she'd been on her knees for him with his dick in her mouth. God, if the bars hadn't prevented her from taking him deeper, Na'tori would have tried to feel him in the very back of her throat. Her core clenched around nothing, and she could feel cream collecting in her panties from just the thought of him. He was potent. The pleasure he could ring out of her was a feeling she wanted to experience over and over again. The idea of having more sent her heart hammering in her chest because she'd known that she would have been mated to him within seconds if he had been released from that cell.

Silas coming downstairs to find her in that compromising position had given her a new perspective. Alaric had been furious and lashed out with his mind at the male but a gentle hand on his chest had calmed him enough to leave Silas be. She knew they were close, close like brothers instead of friends, and once the anger lifted, Alaric might regret his actions in hurting him. Only when she knew he was calm and had his anger under control did she race up the stairs to get her feelings under control.

Alaric made her want things. Not just sexually but in all the things that mattered. He brought out her urge to fight against anything and everything that didn't serve her in the best possible ways. Being around the Eternals was showing her a new way of life.

They fought for humanity, not just for themselves but for those lesser than them. She wanted more of that.

She headed into the bathroom and quickly showered before covering her birthmark once more and pulling on a blue dress covered in butterflies. It fell to her mid-thighs while a pair of comfortable flats covered her feet, and her hair fell down to her waist in a waterfall. It was six thirty at night, and thunderclouds had filled the sky earlier that morning, but there was no telling if it had been the actual weather or if Cairo or Rome had manipulated the weather with their emotions. She could hear the raindrops pelting the windows as she entered the living room to find most of the Guardians up and about, strapping weapons onto their bodies. Their movements were stiff like robots, with hardly any talk or banter between them. For once, Maverick and Akio weren't even arguing.

Rome was at the kitchen island standing between his mate's spread legs as he kissed along her throat, Maverick leaned against the counter with an annoyed expression on his face as he glared at Alondra, and Akio sat on the couch with a laptop on his lap, his fingers flying across the keyboard. Amirishka was sharpening her throw stars and blades on the couch next to Akio, Erick stood stoically at the window as he stroked the pommel of a sword strapped to his side, and Silas leaned against the wall by the entryway that led into the basement as he used a blade to clean his teeth. Cairo sat in a large wingback chair, fire dancing along his fingertips as he played a game on his phone.

Na'tori cleared her throat before she spoke. "Do you guys ever take a night off?"

Akio chuckled and gently closed his laptop before standing; his full-length jacket flowed down to almost his ankles and hid the blades she knew were covering every inch of him. "We only take breaks when boss man thinks there's a real threat to our safety."

"All because of that damn virus you created to knock us the fuck out," Maverick snarled and finally removed his eyes from Alondra to look at her.

She tried not to flinch at his words and failed miserably before

Alara came to her defense. "She didn't know what she was doing. She's explained that already, so let it go, Mav!"

"Fine." He grumbled and crossed his arms like a child throwing a tantrum, but he did it silently.

"So you mean to tell me you guys don't just take a night off just to have time together as a unit?" Na'tori played with the hem of her dress as everyone paused to stare at her with equally confused expressions.

Rome removed himself from the apex of Alara's thighs and turned with his brows raised in question. "We protect humanity from the creatures your family created. Do you think we have the luxury of taking nights off?"

Annoyance made her speak without thinking first. "The Rogue's wouldn't be possible without your blood! All I was thinking was that you each deserved a night off just for the sake of it, but I get it if you can't! Let everything else supersede your peace of mind."

She was storming for the stairs that would lead her to Alaric when Rome materialized in front of her and caused her to pause. He bared his fangs as black wings made of shadows sprang from his back, and his eyes glowed with a level of ferocity she hadn't been expecting. Her heart pounded in her chest, and fear filled every space within her body until she felt sweat perspiring along her skin. Silas was moving towards her to hopefully assist her when an ear-splitting roar echoed through the room and sent Rome to his knees.

"Dammit, Alaric," Rome's wings rippled, and pain filled his voice as he spoke through gritted teeth, "I wasn't going to hurt her. I just reacted, kinda like you're doing now."

"Let me the fuck outta this cell, Romulus!" Alaric yelled up the steps.

Rome climbed to his feet when Alaric released him from whatever mental hold he'd been able to wrap around the Eternal, and everyone seemed to speak at once.

"What the hell is she talking about?" Maverick questioned.

Akio shook his head in wonder. "Did she just say what I think she said? Your blood is the reason those bastards exist?"

"You wouldn't keep vital information like that from us," Cairo shook his head in denial.

Erick's voice was full of resolve as he faced the room. "I always figured that was the case. You were the first of our kind, the first to ever be discovered and sought after, and the first to combat humans on the field where your blood would spill in order to gain access to your DNA." He shook his head ruefully. "It's no wonder Titan wants you so badly. Do they believe you're the only one capable of creating more of us? Is that why they're so adamant about capturing you specifically? I've tested each of our blood samples against a human without the chromosomal pair that would make them Kindred and found that we all have the power to create bloodthirsty fiends. Who is to know what other secrets you might hold?"

Amirishka threw a blade and let her anger fuel her as it embedded within the wall where Rome's face would have been if he hadn't been standing so close to Na'tori. "You and your fucking secrets!"

"I think we all need to take a breather," Alara stated as she made her way through the ground of warriors until she reached her mate's side and leveled Na'tori with a look. "We thought it best not to bring this up because it can't fix anything knowing what an Eternal's blood is capable of." She looked each Guardian in the eye, hoping they would understand where she was coming from. "Knowing would have only made you all stress that much more, and Romulus didn't want that for any of you. He decided to carry the burden alone, and I respected his choice. You should do. What does knowing give you but a sense of defeat and fear?"

"He should have told us." Akio expressed pure anger. "I think I speak for everyone when I say that just because we follow him doesn't mean he needs to carry the full burden of everything on his shoulders. We would have understood, just like we did when we learned about the ability to create more Eternals. We would have understood if given even an ounce of trust!"

Na'tori watched them argue back and forth; all she wanted to do was sink into the ground and disappear. She'd caused this problem. She'd caused the discord between them, and the part of her that was always afraid of disappointing someone made tears fill her eyes, but she refused to let them overflow. She didn't want to keep looking weak in front of these warriors. She wanted to be stronger than this.

"God fucking damn you, Romulus!" Alraic's voice was once again heard over the yelling, along with the sound of slamming metal against metal. "Let me out of this cell!"

Rome tossed the key to Na'tori with a glare. "Go calm him down while I speak to my warriors."

Na'tori didn't need to be told twice to make a hasty exit. She gripped the key with all her strength and headed for the basement as the Guardians continued arguing. The moment she reached Alaric's cell, she promised herself she'd breathe a little easier, but that wasn't the case when she saw the destruction of his cell. The cot was bent and twisted against the far wall, bedding was everywhere, and the man himself stood amidst the destruction with pinkened skin due to the silver of the bars. His chest rose and fell with each harsh breath he took as his eyes glowed a vivid swirl of gray and green that compelled her forward.

CHAPTER
TWENTY-ONE

The moment Na'tori opened the cell door, Alaric pulled her into his arms and checked her over. Being locked in the cell and smelling her fear when Rome had released a burst of raw energy had sent every protective instinct within his body into a riot. They may not have mated yet, but Na'tori was his in every way that mattered, and he planned to protect her from everything, even the man who had become more than a brother-in-law to him. Rome had become his King. He could feel a tether between them, but he would never put him before the woman who would become his mate.

"Are you okay?" He looked her over and tried not to become distracted by the slim-fitting dress that covered her and outlined a body he would know anywhere.

"I'm fine," she replied softly as her arms tightened as much as they could around his waist, "I just wasn't expecting that reaction. I thought everyone knew that Rome's blood was responsible for creating the Rogues. I didn't know I was telling close-knit secrets."

"It's not your fault."

He kissed her forehead and froze when his gaze locked onto the pounding vein within her throat. The smell of her fear was a turn-off, but with every harsh beat of her heart, Alaric was more and more compelled to sink his fangs into her throat. He closed his eyes against the sight and shifted his lower body away from her in fear that she would take this as anything but what he meant it to be.

Comfort.

She stiffened, and he felt her head tilt up to look at his face as her hand rubbed against his back. Her voice only caused the fire filling his veins and loins to heighten. "What's wrong?"

He looked down into her eyes and knew he was about to change their lives from that moment on. The wall in his mind that kept that darkness in check began to crack and fracture as his eyes scanned the space around him. He wouldn't make it past the men and women still arguing upstairs, so his only option was the hallway leading towards a room where he knew they held meetings. He lifted Na'tori into his arms and used the new speed he'd gained when he became an Eternal to enter the room and place her on top of the oval table. His eyes took in the reinforced walls, an old-fashioned globe that had seen better days, a miniature coffee cart, an extensive high-definition surveillance system, and a biometrically sealed weapons cabinet that would fit perfectly in front of the door.

He used his strength to push the cabinet before the door and turned to face Na'tori again. Her legs were still open, showing off bright blue panties, and her eyes were wide with shock, but her breasts told a different story, as well as her scent. Her nipples were pebbled, her chest was rising and falling harshly, and her gentle hands were curled around the wood edge of the table.

"What's going on?" She looked around until her opalescent eyes returned to him, revealing her nervousness.

That dark corner in his head scratched and scratched at his weakened walls. Images flashed before his eyes of pinning her to the table, tying her hands up with the string of his sweatpants, and forcing her legs open until he revealed her core. He shook his head to dispel the images, but more crammed through. She was bent over, back arched, handprints peppered her ass as he fucked her from behind, and a red imprint of fangs marked her throat. He wanted that.

Alaric snarled, launched across the room, and flattened her to the table. Her chest meshed against his own, Na'tori's nails dug into his triceps, and her hot center pressed against his abdomen. Her scent was everywhere, drugging him and pulling him under a spell he didn't think he'd ever want to be released from.

"It's happening, isn't it?" She whispered, "It's okay. I want this, too." Na'tori loosened her hold and trailed her fingers along his skin when he stood.

Alaric glanced between their bodies, saw the hiked-up dress around her waist and the wet spot her cream had left on her panties, and groaned when she spread her legs wider. Blood roared in his ears as his heart pounded like a drum in his chest. When he spoke, he didn't sound like himself. He sounded like a man on the edge of a cliff with nothing to lose.

"I'll try to be gentle."

Her nod was all the confirmation he needed.

His hand curled around her neck, pulling her up until her lips brushed his. "Wrap your hands around the edge of the desk like you did a second ago, princess, and keep them there until I tell you you can move them."

She did as he asked as her eyes dilated with pleasure and the scent of her intensified. He finally closed the distance between their lips and kissed her like a man starving for a taste while his fingers trailed against her arms before gripping the straps of her dress to pull them down until her breasts popped free. He cupped the weight of them and sucked in her gasp as he nipped at her lips and rubbed soothing circles around her areolas. She squirmed against him and mewled into his mouth the longer he teased them both, and his cock hated him for it. It pulsed and dripped with precum, but he ignored his need. He wanted to make this good for her. Memorable even.

Na'tori's thighs trembled the longer he ignored direct contact with the hard points of her tits and smiled when one of her hands gripped his wrist and tried to direct him towards her right breast.

"I've been waiting for you to disobey," he chucked against her lips and nipped her bottom lip before dropping his hands to the string dangling from his pants. The image of her hands tied behind her back drove his subsequent actions as he drew the string out, forced her hands behind her back, and tied her wrists together.

"Alaric," she groaned in frustration and fought against the binding, but it held steady. "What are you doing?"

"Are you comfortable?" He kissed along the shell of her ear, scented the aroma of makeup, but ignored it in favor of trailing his lips down the valley of her breasts until he reached her navel and knelt on the floor.

She nodded frantically. "Yes. Please do something, god, you're driving me crazy."

"I just need to make sure this is what you want." He licked the dampness of her panties and grinned when she moaned and spread wider for him still. "You want this so bad, don't you princess?"

He licked her pussy through her panties again, but he was the one to groan in pleasure when she leaned back and propped her legs up like she had done this so many times before. The thought angered him enough to grip the edge of her panties with his fangs and tear them off. Her gasp was music to his ears when he took her thighs and spread her wider as his tongue finally licked along the lips of her pussy and sucked her clit into his mouth. Her taste burst along his taste buds as he sucked and licked her until her legs were a trembling mess and incoherent words were leaving her mouth. Only then did he stand and lower his sweats to allow his throbbing dick to spring out and slap against her wetness.

Those walls within his mind continued to splinter and crack, but he continued holding that darkness back as he curled a hand around her neck and sat her up again. Na'tori's legs remained open, feet propped up on the table as her lust-filled gaze found him.

"You want this, yeah?" He questioned once more to make sure they were on the same page as he gripped his dick and lined them up to allow his tip to swipe through her folds.

The heat of her center was like molten lava, and he wasn't even inside of her. Alaric couldn't even begin to imagine what it would feel like when he sank into her and permanently marked her so that the world would know who she belonged to. Na'tori's chest was rising and falling rapidly, her legs were still shaking like a leaf, and her beautiful center was slowly dripping cream onto the table's wood. It was such a pretty sight that he continued to run and tease her clit with the mushroomed head of his cock.

"Please," she groaned, "Please fuck me."

"The correct words are mate me." He tightened his hands around the back of her neck and leaned over to give her a languid kiss as he slid the tip just inside of her. "God, you're tight," He cursed. "Tell me to tie you to me, and I will, princess. Give me the words."

"Make me yours, Alaric."

"With pleasure."

He teased her with the first few inches of him, warming her up to the sensation of having something foreign within her as she moaned and creamed on his dick. He needed her to orgasm first. After that, he would give them what they both needed, and he prayed to God that his mental shields would hold because that darkness was wreaking havoc on his psyche and pouring thought after elicit thought into his mind.

Alaric kissed her deeply as he swallowed each and every sound that passed through her lips and made a few noises of his own as he sank further and further into her core until he reached the elusive barrier that determined her innocence. His eyes were brighter than they'd ever been; he could feel them shining like the high beams on a car, and his fangs were sharper than a blade as he caught his bottom lip and poured all of his concentration into this moment alone. He held her open with both hands and glided smoothly between her folds before slamming forward. Na'tori screamed in what could only be described as ecstasy mixed with a bite of pain as her legs tensed and her cunt sucked him in and pulsed around him.

"Sssssh," he kissed her and swallowed every cry as he held himself still inside of her heat, even as she squirmed beneath him. "Don't move, fuck, don't move."

Na'tori groaned. "Untie me."

"Not yet, princess. Look at me." He gripped her chin and waited until her eyes locked on him instead of the area where they were joined. "Are you okay?"

"Yes, now untie me."

"I said not yet. You touch me now, and I'll have no control."

He eased out of her and slammed back in to watch her eyes blow wide as her cry of passion rang in his ears and her muscles tensed around him. He watched her every facial twitch as he fucked her, yet his gaze continuously strayed to the erratic pulse in her throat. He wanted to sink his fangs right into that beautiful space between her shoulder and head as he pumped his seed inside of her to tie her to him for the rest of his life. Alaric wanted to own her in the most primal way of his kind, and although he was just learning the ropes of being an Eternal, he knew this was a fundamental need. He needed to mark her.

Alaric angled his hips until every thrust allowed him to stroke her inner g-spot until she was screaming his name repeatedly. When her orgasm hit, he felt the moisture and release and envied his cock for several moments until logic prevailed. He would taste her again soon, but first…his eyes latched onto her throat, and she tilted her head to the side to indicate that she wanted this just as badly as he did. He gripped the back of her head and fucked her deeper as his heart raced and his balls slapped into the globes of her ass before he ran his nose along the column of her throat. Alaric's moan was throaty and deep as he licked at her pulse point before wrapping his mouth around her jugular.

He went to bite down and growled in frustration when his jaw wouldn't close around her carotid. He tried again and met the same invisible resistance before his hands tightened around her thigh and neck. His hips continued to slam into her as his orgasm climbed higher, and her moans played in a loop within his mind. The moment she came, he met her on the other end of that destruction but cursed every God that existed as his cum pumped into her body continuously. Aggression and anger funneled through him as he pulled out of her tight sheath and trained his eyes on the release that covered his cock and poured from her center. Alaric released her thigh to collect the cum that leaked out of her and pushed it back in. He didn't understand why he couldn't bite her and mark her as his mate. Had those damn Gods lied to him just so he would come back? Was she even really his mate?

He curled his fingers inside her cunt, grabbed a handful of her hair, and forced her to meet his gaze before he spoke. "This changes nothing. You're still mine, princess. Is that understood?"

"Yes," she moaned as his fingers continued to tease her.

Alaric kissed her deeply even as anger carved deep gouges in the shields within his mind, and that darkness began to leak through to wrap around him. He was tempted to just knock the wall down and see what that did for him when his supernatural hearing picked up the sound of someone approaching the room. By their gait, he knew it was his brother-in-law. His time with Na'tori was ending now, but maybe Rome could tell him what the hell was going on because he wasn't willing to accept that she wasn't his mate. He pulled his fingers from her pussy, and watched as discomfort morphed her features before he tapped them against her lips and waited for her mouth to open.

"Suck them," he whispered as Rome's fist began to pound at the door.

"Dammit, Alaric, open the damn door." Rome snapped, "And you better wipe down whatever surface you just used, or so help me, I'll string you up by your balls."

Na'tori's eyes went wide with embarrassment, and she tried to get up, but he still had her by the hair; his hips kept her legs spread wide as she continued to leak onto the desk, and her hands were still tied behind her back.

He tightened his grip on her hair and snarled. "I said suck, princess." He didn't bother whispering because Rome would hear them regardless.

Her pupils dilated with pleasure as she wrapped her lips around his fingers and sucked, her tongue swirling around his digits until she licked up every drop of their shared release. Only then did he release her from his hold and slowly step back. The need to sink his fangs into her still sang within his blood, but he didn't know what to do about that, so he began to reinforce the walls within his mind.

"Alaric!" Rome exclaimed, "You've got two minutes to open this door, or I'm teleporting into the room, so I suggest you both get decent."

Alaric chuckled. There was something about pissing off the king of Eternals that just made him smile. Rome was a prickly bastard with anyone but his mate, and it showed. He pulled the straps of Na'tori's dress back into place, released her wrists from the string, and stuffed her panties within his pocket as he pulled his sweats back onto his waist. Alaric gave her another passionate kiss before he headed for the door to let the nosy bastard in. It was quick work to place the cabinet back in its respective corner before he opened the door to face a furious Rome.

Rome growled low and deep before he spoke. "This is not the fucking room for that shit."

"Would you have let me upstairs?" Alaric cocked his head to the side as he waited for a response and listened to Na'tori as she wiped the desk down.

"You already know the answer to that," Rome replied dryly. His eyes glanced over to take in Na'tori before he frowned and pinned Alaric with a look. "What happened?"

He didn't need to ask him what he meant by that question. He knew he was referencing at the fact that he had been unsuccessful in mating Na'tori. The need to do so still beat at him like a battering ram, but he ignored it. How did he begin to explain what had happened? He could hardly understand it himself, but he still had to try.

Alaric didn't need anyone else hearing his tale and instead sent Rome a mental image of the moment he tried to pierce Na'tori with his fangs. "You tell me what the fuck went wrong because I tried Romulus, but something kept me from marking her. Is she not mine to mark? Did those Gods of yours lie to me?"

CHAPTER
TWENTY-TWO

N a'tori finished wiping up the shared release between her and Alaric as she attempted to calm her racing heart and still the images within her mind of what they had just done. Is that how sex would always be? If so, she wanted a front-row seat to it every single time. Alaric had been everything she had hoped for and more. She wanted to do it again, yet when she shifted, she felt the soreness of her pussy and felt the cum that continued to leak out of her, but there was nothing she could do about that. Alaric had torn her underwear and then dared to shove them into his pocket. She smiled softly, knowing she would never see that pair again, but it had been worth it.

She turned and watched as Rome and Alaric stood in silence. They had to be communicating telepathically, which was fine with her, but Rome's expression made her curious to know what they were saying. He looked shocked, almost like he couldn't believe what Alaric was saying, and she wondered if it had anything to do with the fact that Alaric had never actually bitten her. She touched the side of her throat where his mouth had been and wondered to herself why he hadn't done it. The second she'd seen his intentions to bite her, Na'tori had submitted, ready to take that dive into the unknown and belong to someone other than herself, but then nothing. She'd never felt the pressure, the bite, or the pull she knew accompanied it, and something within her had wilted at the thought.

Had Alaric changed his mind?

Did he no longer wish to mate with her?

She needed to know.

She moved for the door and came to a standstill at Alaric's back, where she placed her palm before she spoke. "Did you change your mind?" She hoped her voice was firm. "It's okay if you did, I would understand."

He stiffened under her palm and looked over his shoulder with a raised brow and a frown. "Did my cum inside of you somehow leak out and leave you with little to no common sense, or were you not listening when I told you that you are still mine? Do we need to reenact the scene again? This time with a witness for you to understand I meant every damn word I said?"

She blushed furiously as her gaze tracked Rome's expression, and her ears noted his chuckle before she shook her head. She was opening her mouth to respond when Alaric turned to face her fully, gripped her by the back of her neck, and pulled her flush against his body. She had no other choice but to meet his gaze as his fingers tightened, and that delicious snarl of his sent shivers down her spine.

"You don't look at him while my cum still leaks out of you, and you damn sure don't show embarrassment."

"So when can I look at him then?"

Alaric snarled again, and Rome laughed heartily before he spoke. "God, you're worse than me; let the poor woman go, and let us figure out why you couldn't mark her so we can move on to something a little more pressing. The others are upstairs waiting so we can run through some sort of game plan for our next course of action instead of hunting every night with no real results."

Na'tori genuinely thought Alaric would ignore Rome's comment and was mildly surprised when he didn't. Instead, he kissed her forehead before releasing her. She continued to run a hand down his back even when he turned back to Rome and spoke.

"Is it possible the Gods lied to me about who my mate is? Are they even capable of granting me what I demanded?"

Rome pondered the questions, then froze and glanced over his shoulder to look back toward the hallway and staircase leading to the upper levels. "Excuse me for a moment." He disappeared in a plume of black shadows, leaving Alaric and her alone once more.

She glided her hand over the muscles of his back and bit back the moan that rose to her lips when her pussy pulsed and the feeling of his cum slowly slid down her inseam. "I think I'm going to go take a shower."

Alaric whipped around, tangled a fist inside her hair, and pulled her body flush against his own as his voice caused her heart to beat wildly with excitement. "Are you trying to wash me away, princess?"

"No," she whispered as her hands held his waistline, and she licked her lips and stared into glowing eyes, "This is new for me, and it's not very comfortable. You took my panties, and it's...I mean, we're dripping down my legs, and I'm a little sore."

He loosened his grip on her hair and expelled a breath as if he had been holding it. "I was too rough, wasn't I?"

"It was perfect."

"Take a bath. It'll soothe your muscles and help with the soreness." His eyes lost their glow before he pulled her into a drugging kiss that made her lose all thought and reason.

"Come with me," she pleaded.

What was it about this male that made her putty in his hands? Having sex with him hadn't been enough. She wanted so much more. With Alara and Rome, they made it look so easy and peaceful to be mated, to have the one person meant to be yours. Na'tori wanted that. She wanted it with Alaric.

"If I come with you, I'll fill you again." He replied as he pressed his growing erection against her, letting her know that he was deadly serious. "Besides, I don't think Rome trusts me leaving the lower levels."

Rome's voice cut through their talk. "I was only worried because

I thought the drive to feed would make you do something you'd regret, like bleed her dry. I needed to protect you both, and you seem okay. But, if you show signs of aggression towards her or anyone else, you'll be right back down here until you have that shit under control. Is that understood?"

"Crystal."

Alaric lifted her into his arms and used his supernatural speed to get them to the bathroom before placing her on the sink and locking the door behind them. Na'tori watched him start the shower and check the temperature. His muscles flexed with every movement he made, and the temptation to touch him was overwhelming. She climbed down from the counter and removed her dress. Her skin began to tingle as her heart continued to race in her chest. Alara hadn't lied when she said she would have this ungodly attraction to Alaric if he was her fated mate, but that didn't explain why he hadn't bitten her. They needed to make that happen to solidify their bond, but how?

Alaric glanced over his shoulder and froze as his eyes dropped to her breasts and then the valley between her thighs. "I see that you're ready." He gestured for her to enter the shower and tugged down his sweats. "The water should be warm enough."

She watched as his abs rippled and his cock bobbed up and down as if to say 'come closer' before she crossed the room and entered the shower. She made sure to put an extra sway in her hips and groaned in pleasure when the water beat against her chest. She turned to watch him enter the shower and smiled when he slid the shower door behind him and stepped right up to her. She tilted her head back and moaned into his mouth when he took her lips in a searing kiss. His hands felt like hot brands when he cupped both of her ass cheeks, and she hissed when he spread them and nipped her bottom lip with his teeth.

"You're such a fucking temptation." He skimmed his lips to her ear and nipped it as well, "You're supposed to be showering, not fucking me with your eyes."

Na'tori chuckled, felt the water pelting her everywhere as her eyes slid closed on a moan when his finger ran between the globes of her ass and skimmed over her forbidden hole. "But you're so nice to look at," she whispered.

"Let me help you since you seem so distracted, and then we can get to the fun part."

She was waiting for him to take her lips in a bruising kiss once more but instead found herself shoved under the showerhead as Alaric's throaty laugh echoed around her. She sputtered and slapped at his chest after wiping the water from her eyes to glare at him, but he was already lathering up a loofah with a smirk. Na'tori wanted to waterboard him until he was choking on water, too, but when his hands, coupled with the loofah and soap, began to run over her body, she forgot all about it. His hands were gentle as he scrubbed every part of her front before he turned her away from him and began the slow process of rubbing her down.

She placed her hands against the shower wall when he lifted her feet one by one to scrub at the bottoms before his hands glided up her legs. She heard the soft splat of the loofah hitting the ground before Alaric gathered her hair and tugged her head back. He ran his lips across her cheek as his erection slid between her legs and nudged her clit.

"Please," she groaned as he rubbed against her clit and used his other hand to tug at the tight peak of her nipple, "please, more."

"Only after you're clean, princess; besides, I thought you wanted a shower, and you were feeling sore."

Alaric toyed with her for several more moments before he stepped back and grabbed the shampoo to lather her hair. She moaned for an entirely new reason when he kneaded her scalp and ensured that every hair follicle had a healthy application of shampoo. He helped her rinse, immediately applied the conditioner, and even detangled her hair before rinsing it again. Na'tori was at a loss for words. This was something she'd never expected to experience from any man, let alone Alaric. He was so gentle with her that every touch made her heart flutter, and every kiss delivered to her flesh made her question if she was really alive and if this was actually happening. She was moving to turn and return the favor when he gathered her hair again but froze.

His hands tightened painfully on the roots of her scalp, and the hand on her waist kept her still as his fingers dug into her skin. His hold was no longer gentle; it was painful and nerve-wracking because she could feel this new anger. She didn't understand where it was coming from until he removed his hand from her waist to caress the mark on the back of her neck. His snarl sent the hair along her body, standing up as genuine fear coiled within her gut. She reached back to grip the hand that held her hair and dug her nails into his skin when he pushed her body into the unforgiving tile wall.

"You were there that night," he snarled, "You're the one who saved him, aren't you?"

"I-I-I'm not sure what you mean." She fumbled over her words, "You're actually scaring me, Alaric. What's wrong?"

He pressed his slick front against her back, and his lips skimmed her left ear as he whispered his following few questions. "Were you there the night they burnt your brother's other facility to the ground? Are you the one who saved his life?"

The events of that night looped through her mind, and the realization that they had genuinely tried to end her brother's life hit her squarely in the solar plexus. Now that she knew what her family really did for the company, she couldn't say she blamed them. She understood their need for violence. She disagreed with the actions of her family, but she didn't think she'd want to see her brother dead. Or did she? Na'tori released her hold on his hand and became pliant within his hold. She felt his erection become harder at her submission, but she forced herself to ignore it. They needed to get through this moment. She needed to de-escalate the situation before he assumed the worst about her.

"Yes, I was there but didn't know what I know now." She finally replied when she found the right words to use. "Whatever took place that night, I knew nothing about it; all I saw when I walked into that room that night was my brother dying and bleeding out. I didn't know about the atrocities he'd committed. I don't even fully know what took place that night to have you and your people burning the place down, but I couldn't leave him to die. Alaric..." she closed her eyes when the urge to cry hit her unexpectedly, "you have to believe me."

He was still for several more moments before he loosened his grip and kissed the shell of her ear. "I believe you, princess." He kissed the side of her throat and sighed heavily as he rubbed at her burning scalp before he released her and took several steps back, "I apologize for handling you so roughly. I was caught off guard."

Na'tori rested her forehead against the cold marble tile and blindly reached for the handle to turn off the shower. Her legs still shook, her heart continued to pound within her chest at a brutal pace, and the urge to cry was still consuming her emotions. Whatever her brother had done had to be worse than whatever she knew. The anger in which he'd handled her made that very clear, but what was it?

She turned to face Alaric and found him watching her warily as his hands flexed at his sides. "What did he do?"

"It's not my story to tell."

"Then whose story is it?"

He shook his head slowly as his eyes took her in from head to toe. They began to glow once more as he cautiously stepped back into her space and lifted a piece of her hair before inhaling softly. "Do you forgive me for my rough treatment of you?"

She could see in his expression that he was actually remorseful for his actions, and she was convinced Alaric wasn't a man who often apologized. She pressed her palm flat against his chest and pushed lightly to see if there would be any give. He surprised her once more when he did and allowed her hair to drop, the weight of it smacking her hip lightly. Na'tori could see the need within his eyes. With a rock-hard cock and the occasional flash of fangs, she knew he wanted to seek pleasure in her body and not just gain her forgiveness.

"I'll forgive you on one condition." She leaned back against the wall and chuckled when his expression turned curious.

"Are we bargaining once again, princess?"

"You bargained with me before, but I'm getting what I want this time."

"Name it."

She wasn't a seducer. Sex was still very much something new for her, but she wanted to try so many things, and now that the tense moment was over between them, what better way to ease the rest of whatever was in the air between them. It wasn't just him that needed her. She needed him as well, maybe even more than they both realized.

"I want you to do what I did for you in the cell." She stated hesitantly.

Alaric shook his head softly and rubbed his thumb over his bottom lip as his eyes ate her up with his stare. "Say the words, don't be shy. All you have to do is ask, and I'll do it."

She blushed. Na'tori knew her cheeks were the color of a red neon sign before she worked up the nerve to ask for what she wanted. "I want you to go down on me, but..."

"But what?"

"But I want to know what it feels like from the back."

You could hear a pin drop with how silent the room became, but she refused to look away from his gaze until he lifted his hand and twirled his finger. It was a clear indication that he would give her exactly what she wanted, but first, she needed to get into the position she'd requested. The look in his eyes had turned feral, and his fangs were a lot sharper than they'd been several seconds before. Na'tori wanted to drop her eyes to the erection she knew was pulsing between his thighs, but when his head tilted to the side, she knew he was running out of the patience he had to let her drive this boat to whatever destination she had in mind.

She turned her back to him and moved to look over her shoulder when Alaric fisted her hair and pressed his other palm into the space between her shoulder blades until her chest and cheek were pressed against the wall. His voice was rough and needy when he spoke.

"Place your hands against the wall and don't move them until I tell you to, and I'll reward you."

She wasted no time placing her hands against the wall before feeling Alaric drop behind her. Spreading the globes of her ass and simply breathing on the lips of her pussy was not something Na'tori had been expecting, but with the first puff of air against her wet labia, her core clenched, and her legs shook slightly. The anticipation was killing her as he continued to inhale and exhale roughly behind her as his hands massaged her ass.

"Alaric?"

A slap resonated within the room, and a sting traveled through her left cheek before she realized what had happened. He'd spanked her and was now rubbing a soothing hand over the abused area. Her breath was trapped in her throat as she waited for words, actions…anything. She was opening her mouth to speak again when his tongue curled around her clit and sucked. Na'tori came up onto the balls of her feet with a squeal before his tongue slid down to plunge into her center. He did it repeatedly, never giving her enough time to relax into it as he devoured her pussy until she was a weeping, screaming mess.

Na'tori's voice was raw from screaming, her pussy felt sensitive to the touch, and her legs shook like a newborn calf when Alaric finally stood up. She wasn't sure how many times he'd pushed her to the edge only to deny her that plummet, but she wasn't sure how much more she could take of his oral torture. His hand slid up her back and fisted in her hair. God, his obsession with her hair was causing her nerves to be so sensitive and triggered her to respond whenever he gripped the long tresses. She moaned softly when his dick rubbed the hotspot between her legs, and his hand held her hip while his lips moved across her throat in lazy circles.

"Princess," he whispered and then chuckled when her body shook against his own, "Did I give you what you needed, or did you actually want to cum? Because you didn't specify, and this tight fucking cunt of yours feels like it really needs to." He punctuated each word with a shift of his hips that caused his dick to rub against her dripping center.

Her calves hurt from how long she remained balanced on the balls of her feet, yet every time she tried to relax, he took his cock and slapped it against her clit. She moaned and closed her eyes when, once again, she felt her orgasm teeter tottering just out of reach.

"Cum," she groaned, "please let me cum."

"Will we keep that mark of yours to ourselves?" He questioned as he notched the mushroomed head of his erection at her center and gently pushed past her sensitive folds.

"Fuck," she screamed and nodded frantically just as a climax the size of Texas slammed into her and robbed the breath from her lungs.

Her entire body felt weightless and boneless as Alaric's hips continued to pound and fuck her into oblivion. With each thrust, that chasm of need opened wider until she was craning her neck and practically pleading for the feel of his fangs sinking into her throat. He licked and sucked at her throat, but the bite never came. Only the feel of his dick splitting her open registered in her mind as his curses filled her ear, and a load of cum bathed her inner walls several moments later.

Alaric groaned and cursed louder as load after load of cum shot into her before he slowly eased out. She hissed when her sore muscles attempted to hold him inside and almost allowed her legs to fall out from under her. He scooped her into his arms and carried her over to the sink before placing her down and cleaning the area between her legs. His eyes never strayed from his task, but it was becoming hard for her to keep hers open enough to focus on everything he was doing. She finally allowed his last few words to register in her mind before she spoke. "Why are we keeping my birthmark to ourselves?"

"Because I don't need the rest of them knowing that you helped Lukas that night...at least not right this second. We need a win first." He replied. "Just know I'm still mildly upset about your part. Trust me, I know why you did it, he's your brother, but shit happened that night that can't be undone, and I want my revenge on the people involved. Unwittingly, you were a part of that, so I need time to control the rage funneling through me."

Her voice and eyes went hard as the reality of the situation settled around her. "So then, why did you just fuck me like that?

Why did you agree to what I wanted?" She reached over, snagged a towel from the rack, and wrapped it around her body as she glared.

"I was apologizing for hurting you. The rest is irrelevant for now."

He took a piece of her hair and rubbed it between his fingers in a soothing gesture, but she knocked his hand away, climbed down from the sink, and shoved him with all of her might.

"Fuck you and shove the secret up your ass," she snapped and moved for the door.

He didn't follow her when she stormed into his bedroom and slid between the bed sheets. She thought he would follow and question her, but he never came. With how worn out her body and now mind were, Na'tori didn't fight sleep when it dragged her under. Instead, she pulled the covers over her head and succumbed to the call.

CHAPTER
TWENTY-THREE

Alaric tied a towel around his waist, gripped the edge of the sink, and stared at his reflection as if the man staring back at him was his worst enemy. He wanted to go after her and make her understand what he meant, but his anger was a new beast for him. Being an Eternal meant heightened emotions that were a struggle to contain. His eyes were beaming so brightly within the reflection that he was at risk of becoming disoriented when a twinge of pain came from his side. Alaric frowned, placed his hand against his side where he had previously been shot, and groaned when the feeling of blades stabbed at his brain and caused him to gasp in shock. He didn't make a peep when that pain morphed and spread to the nape of his neck, although he wanted to scream at the sensations that were spiraling through his head and neck. He was used to screaming in silence after years of pain conditioning within Titan.

He gasped when another sharp pain made him close his eyes in an attempt to take stock of what was happening around him. He could hear someone walking down the hallway, and by the sound of their tread, he knew it was Alara. Noises were louder to him now, so when his sister rounded the doorway and spoke, it was like nails raking across a chalkboard.

"Alaric, what's wrong? Let me see." Her hands grasped the side of his head before she hissed in pain and drew back from him. "What the fuck?" She murmured as she stared down at her hands quizzically.

He heard her call for Rome, but he couldn't focus on their words when the larger male appeared at her side; all he could pay attention to was the crippling pain spreading through his head. With his eyes closed and his teeth clenched to hold back the screams that wanted to bubble forth, Alaric felt a heavy hand on his shoulder before a feeling of weightlessness filled him. He finally sagged with relief when the pain subsided and popped his eyes open to look around in surprise when he found himself stretched across one of the beds in the basement. Erick was at his side; his expression was filled with curiosity as he looked something over on the monitor beside him.

Alaric frowned when he noticed an IV needle was injected into his arm, and electrodes were attached to his chest and head. How the hell had they hooked him up so fast? He looked beyond the men and women that filled the room, focused on a clock hanging on the wall, and paused in shock. An hour had passed since his time in the bathroom with Na'tori. How was that possible? He looked at Alara, her worried expression portraying every fear imaginable as he pulled the electrodes from his body and sat up. No one objected, so he figured it was okay to do so.

"What happened?" He finally questioned when everyone continued to stare at him in silence.

Alara stepped forward, hesitantly placed her hands on the sides of his head, and gasped in pain before Rome snatched her away from him and ensured that she siphoned from him to help her heal the burn marks that had appeared on her palms.

"I had to give you a serious blood transfusion as well as an EEG scan to monitor your brain waves," Erick commented. "Alara, Rome, and even Alondra attempted to check you to see what was causing you so much pain, but no one could touch you to heal you without suffering minor burns."

His gaze shot to Rome. "Show me."

Rome was the most powerful being on the planet—to their knowledge—if he was hurt when touching him, then what did that mean? He could hear and feel his heart leaping in his chest and watched as Rome reached up. Alaric felt the exact moment his hands were placed against his head. His skin tingled before his brother-in-law jerked his hands back and revealed his palms that now looked singed as if they had been placed against a hot surface.

"Touching you feels like touching a hot flame," Rome stated as his flesh healed within seconds. "Erick is running bloodwork to determine the cause because we can't touch you long enough to decipher the problem. If you hadn't calmed down on your own, we would have needed to knock you out. It almost looked as if you were having a seizure."

Everyone looked to Erick when the monitor beeped, indicating the results. He pulled the information up, and his expression became paler than he already was before his eyes shot to Alaric. Red eyes glowed like rubies as he looked Alaric up and down like a puzzle he was trying to solve. Or maybe even an experiment gone wrong.

"God," Akio grumbled, "the anticipation is killing me. What's his issue, doc?"

Erick rubbed the back of his neck, closed his eyes, and sighed heavily before once again pinning him with a stare. "I hate being the bearer of bad news."

"Fucking spit it out." Alaric snapped, tired of waiting to hear what clearly would be life-changing results.

"Simply put, your entire body is infected with the virus that was killing you previously. Your blood is filled with the stuff, which could explain the seizures. On the other hand, your brain waves look... unusual, to say the least. I can't tell what the issue is, but something is wrong, Alaric, and I think that something...is death."

Everyone began to talk at once, yet Alaric ignored them. Instead, his mind focused on his conversation with the Gods. He felt his anger bubble forth. Those bastards had known. They'd known that the virus would still be present, but instead of flowing and attempting to reach every cell and organ in his body, it would corrupt his entire being. He stood swiftly, shoved Erick out of the way, and scanned the results the computer had spit out for him. He couldn't read medical jargon, but from the video of his blood under a microscope, he could make out the difference in the blood test Erick had run on him several months ago.

"What does this mean?" He found himself asking.

"You're dying." Erick stated plainly, "I don't know if anything can stop it. When I gave you the blood transfusions, I figured it would combat the virus that's eating away at your cells, but all that did was feed it. The virus fell still after a few blood bags, allowing the new source to spread through you. It's almost as if…God, I hate to say it…but the virus is causing your body to feed on itself. It's similar to the decomposition of Rogue's when they are reduced to ash but a slower and more painful process." He paused. "Can you tell me what you're feeling right now? Maybe we can find a silver lining in the situation and figure out a way to stop this and reverse it."

"Is Na'tori aware?"

Alara strode forward and forced him to turn until he stared down into her teary eyes. Fuck. He was sick and tired of seeing her cry, but there was nothing he could do about it.

"Don't say what I think you're going to say." She gripped his hands within her own, "Don't do this."

Alondra spoke from her position behind Rome but approached as well. "Do what?"

Alaric kept his face impassive. He was still upset with Alondra for the secrets she kept to herself, and he still wanted to know what they were, yet a part of him understood. Especially if the secrets were in the name of protecting someone else. He wanted that to be her reasoning because if it wasn't, then he wouldn't see the justification for the act.

With both of them staring at him, Alara with her tears, and Alondra with a curious expression that screamed more anger than any other emotion, he felt he had no choice but to come clean. If anyone deserved an answer, it was the women that he'd done everything to save, but what he wouldn't have was an audience. He pulled his eyes away to greet Rome's cold stare.

"I'd like to speak with my sisters alone."

"We're a family," Silas frowned, "whatever you plan on saying to them, I think we each have a right to know as well."

Alaric looked around the room and took in each and every expression that stared back at him. They didn't want to know to be nosey; they wanted to know because they cared. With his incessant need to make jokes, even Akio was blessedly silent, just waiting to hear what he had to say. Silas was right. This was his family, and they deserved to know just as much as his sisters did. He sighed and ran his hand over his face as frustration poured through him. Alara's hands gripping his own usually calmed him, but he didn't feel that calm for once as she held onto his hand like a lifeline. Instead, he felt an insurmountable rage with no way to release it, and that door in his mind shuddered as the darkness he knew lay beyond pushed and attempted to break it down. He fortified his mental shields and spoke.

"I'm okay with dying. I don't want or need anyone going to extraordinary measures in an attempt to save me. I'm okay."

Silas stalked forward and shoved him with enough force to loosen Alara's hold before he pinned him to the wall and snarled. "What the fuck are you even saying right now? You're not just going to accept death."

"I never wanted this life to begin with." Alaric pushed him off, felt his fangs drop in aggression, and snarled. "I came back because I wanted a mate. I wanted Na'tori. And guess what, Si, I can't fucking mate her! I've tried and nothing. Those damn Gods of yours lied to me, and to top it all off, I'm still dying from the same shit I was dying from before. Being an Eternal has changed nothing for me but made me more aggressive and unhinged than I was before!"

"Maybe it's because of this virus," Alara interceded.

She attempted to move back into his space, yet Rome pulled her back and placed her behind his back, and his eerie blue gaze observed Alaric. "Si, step back right now." He ordered, "Something's wrong."

Alaric watched as his closest friend did as he was told while a ringing seemed to fill his ears. He slammed his hand against the side of his head when that damn door in his mind creaked open, and darkness crept through.

"Erick...do something now!" Rome exclaimed as a broad sword appeared in his hands.

Alaric wasn't sure what was happening, but the ringing in his head got louder, and the need to crush something with his mind whipped through him. It was like being hit by lightning. He grit his teeth when the pain from earlier returned and dizziness slammed into him from all sides. He heard a curse before something pierced his neck, and he fell into darkness.

CHAPTER
TWENTY-FOUR

N a'tori woke slowly and stretched, her hand reaching for the other side of the bed in search of Alaric, but instead, she encountered cool sheets. Her eyes flew open, the sun bled through the shades from the window, and the events of last night played back in her head. She looked around the room, hoping to see any trace of him, and paused when her eyes landed on someone she didn't expect to see. Alara was leaning against the closed bedroom door; her eyes looked sheltered yet filled with pain as dark bags sat beneath them. It looked like the woman hadn't slept for days, which worried Na'tori. Before she could question her, Alara spoke. Her voice was small and cracked as if she had been using it to scream at the top of her lungs, and now it was rubbed raw.

"I need you to save my brother. We don't know each other well, but I believe you can help him. Not just because you're a scientist or doctor but because I know you care about him." Alara wiped the fresh tears that had begun to pour down her face. "I don't even think he wants you to be aware of this, but I don't think I should keep you from this because you might be the only one who could help him. The virus didn't only progress; it has infected his entire body, and he's going to die, Tori. I just know it. I can feel it through whatever bond we forged in the womb. I don't know what's going on with him, but his abilities are so much stronger than before. He has no control over it when his emotions are heightened, and the pain makes him…unhinged. Erick just had to sedate him because Rome could feel the power growing within him. I-"

Na'tori cut her off as she came to her feet beside the bed, sheets wrapped around her body to hide her nudity. "Wait, so Erick gave him what exactly? And what do you mean his entire body is infected now? I thought becoming an Eternal was what was going to help him get rid of it. What happened while I slept, and why did no one come and get me?"

"Eternals can't become influenced by any drug or alcoholic drink by any means, but if you administer human blood that is filled with the drug or drink of your choice and inject it directly into a Guardians bloodstream, then they're easily influenced. In this case, Erick shot him up with some Ambien-laced blood. Hopefully, he'll sleep until the afternoon, and by then, maybe you could help me come up with an answer on how to save him. Everyone involved knew that changing him wasn't a fix. None of us knew what carrying the virus you created would do once he became an Eternal. This is something new for all of us to unpack."

"So he really is dying still?" Na'tori whispered as she retook her seat on the bed. "How am I supposed to help him? I know nothing about the genetic makeup of an Eternal. I've never…God…"

Tears flowed uncontrollably at the thought of losing Alaric. She couldn't for the life of her understand why it was hitting her so hard. They were still in the stage of getting to know one another, but he was the first man to treat her as if she were more. He saw her. She had to believe he saw her because she saw him so clearly that it scared her. She could fall in love with him. Shit, maybe she already had. Na'tori had been okay with the mating. Even knowing so little about the man who had come into her life like a runaway train, she had wanted his bite. She wanted him.

Cold hands gripped her own, and she focused enough to find Alara beside her on the bed with a teary gaze that matched hers. "I need your help Na'tori." She pleaded. "I'll do whatever, just help my brother."

"You don't have to try to convince me," she replied, "I would have helped him regardless. Alaric and I may not yet be mated, but I see him as mine, so please, the next time something is going on with him, can you come find me so that I can help when everything is going on instead of coming when it's all said and done."

"We weren't trying to keep you out of anything; it's just that so much happened within a short amount of time that we didn't think about it." She rubbed her palms as if she still felt the burns that were caused after touching Alaric, "Trying to heal him was like placing my hands into a pit of fire. Rome was even unsuccessful. I figured maybe I could get Rome or any of the others to be a base-line for what's considered normal readings for you to work with Erick to do whatever you need to do to heal him."

Na'tori nodded in understanding before she stood and crossed the room to dress in something presentable. She didn't know how fast the virus was progressing in him now that he was immortal. Maybe she had more time to find a definitive cure now, or perhaps the time of death had been sped up because of what he now was. There was no telling until she tested his blood and looked every-thing over. Earlier, she had cared about modesty, but now she just wanted to get down to Alaric as fast as she could, so she dropped the sheet and quickly pulled on a pair of sweatpants and one of Alaric's shirts.

"I need you to promise me something," Alara stated with an expression that Na'tori couldn't figure out.

"Promise you what?"

"I need you to promise me you won't hurt him. Don't put him through anything that isn't needed, and don't be like your brothers."

Na'tori didn't want to ask, yet she knew she needed something. She needed to know how bad it was and how bad her family had treated her. She knew they did evil things, but the way Alara looked at her now and the fear she could see on her face told her that things were so much worse than she'd initially thought. They'd done something terrible. Clearly, her brothers had hurt this woman, but what could she do to help her?

"What did they do to you?"

Alara smiled weakly. "It doesn't matter. I've found myself in a better mindset and don't want to rehash the past, but I do think that if you knew what happened to me, it would make you see that there's nothing worth saving when it comes to Lukas Titan. I can't say anything about the other brothers because I've never met them, but I'm sure they're just as bad, which is why you surprised me. You act nothing like him."

Na'tori crossed the room after tying her hair into a ponytail and retook her seat beside Alara. She moved to reach out and hold her hand and thought better of it. They weren't close. Shit, she knew her even less than she knew Alaric; she didn't want to overstep and make her uncomfortable, but Na'tori also wanted her to know that whatever she had to say, she would be there for her. The thought and patience Alaric's sister had given her since she arrived here was a blessing she hadn't realized was needed, and she wanted to show that same support and understanding. She thought she would have to ask Alara again what Lukas had done to her but paused when she spoke.

"The night Cairo burned the last facility to the ground was the night my sister made a mistake. She took me back to Titan in order to help lure Rome there, and your brother took what wasn't his to take. He raped me because he wanted me to bare his children. Rome tried to kill him and his guard with his blades, and when we found out he lived..." her eyes closed briefly with her hands fisted within her lap, and her breaths came easier. "When we found out he lived, a part of me was glad because I wanted to be the one to kill him. I still do, but I don't just want to kill him for what he did to me. I want to kill him for doing the things he's done to hurt my family. I want to kill him for putting Alaric through this."

It was hard to digest what she was hearing. Her brother had

done what? She wanted to throw up. Her stomach churned as nausea swam through her, but she wasn't just sick; she was furious. She had helped him get away. Without her, he would have died in the facility, but because she had wanted to save her brother…fuck, she was just as much to blame as Lukas. How could he have done such a thing? How could he do something so heinous and wrong and then just go about life as if he hadn't just ripped a woman's choice and world apart? Na'tori stood and crossed the room to stand at the window. Pushing the shades back to allow the sun to kiss her skin, she stared out towards the city, her emotions and mind fighting to make sense of what she now knew. She wanted justice. Not just for Alara but for every individual who had ever been hurt by her family. How could she do that for them?

She pressed her hand against the warm glass as tears filled her eyes. "I helped them hurt so many people," she whispered, "what does that make me?"

"Don't look at what you did before. Look at what you're doing now. You've already proven to me that you can be better than the rest of your family."

Na'tori shook her head, more tears fell down her cheeks, but she furiously wiped them away and turned to meet Alara's stare. "That night, I helped him. I'm why he's still alive, but I didn't know that he…I don't think I would have helped him had I known what had just occurred."

Alara didn't speak for several moments, but when she did, there was no anger in her tone, just simple curiosity. "Alaric knew, didn't he?"

"Not until recently. He didn't want anyone to know just yet, and now I know why. He wanted to protect you from the truth."

"He wasn't protecting me, Tori; he was protecting you." She wiped her tears as she came to her feet. "And now I need you to protect him. Help me save his life. By any means necessary, we need to save him. He doesn't deserve this."

"Lead the way."

She followed Alara from the room and hoped that she could do what she was asking of her. She hoped she could save Alaric's life.

Six hours later, Na'tori sat at Erick's desk in the infirmary with her head buried in her arms. Nothing. She'd come up with nothing. No matter how many tests she'd run, Alaric's results were still the same. He was dying. There was a possible move she could make, but fear held her immobile. Could she do it and get successful results, or would she be right back where she started? She didn't want to keep failing.

She looked up to watch the rise and fall of Alaric's chest as he lay unmoving atop one of the beds with IVs and monitors hooked to his body. Although the sun had fallen from the sky half an hour ago, he had yet to wake up. All the Guardians except Silas had gone out for a hunt, leaving him to watch over Alara, Alondra, Na'tori, and Alaric. She knew Silas had stayed behind to ensure his best friend woke up, and she couldn't blame him. If not for Rome telling everyone to head out, they would have stayed to ensure Alaric awoke without problems, but Na'tori had promised she could handle him alone.

She turned back to look over the results of the last blood test she'd run and groaned in frustration. The virus had corrupted his cells so thoroughly that there was no telling if she could reverse it. They just kept multiplying. The blood Erick had provided him with had long since dissipated, and she feared that when he awoke, Alaric would be just as volatile as he'd been before.

She pulled a packaged needle off of the tray beside the desk and quickly drew her own blood before she could talk herself out of it. She bit her nails nervously after placing a mix of her and Alaric's blood into a tube within the bio-mixer Rome had brought in for her. As she waited for the results, her eyes scanned the room. The cells in the back of the room were blessedly empty; only Alaric occupied one of the three hospital beds within the infirmary, and the cabinets and tables were fully stocked with medical supplies that could help them in any situation. The bio-mixer beeped to indicate it had finished the cycle, but before she could check it, a gust of air blew against her, and the feeling of someone standing over her registered throughout her body and within her mind. She didn't have to look towards the bed to know that Alaric was up and now standing behind her; she could feel his unique energy rubbing against her own. A hand fisted her ponytail and pulled her head back until she stared into his questioning gaze.

"What's going on, princess, and why do I scent blood?" He inhaled and groaned, "Please tell me that's you that smells so mouthwatering."

"I needed to test your blood and mine together. Maybe that would help the virus and help me learn why you haven't been able to mate with me."

"And who told you about the virus? Alara, I'm sure, she's so adamant about saving me. You want to know what would really help me?"

Her saliva dried up in her mouth when his tongue peeked out to lick across his lips. She moaned softly when his hand tightened, and the other trailed a burning path down her chest to cup her right breast. This sexual connection between them had spiked and bloomed into so much more since their last sexual encounter. She always wanted him now, but she hid it better than Alaric. For Alaric, he simply reacted no matter where they were or who they had the potential to be around. When he wanted her, he acted, and she followed his lead.

"What would help you?" She whispered, sure she already knew what answer he would give her.

Alaric tugged on her ponytail, causing her to come her feet before he kicked the chair away and bent her forward until her breasts and face were pressed against the desk. His erection dug into her, causing a soft moan to part her lips as he leaned forward and kissed her cheek before he trailed a hand down her back. She pushed against his hand and groaned when a sharp slap was delivered to her ass.

"Stay still," He ordered, "let me help myself feel better."

She knew that at any moment, one of the others could make their way downstairs and find them in a compromising position, but when Alaric tore the sweats down her legs and gripped each of her ass cheeks within his hands, she was past caring. He crouched behind her, latched his mouth onto her clit, and sucked before plunging two thick fingers into her wetness. She moaned loud and long when a small orgasm flowed through her, causing her legs to shake and her eyes to fall closed in ecstasy.

"You taste so good, princess," he groaned, "now let's see if feeling you wrapped around my dick helps."

It took a few moments to register what he was saying, but by the time she did, Alaric was sliding the thickness of his erection into her. She went onto the balls of her feet and moaned when his hand slapped against her ass and caused her to plant her feet once more on the floor. His answering groan sent her pulse skyrocketing, yet he didn't move. He wasn't thrusting into her, he wasn't owning her. Alaric stood behind her, dick buried in her pussy so deeply that she could nearly feel him in her gut, and all he did was caress the globes of her ass as she shuddered around him. Na'tori feared opening her mouth and shattering whatever this energy between them was, but she needed him to move. With him touching her, it didn't take much to have her on the precipice of another orgasm. She could feel it sitting, waiting, and hoping to climb higher, only to wash over her in a blurred release that would leave her like jello at his feet.

"We're going to make a deal." His voice was deep and choked as if he struggled with his words.

"What deal?" Na'tori smiled when his hands trailed up her back, pushing the shirt up as he went.

"You get one chance at saving me. One chance only, and then you leave it alone. I don't want anyone risking anything to save my life, and I don't want you beating yourself up when you realize there's nothing to be done." He laid across her back and nipped her ear playfully, "In exchange, I will manage my anger better to ensure no more flare-ups, as well as guarantee you repeated orgasms for the rest of our time together."

How he could discuss such a sensitive matter at this time was beyond her. Why would she agree, and why did he want them to give up on him so quickly? Did he really feel so undeserving of life? Of happiness? Love?

Na'tori pushed back against him and moaned when he went a lot deeper than she'd intended. She'd assumed the whole thing was already inside of her, but she'd been wrong. God, he was huge. Her hands clenched into fists when he hissed and slowly slid out until only the head of his dick remained. The weight of his chest was gone, and her eyes slid closed on a moan when his hips slapped against her own when he sank back inside and paused. She had to know how he was keeping his composure while she was slowly losing hers. Her entire body felt like a livewire, trembling in anticipation of the orgasm she knew would take her breath away.

"Don't do that again, princess," he took hold of her ponytail and pulled her up until his lips hovered near her ear. His following words were whispered into her ear as he fucked her slowly. "All that's left to do is agree."

"W-why do you f-feel unworthy of living a full h-h-happy life?" She gasped and struggled between words but still got her question out.

"Because the things I've done in my life have tainted my soul and mind so thoroughly that nothing could cleanse me from the evil I helped your family do. If death is my fate, then I accept it. You should, too."

"I get one chance?"

"One chance." He groaned and tightened his hand within her ponytail as well as the hand that gripped her ass like a lifeline.

With every slide into her, Na'tori felt the walls around her heart fall. She could feel his aura caressing her skin, amping her higher towards the peak of oblivion she desperately wanted to reach, yet the part of her that cared about his life edged her towards their reality. Her walls came back up, and yet the words that left her mouth belied her true feelings. Her words cemented what she didn't feel.

"One chance." Na'tori agreed.

Alaric growled with approval and she knew that if she could see his expression, his eyes would be feral as he watched their joining, and his fangs would be peeking from beneath his lips as he attempted to keep himself in check. The noises that came from them both were a symphony of its own making as her cream coated him and ran down her inner thighs. When his hand slid around to her hooded clit Na'tori's eyes rolled into the back of her head, her toes curled, and her body tensed like a violin bow as an orgasm so intense slammed through her and robbed her of sanity and breath. Alaric's answering groan and the feel of his cum filling her was enough confirmation of a deal sealed as he allowed her body to rest once more against the desk.

CHAPTER
TWENTY-FIVE

Three days later, Alaric found himself shoved against the brick wall of a building with Silas's forearm pressed into his throat, cutting off his air and effectively stopping the darkness from tearing down the rest of the walls within his mind. Only when he tapped frantically against his best friend's ribcage did Silas back away gradually, and yet his eyes watched him like a hawk.

"Are you sure you've got whatever that shit is under control? I'd hate to have to get Rome to take your ass back home." He commented, his face full of exasperation and wariness.

"I'm fine," Alaric replied, "I've got it under control."

He didn't know how factual his response was, but he didn't want to be confined to the house again. He wasn't sure how much longer he could have been within the walls of the house he called home without taking Na'tori on every hard surface he neared. His control was frayed. In fact, there was none left. With every sexual encounter they had, he fell more deeply into the hole of need that he was unsure how to climb out of it, and the frustration of not being able to sink his fangs into her as he fucked her into oblivion wasn't helping him any. No matter how much he worshipped her body and brought them both to completion so filling, he couldn't mark her as his mate.

It wasn't just the sex that pulled him in. Na'tori's giving nature and how she seemed to get along with his sisters—although he still questioned her and Alondra's relationship. She put her heart into everything she did, easily and without fear of being hurt. Alaric could see how she trusted his newfound family and could sense her love for them as if it was simply second nature for her. Just the other day, he'd walked in to find her and Erick with their heads together as they talked over new devices she was attempting to create to assist them in battles with the Rogues. Anger had initially tightened his gut until he'd seen the respectable distance between them.

Everyone seemed aware of the tight leash he was attempting to keep around himself. With every snarl and rumbling growl, the rest of the house observed him to gauge his mood, yet only one person could fix it. The object of his obsession, Na'tori.

"Fuck, that better be for Tori and not because I just gripped you up." Silas scoffed as he turned back to watch the people milling around the bar they were supposed to be watching.

Alaric tried not to feel embarrassed as his erection dug against the zipper of his jeans. He was in a perpetual state of arousal, and it damn sure wasn't because of what had happened moments ago. No, he was rock fucking hard because no matter how often he gorged on Na'tori's body, he wasn't satiated.

He shoved Silas in the back and attempted to change the subject as he prayed for his dick to soften. "What makes this bar so special?"

"Akio recently heard chatter from whatever part of the black web he frequents that Titan soldiers regularly visit this bar. I offered to see if the rumors were true. You're here because Rome wanted you out of the house. You're making his mate uncomfortable with all the sex you and Na'tori seem incapable of silencing. Still, I was told you aren't to reveal your Eternal side, so you have no supernatural speed or strength, and you damn sure don't show off your ability to heal. Titan doesn't need to know that Eternals are possible to create. Got me?"

It wasn't often someone could make him feel embarrassed, and yet here he was once again, feeling the warmth upon his cheeks as he blushed. Knowing his sisters could most likely hear the sexual antics between him and Na'tori had never registered for him, but now that it did, he promised himself from here on out, he would control himself better. The Eternals hearing him was to be expected because of their heightened senses, but if Alondra and Alara could hear them as well, then that was mortifying.

"I'll refrain from being so vocal." He turned to watch the bar across the street when Silas chuckled. "What, Si?"

"Does this include the free show I saw in the hallway last night?"

Alaric snarled at the thought of the night before. He'd been told once again that he couldn't leave the premises, and anger had funneled through him at the thought, but before it could fester and boil over, Na'tori had dragged him into the hall and shoved his cock so far down her throat he'd seen stars. He'd only noticed Silas leaning against his bedroom door when the bastard had chuckled darkly and shifted the damn erection he'd witnessed behind his friends' jeans. The last time Silas had similarly caught them, Alaric attacked him, but last night had been different. Oh, he'd still been angry but not angry enough to stop Na'tori in her ministrations, and she seemed to like it. After swallowing his load, she turned to Silas and smiled before heading toward the basement to work some more.

"It was a hallway," Alaric finally grumbled, "you had just as much freedom to be there as we did. I'll try to corral her into a room the next time something like that happens. Now can we please fucking focus so this damn erection in my jeans can go away? I need to kill someone."

Silas smiled. "By all means, keep the shows coming...I like to watch." He shrugged. "I nearly forgot. This is your first time out since your transition. The killing won't help to kill your sex drive. Sorry to disappoint you, brother, but if anything, you'll want to get home to her and enact whatever filthy thoughts are flowing up there. If you decide to be an exhibitionist, let me know, and I'll pull up a chair."

"Shut the fuck up and quit teasing me about this!"

Alaric watched the bar's front door and tuned Silas out as best as he could, yet he could feel his stare drilling into the side of his head, and he somehow snuck through the barriers within his mind. *"Who says I'm teasing?"*

Before he could form words to respond, the door to the bar burst open, and three men filed out. One was being held up between two as he stumbled and slurred incoherent words. To anyone else who might be paying attention, that's what it would sound like, but for Silas and Alaric, they heard the words perfectly.

"We gotta catch those damn freaks and eradicate them from the world. Lukas doesn't know what the hell he's talking about. I say we get the government on board to run a blood test on every citizen in Van Scive. They wouldn't be able to hide from us, and we wouldn't need that stick-in-the-ass sister of his on missions with us."

"Clyde, would you shut the fuck up before you get us all killed?" One of them snapped as they threw him into the back seat of a four-door truck that had clearly been government-modified.

Alaric snarled and sent Silas a telepathic message. *"Please tell me we're killing them."*

"Not here," Silas replied.

They waited until the truck was down the street before they burst from the shadows and ran after the vehicle. They tried to stick as closely to the shadows as they could while keeping eyes on the truck as they went, but a shadow wasn't always promised, and if they happened to race past a human, the most they would notice was a blur of motion to accompany the gust of wind that would flow against them. Humans were easy to trick with the eyes, but if they ran past a Rogue, they would see them. Luckily, they ran into none as they made their way across town until they reached an apartment complex several blocks from the Titan warehouse.

Alaric watched the truck pull into a parking spot before the men once again carried their drunk man inside. From the outside, Alaric could tell they had entered an apartment on the third floor when a light flickered on, and three forms stumbled past the closed shades in what had to be the living room.

"So, how do you want to play this?" Alaric questioned as he itched for a fight.

"We wait until they sleep, and then we creep inside and get the answers we need by sifting through their thoughts. No need to go up, be spotted, and find ourselves fighting and garnering attention from unwanted eyes. If another human hears a fight, they will likely call the cops, and we can't have that." Silas replied as he pulled a blade from his jacket and cleaned his nails with the sharp edge.

"And why can't we just read their thoughts from here?"

Alaric didn't want to wait until the bastards fell asleep. He wanted to act now before the darkness could start building and pushing against his mental shields once more. Holding that darkness back when it rose within him was becoming harder and harder to contain. Only when he was buried in a part of Na'tori's body or when he was close to losing consciousness did that darkness bow down to him long enough to shove it back behind the door he'd built for it. He didn't know if Silas choking him would work this time. His skin was itching at the thought of killing the men responsible for his family's hurt and pain. He didn't recognize the two guards who had helped the drunk, but he knew the drunk well. Had worked with him on many occasions. He was a man he would love to kill.

"If I attempt to read them from here, I'll only be successful in maybe reading one of them, but it would take time. Their mental walls are strong." Silas shook his head and grinned when he removed something from beneath his nail before he finished his statement, "Clearly, Titan's been practicing since you left them. This isn't the first time I've encountered strong blocks. Give me thirty minutes to an hour."

Alaric frowned and searched the minds of everyone within the building until he found the men he desired. Breaking through their mental shields took less than a minute, but when he did, a crack formed within the door that held back that thrashing darkness that steadily beat at him. He ignored it and focused on the task at hand, even when the weight of Silas's hand registered on his shoulder. He ignored that, too.

The first man was easy. He was young, new to the company, and learning the ropes. He didn't have vital information—not like Clyde and the other male—so he forced him to sleep after erasing his mind of everything having to do with Titan and planted a new objective for him. He was innocent, at least for now, but if he stayed with Titan, he would become their enemy once they corrupted him and taught him a way of life that would get him killed. When he woke, he would be headed for a plane in search of a new life far away from Titan's clutches, but when he slid into Clyde's mind and the male still holding him up, their future looked very different.

"Alaric, whatever you're doing, stop this!" Silas slid between the cracks within his mind and paused in shock. *"How are you doing this, and what the hell is that dark matter?"*

Alaric shoved him out before he could get a good look around and continued to pick apart the memories of the men inside. It was like watching a horror story unwind. Every rape, torture, and death they'd participated in over the years played within his mind until he paused on a memory of Na'tori. They were together, watching his woman like a piece of prime rib, and the thoughts that they shared about her sent him into a rage so deep that he didn't think about his next actions. No, that wasn't right. He thought about his actions, but he didn't give a damn.

He was racing across the street, all his thoughts on personally tearing their hearts from their chest when Silas slammed into him and pushed him up against the side of the building.

"Rein it the fuck in Alaric!" He struggled to hold him back when Alaric jerked forward and snapped his fangs in front of his face with a vicious snarl. "God, don't make me do this, brother."

Alaric felt the weight of Silas's forearm against his throat and slammed a fist into his ribs to loosen his hold, but he didn't release him. With his mind still connected to the bastards upstairs, he fell deeper into the depths of their depravity and went feral. His mind tore through their memories at a rapid speed before he slowly cut off the parts of their brains that told the body to function. He made it slow and painful even as he fought against Silas's immovable chokehold until Clyde was gasping for breath, and the man beside him was bleeding from every orifice his body possessed.

Blackness edged his mind seconds before Silas released him and snarled.

"Dammit! God fucking damn you. You told Rome you could handle this, but clearly, you can't. Now, there are two dead bodies we need to get rid of before they are found because you turned into a rabid animal. Is that what you fucking wanted?"

"No," Alaric replied with a calm that scared even him, "I wanted their beating hearts in my hands, but I suppose their gasping breaths and the scent of their blood will do."

Silas shook his head and stormed away without another word. Alaric followed, a grin stretched across his face as he licked the tips of his fangs in agitation. A new huger was burning through him, and he wanted to get home to his woman.

CHAPTER
TWENTY-SIX

No matter how many times he ran the test, he kept getting the same results. The decline was evident. There was nothing he could see that would work and save him. He would die.

Erick crumpled the test results in a fist and threw them into the trash. All his life, he had saved lives. Even before he became an Eternal, he was a doctor. Someone who valued life above all else, and now he was useless. No amount of medicine would cure the problem running through the blood that sat beneath his microscope. He ran stiff fingers through his waist-length snow-white hair, frustration and anger filling him to the brim as he listened to his family moving about upstairs. He should have been up there with them in preparation for the hunt tonight, but he couldn't focus.

After Alaric had lost control the night before, everyone was hesitant to allow him out for the night, although he'd brought back vital information. They now knew that Titan was beefing up their Rogues with some kind of injection created by Dr. Salazar, and now they were trying harder than ever to impregnate Kindred women in the hopes of breeding more Kindred. The information had infuriated them enough that Rome hadn't cared about the slaughter Alaric had committed. That didn't mean they weren't still worried.

Erick was worried about another matter entirely. With every use of his ability, he lost his fight with the land of the living. If what Silas had described about the labyrinth within Alaric's mind, then there was no telling if that darkness within him would corrupt him and drag him into an earlier grave.

"Hey, you alright?" Akio questioned as he stood at the foot of the steps.

Erick had never even heard him come down. He was so lost in thought that even his senses were failing him. He came to his towering height of six foot eight, grabbed his sword off the desk, and headed for Akio.

"Everything is fine." He replied as he met his brothers' eerie black gaze.

Akio watched him curiously and tucked a blade into the many pockets inside his black leather overcoat. "You know that Rome has paired us up for the night, right?"

"I'm aware."

Erick attempted to step around him but paused when Akio pressed a palm against his chest. "Promise me you're at your best because you won't be getting me killed out there because your head isn't screwed on right."

He stared at Akio's hand until it dropped, then stepped around him without saying another word. He was fine. He had no choice but to be.

CHAPTER
TWENTY-SEVEN

"Don't you ever feel like you should be out there too?" Na'tori questioned Alara as she helped her clean up the kitchen from the marathon of cooking they'd done in the last few hours.

Dishes of Lasagna, garlic bread, salad, pies, and cakes lined the countertops. Every night, Alara cooked for the entire house while they were out for a hunt, and since Eternals were still capable of eating solid foods, unlike Rogues, she ensured they got a good meal every morning they returned. It was thoughtful on so many levels, yet Na'tori couldn't help but wonder how a woman of immense power preferred to wait on the sidelines every night instead of being by her mate's side in battle. Na'tori would have been trying to convince Rome to let her join them if not for her vigilance in trying to find a cure for Alaric. Alaric wasn't her mate by bond, but she accepted him as such. A bite changed nothing for them.

Alara placed the last dish into the dishwasher before starting it. "I stay here because Rome would lose his mind if I fought beside him."

"He would do more than lose his mind," Amirishka chuckled.

She was leaning against the counter, piece of pie in hand, watching them.

"But you're nearly as strong as him, aren't you? And I know you spar with Amirishka and Maverick." Na'tori wiped the countertops down and sat on one of the stools in front of the island. "If you can hold your own against them, then surely you can handle a few Rogues and the humans that accompany them."

"That's not the point." Alara dropped a plate of food before her and looked towards the clock to check the time. "If I go out with him, he'll do nothing but worry. He won't be able to help it. It's in his genetic makeup to protect me at all costs. It doesn't matter how strong I am or what I can do. To Romulus, I'll always be looked at as something to protect, and the rest of them can sometimes be worse because I'm considered their queen."

"Not considered our queen," Amirishka scoffed as she plated another piece of pie, "You are our queen."

"So you see…" She smiled softly, "Staying here ensures that they aren't distracted, plus I'm perfectly safe here."

"Okay, that makes a bit more sense."

Amirishka finished her pie, wiped her mouth clean, and watched Na'tori with a curious expression. It looked almost as if she didn't want to voice what was on her mind before she spoke. "Do you think your brothers are looking for you, or do you believe they could care less?"

Na'tori opened her mouth to respond but froze instead when a red dot appeared over Alara's chest. She didn't think; she vaulted over the counter, knocking dishes and platters to the floor as she tackled Rome's wife to the ground. The sound of bullets hitting the window registered, yet no glass broke.

Amirishka snarled like a beast as she headed for the front door and removed her throwing stars from their hidden pockets before she spoke over her shoulder. "Get Rome here now, Alara, and find your sister!" She walked out the front door, deflecting bullets with her blades as she went.

The door closed behind her, and Na'tori found herself breathing easier when she looked at the windows in the living room. Dents filled the glass, but there were no cracks or proof that it would have shattered.

"It's bulletproof glass," Alara stated as she rose to her feet and grabbed Na'tori's arm to pull her towards the location of the bedrooms, "Come on, we have to get Alondra."

Na'tori tugged against her hold. "We can't just leave Amirishka! We have to help her."

"Trust me, she can handle herself. Now let's go."

She wasn't sure what happened. One moment, she was sure she was heading for the door to help Amirishka—even without the blade she typically carried—and the next moment, she was pulled behind Alara as they headed for Alondra's bedroom. Her body felt weaker somehow, making it easy for her to be dragged along, and when she looked at Alara, it was to find her aura pulsing and thumping with so much life and energy that it was clear to see that she had siphoned from her. Na'tori yanked her arm away and stumbled back just as they reached her sister's room. She was dizzy for several moments before she could see straight again.

Alara looked back at her and snapped at her with a quick lashing of words, "We don't have time for this, Tori! Titan is here. They are at our doorstep, and that has never happened before. They've never attacked us without the Guardians present, which means they've been watching the house, and they specifically waited until nearly everyone was gone to launch this attack. This is bad because I can't reach Rome. Something is blocking me."

"Then we need to help Ami. She's fighting, we don't know how many guards, and we're cowering in here." Na'tori shot back as she moved past her and into the room where Alondra slept, utterly oblivious to the danger lurking around her.

She approached the window facing the front street while Alara attempted to shake her sister awake before she gasped at the sight that greeted her. Several guards lay on the harsh ground with blood pouring from multiple stab wounds while Amirishka used her unnatural speed to avoid the tranq darts and bullets from piercing her. She watched as a guard was tackled to the ground behind an armored vehicle before Amirishka sank her fangs into his jugular and sucked greedily. Her aura pulsed and whipped around her, growing with each pull of blood that she seemed to gulp down before she stood to her feet. Her mouth was moving, yet she couldn't hear her words.

Na'tori watched with bated breath when the remaining six guards paused simultaneously, turned their guns around until the barrel was pressed against their skulls, and pulled the trigger. Blood and brain matter flew through the air, the bodies crumpled to the ground, and Amirishka swayed on her feet before she stumbled and looked up towards the window. Pure, unadulterated fear stared back at Na'tori seconds before the Eternals' eyes rolled into the back of her head, and she fell face-first into the pavement.

"Oh God," Na'tori whispered as her eyes scanned the street for more guards.

"What? What is it?" Alara questioned from behind her before she gasped in shock, "We have to get her out of the street. We have to do it now!"

She raced from the room before Na'Tori could utter a single word. She couldn't even move an inch as the reality of the situation dawned on her. She'd been behind these walls all this time, forgetting the danger her brothers presented to every Eternal and Kindred that walked the earth. They were willing to shoot up homes and rape women. When would it stop? When would they be safe?

Na'tori turned and headed for the door to help Alara, yet paused when her gaze caught and held onto Alondra's still form. She squinted and called on her ability. Alondra's aura was the weakest she had ever seen, causing concern to fill her and indecision that made her glance between the woman lying across the bed and the woman passed out on the pavement outside. Did she help Alondra or help Alara with Amirishka? Titan reinforcements had yet to arrive, but that didn't mean they weren't on their way, and Alaric's sister didn't just look asleep; she looked deathly sick. She was teetering on the edge about what to do when shadows surrounded Alara outside before Rome appeared with a broad sword in hand and fangs bared.

She didn't wait to see what she would do. Instead, she moved for

Alondra, placed two fingers against her pulse, and frowned when a weak beat greeted her. She tapped her cheeks furiously as she spoke. "Alo, wake up, sweetheart, and tell me what's wrong."

She remained still, and Na'tori knew without a doubt that Alaric's sister was still suffering from the problem she'd attempted to help her with only a few years ago. She raced to Alaric's room without a second thought, rummaged through the dresser she'd labeled as her own, and bypassed the injectors she'd been hiding from Alaric before pulling out a syringe she'd hoped to never have to use again.

Since seeing Alondra again, Na'tori had dreaded this moment happening, but she'd known that it might. She'd known that her body might weaken and leave her in a nearly catatonic state. She had known, and she had kept it secret from everyone. No one else had noticed Alondra's absence in recent days. No one had seen the bags under her eyes, the constant naps, the chills, and even those rare moments when she seemed almost subdued instead of the usual spitfire she was, but Na'tori had. Na'tori knew she was getting sick again and, in secret, had made a batch of drugs that would curb the problem. At least until she figured something else out.

When she reentered Alondra's bedroom, she didn't pause or stop to think about what she was doing. She knew this was the only way to help her. She tugged the shirt down and jabbed the long spinal needle into Alondra's chest, hoping and praying she was placing it correctly before injecting the substance directly into her heart. She had no clue if it would be fast-acting or gradual, but she could breathe easier for now. At least she'd done something.

She moved to climb from the bed when Alondra's arm shot out and wrapped around her throat. Her grip was firm as she sat up and produced a thin blade from beneath the sheet. Na'tori froze, even though she could have fought back, but they weren't enemies. With the cool metal pressed against her jugular, she stared into grey eyes that carried streaks of light blue like her sister's. Confusion filled her gaze.

"Alo," Na'tori whispered, "It's me. It's Tori." She held her hands loosely at her sides and waited.

Alondra glanced around the room and seemed to realize where she was before she slowly unfurled her hand and sat back with a heavy sigh. "I'm sorry, I-i-i guess I forgot where I was. Did I hurt you?"

She shook her head and rubbed her throat softly as she came to her feet. "You didn't hurt me, but where did you think you were, and why didn't you come to me before it got this bad? You know I would have helped you."

"Yeah," she scoffed, "And risk them all learning my truth. No, thank you, but no. Now, where is everyone?"

"Shit!"

Na'tori left the bedroom without another word and searched for Rome, Alara, and Amirishka. She prayed that the Eternal was okay and hadn't been severely hurt by the guards. There was no telling where this fight between Titan and the Eternals would go, but she could feel a sense of doom looming over her. Something terrible was headed their way, and she needed them to get in front of it.

CHAPTER
TWENTY-EIGHT

Alaric punched a hole in the chest of the Rogue he was fighting, ripped his heart out, and watched as the body slowly began to eat away at itself until all that remained were ashes. He felt the fiend's heart deteriorate within his palm before he grimaced and wiped his hand across his blood-soaked jeans. He glanced around the alleyway he and Silas had found themselves in and saw the blood splatter and clothing that hadn't joined their enemies in the afterlife. A few Titan soldiers littered the ground as well, bite marks in their throats after he'd gorged on their blood in an attempt to curb the dark urges that were coursing through him. It wasn't just his clothing that was soaked in blood. He could feel the sticky substance sticking to his chin from when he'd fed; he could feel it beneath his nails, and he was sure he also had it within his hair. The scent of the stuff filled his nostrils and made him wish for more. He wanted more bloodshed, more piercing screams, and more of his enemies crushed beneath his boots.

"Can we talk about what the hell is going on with you now?" Silas questioned from his position at the opening of the alley.

He didn't want to get into this. He knew what Silas wanted to know. It's what everyone in the house wanted to know. Why was he so feral? Why didn't he want to fight to live? The first question he could answer easily enough. He couldn't mate with Na'tori, and each time he devoured and worshipped her body, he fell deeper and deeper into the darkness that pulled at his mind because no matter how hard he tried, he couldn't bite her and inject his essence into her as he fucked her. It was making him unhinged, tearing apart his mind until all he thought of was the heaven between her thighs or the blood he could shed from his enemies. He was obsessed.

The second question was a lot more complex. It's not that he wished for death. No, he very much wanted to live, but for what? What was living a life of craving and yearning for a woman he could never have the way he wanted? He didn't want to continuously fight the demons within his mind only to risk hurting the ones he loved when he finally broke. And he would break. He reinforced the barriers within his mind daily, and each time, his resolve weakened as a part of him wondered why that darkness called to him on such a visceral level. Yet each time a bit of it leaked through, he acted like a raging animal that knew no control.

"Alaric!" Silas snapped, "Talk to me. I'm your friend. I won't judge you for whatever it is that is eating away at you, but this," he indicated with his hand at the slaughter within the alley, "this can't keep happening. I won't keep covering up this madness of yours from Rome."

"Then tell him," He replied as he began to collect and search the Rogue's clothing before tossing them into a dumpster. "I never told you to keep anything from him."

"He'll lock you up again, and you don't deserve that."

"If you could see what I'm struggling with, then maybe you wouldn't be so quick to say that. You don't know what I deserve, Si."

Silas pushed away from the building and approached him with a snarl. "I would know if only you would speak your fucking mind. Dammit, Alaric, I literally watched you lose your shit. Do you even realize that you killed all seven of them...alone! I didn't lift my finger to help you because you were on a warpath, and I figured maybe you needed this, but then you started guzzling their blood. You started feeding from them, not just from the humans but also the

Rogues. So tell me now, brother, what the hell is going on with you? Let me help you."

"You want to help me?" He met Silas's gaze and smirked, "Then help me get rid of these bodies, and then maybe do us both a favor and tell Rome the truth because if you really care, then you'll protect everyone from me. Especially Na'tori. You promised me a quick death if I started to become uncontrollable, and I'm telling you now, brother, it's happening whether we want it to or not."

Alaric shifted his gaze to the alley entrance, heard multiple humans' footsteps, and slid into their minds as he coerced their thoughts to keep walking by no matter what they heard and keep their eyes forward. For the last thirty minutes, that's what he assumed Silas had been doing as he'd slaughtered Titan's men, but now his friend was so distracted and enraged that his focus was split.

Silas gripped his shoulder and sighed heavily. "I can't believe I promised you that, but I need you to tell me the truth, Alaric. Do you truly wish for it? Do you want death?"

"If Na'tori isn't mine then the world would be better without me."

"You hardly know the woman."

He tried not to let his words affect him and stepped back, allowing Silas's hand to fall. "I can't explain what I feel for her, Si, but I know she is meant to be mine. You're eight hundred and twenty-six with no mate. You may be okay with that lonely existence, but I, on the other hand, am not."

Silas's expression became sheltered as shadows spread throughout the space around them seconds before Rome appeared. His expression was a thundercloud of anger, power leaking from his pours as a torrent of rain began to pour around them.

"House. Now." He spoke through fangs as sharp as knives.

"We have clean up, sir." Silas tilted his head in the direction of the human bodies that still littered the ground. "We can't risk anyone stumbling upon them."

With a wave of Rome's hand, blue flames engulfed the human bodies and reduced them to ash in a matter of seconds before he gripped Silas and Alaric by the shoulder and transported them home. They appeared within the lower levels where Amirishka lay unconscious on a hospital bed as Erick ran her vitals and looked her over. Alara and Alondra stood off to the side, Alara with tears in her eyes and Alondra with an expression Alaric couldn't decipher. When his eyes landed on Na'tori, his heart took off in his chest, and the urge to go to her and pull her into his arms nagged at him. He chose to ignore it.

He could hear Maverick upstairs cursing and growling along with Cairo's eerie silence, and the sound of Akio's fingers flying over his keyboard told him that he was also up there. The whole gang was here, and yet there were hours of darkness left for them to hunt.

"What happened?" Silas questioned, his voice full of concern as he looked Amirishka over.

"My brother's guards attacked," Na'tori commented as she looked something over on the computer she stood before. She still had yet to look at him. "Ami went outside by herself and killed them all, but she was shot up with the tranq as well as a few bullets. I never saw them hit her, but then again, she was moving so fast that I just didn't think it was remotely possible. Her blood results tell a different story, though. She was definitely hit."

"I tried healing her." Alara spoke up, her eyes steadily clinging to Amirishka's still form, "I don't know what's happening. She isn't waking up."

Alaric tried not to react to the fact that Na'tori still hadn't noticed him, but he knew it was because she was desperately trying to get answers as to why Amirishka wasn't responding. He looked over at the female guardian and quickly slipped beneath the layers of her mind before he met utter silence. He didn't need to dive through memories or tear his way through inconsequential thoughts. She was simply blank, and he knew that wasn't possible. She was still blocking him somehow, but he knew it wouldn't take much to knock the wall down.

"Ami?" He questioned.

"Alaric?" Her voice was soft and confused, "why are you in my head?"

"Because we need you to wake up."

"I don't want to. Just leave me be."

Now, it was his turn to frown as confusion filled him. "Tell me why, or I'll tear through this facade you have going on. I know you're blocking me from seeing your truth, and that's fine. I can respect your need for privacy, but what I won't accept is you forcing yourself to stay within your mind. Especially not while everyone is attempting to wake you up."

At first, Alaric thought he would have to tear through whatever barrier she still had left, but she spoke, and his brain took a moment to process her words.

"I remember being hit with the tranq. I could feel the drug sliding through my veins, but there were still too many guards, and I knew I would lose consciousness and they would take the women, so I drained a guard and forced the rest of them to kill themselves. Something happened when I used my ability. It was something I'd never felt before."

"I think you should wake up and tell everyone that. Explain to Rome what happened; don't hide away here."

"Coming from the man, that's okay with simply dying."

He withdrew from her mind without another word. He wasn't touching that comment. Their circumstances were different. He didn't know exactly what her deal was, but she would be waking up, or he'd be diving back into her mind to lay all of her secrets bare.

"Alaric, my God, what happened to you!" Na'tori exclaimed when she noticed him and rushed over to his side.

As soon as she was close enough to touch, her mouth-watering scent curled around him and nearly pulled him into a trance. Her eyes speared him with a look of genuine concern, her hand lifted as if she planned to touch him, yet he knew she wouldn't because of the blood that still coated him.

"I'm okay, princess; it isn't my blood."

He curbed the urge to lick at the dried blood he could feel clinging to his lip as a swell of need roared through him. God. He wanted to see what she would look like riding his cock into oblivion. His hands clenched into fists as he imagined her breasts jumping with each thrust and how the position would allow him to slide so much deeper into her center. He felt his chest rumbling with what could have been described as a purr when Amirishka sat up swiftly and trained her gaze on him.

"Thank God," Alara jerked forward and hugged the female

guardian fiercely. "What the hell, Ami! Why wouldn't you wake up? You worried me to death."

Alaric watched Amirishka over Na'tori's head as she threw her legs over the edge of the bed. Her medium brown complexion had whitened slightly, but now that Alara was touching her, she was regaining her color. Rome was watching her closely, along with everyone else in the room. The woman standing an arm's length away was the only one still pinning him with their gaze. Na'tori was watching him warily. The feel of her eyes scanning him from head to toe made his heart race disarmingly faster.

Rome's voice broke whatever spell Na'tori was under as she turned and returned to the desk without another word. "What happened, Ami?"

Amirishka cleared her throat and met her king's unwavering stare as she spoke. "Titan attacked, I handled it, but I was hit multiple times with the tranq drug. I couldn't risk them going after the women, but when I used my ability, it felt like I was losing it."

"Explain." Erick interrupted as he removed the IV from her arm.

"I can't feel it anymore." Amirishka's voice was soft and nearly unrecognizable.

Rome stepped into his warrior's space and placed his hands around her head before he closed his eyes. Alaric didn't need to dive into their minds to figure out what he was doing. He knew Rome was seeing if what she said was true, and if by the look on his face, when he stepped back his words confirmed it even more that she wasn't lying.

"It's there, Ami, but it's drained. Your ability seems to have lost its potency. I'm unsure if it'll ever return to how it once was. It's nearly dormant."

Akio made his way down the steps with his laptop in hand as he spoke teasingly. "Does that mean she can't seduce us with that voice of hers anymore?"

"I can still stab you in the throat if you'd like." She smiled sweetly, yet her eyes spoke of uncertainty.

Alaric only noticed. After all, he watched everyone closely to ensure that no one was paying attention to him because he was slowly losing it. Whatever this little meet-up was, he needed it to be over with so he could get as far away from here as possible. The walls and doors within his mind that held that darkness back had begun to crack and shudder against the pressure being applied. His gaze slowly traveled the length of Na'tori's body before landing and holding firmly on her ass as animalistic growls rippled from him. His dick felt like a metal pipe in his pants, and the blood that still clung to him ramped his thirst for violence even higher.

Had he indeed been reduced to such depraved thoughts? If his mind wasn't on fucking Na'tori six ways to Sunday and back then, it was on tearing out the hearts of his enemies and feasting on their blood. Maybe he did need Rome to lock him up, or perhaps he should just have Silas put him down now because when his eyes landed on the pulsing vein within her neck, he felt that violence and need mix together to become one. He wanted to launch himself at her, sink his fangs into her throat and fuck her as deep as he could, yet he held himself back because he could feel multiple eyes on him. Alaric had zoned out, and now everyone was watching him hesitantly. Even Maverick and Cairo now stood at the foot of the steps, both wearing expressions that said they would take him down instantly if he made the wrong move.

"Alaric," Na'tori's soft voice caused his eyes to swing back and meet her gaze head-on. "Are you sure you're okay?"

"I'm fine." He lied even as the eyes of his closest friends, whom he now considered family, watched him.

She stepped up to him, opalescent eyes watching him hesitantly as her teeth tugged at her bottom lip. "Maybe you should get cleaned up."

He nodded. He would do precisely that, but he wanted her to be with him. His gut told him that he needed her near him, and it was vital to keep her within eyesight. Or maybe that was the massive erection uncomfortably filling his pants. Still, she was coming with him.

"Wait," Akio chuckled, "she can't go with you just yet, brother. I need to know what she knows about this." He held up a small device, no bigger than a flip phone, with a green light that flashed beside an on-and-off switch. Na'tori took it from his hand and looked it over before she shook her head.

"I don't think I know what this is."

"I say we turn it off and see what it does," Akio suggested.

Rome held his hand out and waited for Na'tori to hand it over before he, too, inspected the small device. He even sniffed it before he frowned and simply flicked the switch off. Alara gasped and stared at Rome like she'd seen a ghost seconds before he crushed the device within his hands and snarled like a beast gone mad.

"It cuts off telepathic communication." He stated. "I only showed up here because I couldn't contact Alara. That's how I knew something was wrong. I could no longer feel her within my mind, and the only time that's happened before was when she was captured and when she thought she needed to protect me from what had happened within the walls of that fucked up facility. We vowed never to close each other out again if we could help it."

"Then how was Alaric just in my head while that device was still on?" Amirishka questioned as she jumped down from the hospital bed.

Once again, all eyes fell on Alaric. The only person who looked deep in thought, eyes still locked on the pieces of the device that now littered the floor, was the woman he desired most in this world. What he couldn't understand was how they didn't see it. What he could do shouldn't have been possible. He was stronger than ever, and his abilities continued to climb daily. Sooner or later, he would be terrified of his own mind if it kept reaching and surpassing what should be possible. How didn't they realize that it wasn't his control he was losing? It was his mind and the darkness he kept locked away inside.

"His telepathic abilities surpass Silas's power and even my own," Rome announced.

"How did they create it though?"

"It was a prototype," Na'tori whispered, yet she never took her eyes off the crumbled pieces of the device. "It was an idea that never came to fruition because I wasn't sure what it benefitted besides possibly affecting and injuring someone's brain waves. I cut the project myself when I realized the potential. I guess they reopened it, and Dr. Salazar tweaked it because this isn't what my device looked like." She finally raised her eyes to look around the room at everyone gathered. "If I could take my involvement away, I would. I never knew my ideas would help them in a war that shouldn't even exist. I'm sorry."

"We don't blame you, Tori." Alara comforted her with a smile.

"I blame myself."

Alaric pulled their attention away from his woman by speaking. "What does this mean now?"

"I can work with Erick to create a device to combat it along with whatever he's juicing the Rogues with, but until I get a blood sample from one of them, I won't know how to do that." Na'tori replied with a frown, "I can possibly even help Ami with her problem."

Everyone seemed to agree with her statement before they each started talking about their nights and how a few of them thought it best to find a new place to move to. They needed to go somewhere Titan would have difficulty finding or entering. Somewhere where there was more security, possibly even more guardians to protect what was quickly becoming a large family. Alaric wanted to stay and discuss more options with them, but the blood sticking to his skin had now started to itch, and his damn erection still refused to deflate.

He stepped behind Na'tori and whispered into her ear as Rome, Silas, and Maverick went back and forth over what they should do about security in the home. "Come shower with me, princess. I need you to reach my back."

"I think we should—"

He cut off her words with a nip to her ear before directing her towards the stairs. No one stopped them or even acknowledged their departure. His hands were gentle as he pushed her forward, but his hardness pressing into her lower back was not. It was pulsing like it owned its own heartbeat, and he couldn't wait to slide it into her heaven until he could feel hers beating along with his own.

She tried again to speak. "Alaric, I think we should help them game-plan something."

"They were doing this long before we ever came into the picture." He kissed the side of her throat and felt her body relax into his own as they continued up the stairs and down the hallway towards the upper floors where his bedroom lay. "I don't just need a shower, Na'tori. I need you. I'm barely clinging to my sanity, and your pussy is just what I need to fix it. Besides... you've got the blood of our enemies touching you now; you might as well join me."

She groaned playfully and glanced at him over her shoulder. "You did that on purpose!"

"And I'd do it again."

TWENTY-NINE

From her position in the bathtub, Na'tori could make out Alaric's body through the fogged glass of the shower as he finished washing the blood from his skin. He turned off the faucet and headed for the tub she was relaxing in. She watched his muscles flex, especially the muscle between his legs, as he slid beneath the bubbles with a smirk on his face.

"Do you see something you like, princess?"

His deep voice called to every feminine part of her, but instead of letting that show, she held back the pleasurable shudder that wanted to race down her spine and splashed water at him as she spoke. "I'm just glad you washed the blood off before you got in."

He growled playfully before yanking her into his arms until she was straddling his lap. Na'tori felt his erection resting between her thighs, felt the hardness of his body against her softness, and melted into him as she tunneled her fingers into his hair.

She smiled softly. "Is this the part where we get to know each other on a deeper level?"

"I would definitely like to go deeper." He chuckled as his hands slid down her body to cup her waist. "What would you like to know? I'll answer it, but after," his eyes trailed to her breasts before he leaned forward to capture a nipple between his lips. He sucked softly until she squirmed and moaned atop his lap before he relaxed once more against the slope of the tub. "After… you'll let me do what I want with this body."

She leaned over and captured his lips in a kiss that made her pulse leap in her throat as his hands slid to the globes of her ass and tugged her closer. She spoke against his lip. "Should I start easy?"

"Start wherever you'd like, princess."

She wanted to know more about the man who filled nearly every thought she possessed, yet she wasn't sure where to start. She wanted to know about his childhood and how her family had treated him, yet a part of her was nervous to learn the answer. Then there were his sisters. Where did they place in his life? She could tell by their interactions that Alara was much closer to him than Alondra, but how close? Na'tori and her brothers had never been close, but Evan had almost gotten close until Ezekiel had put a stop to that.

She thought over all the questions and files of information filed away in her head and settled on something that tickled at the back of her brain like an annoying mosquito bite. "How did you get out and away from Titan? Was it that night when the building burned down?"

Alaric continued to rub circles into her ass as his eyes watched her closely while he spoke. "I got Alara out, followed by Alondra and myself nearly a year ago. It took me several years to accomplish that feat because I needed to gain your brother's trust. I needed him to never doubt me. I screwed up in the end. It got a little messy, and before I could cover my tracks, it was too late."

Na'tori frowned. This wasn't making sense to her. "But Lukas said that—"

"I'll stop you right there," he placed his thumb over her lips and chuckled, "We both know your family will lie to you if it means getting you to do as they please. I'm sure Lukas spun a story about my sisters and me to put him and his company in the best light, and I'm sure your other brothers played along. Let me paint a picture for you, princess. Your family has kept my siblings and me captive for our entire lives. Since birth, they have kept us under their thumb; they have made us accomplices in their acts. That was until I learned who they were and their capabilities. I figured that out when I was sixteen, but I now had a part to play. I needed to play that part until I could get my sisters free, especially when I learned what they wanted from my sisters, and I wasn't going to allow them to take that from them as well."

"So that's why my brother labeled you as an enemy? Because you got your sisters and yourself free? It wasn't because you were out destroying everything they built?"

"I'm definitely out to destroy them, and you should be just as determined to as well." He reached up to remove the tie that kept her hair in its ponytail before gripping the long strands in a gentle hold. "You know what they're capable of, so I'll stop at nothing to burn the entire corporation to the ground, and Lukas will die by my hand after what he's done. I know he's your brother, but he isn't worth saving."

"I know," she whispered. She wouldn't meet his eyes as she ran her hands down his chest and back up to his neck repeatedly as she spoke. "Lukas and Ezekiel have done terrible things. Your sister told me what Lukas did to her. I can't stop his karma from reaching him, and I wouldn't bat an eye if Zeke never breathed again, but Evan... Evan can be saved. He deserves another chance. He's not like them."

"I'm unfamiliar with him, but I'll see what I can do."

"Truly?"

"If I search his mind and find that he is, in fact, innocent in duplicitous acts against my people as well as the Kindred, then I will speak on behalf of him to Rome."

Na'tori finally looked into his eyes and knew he had spoken the truth. If he could, he would save Evan. She couldn't help but smile at the thought. His hands tightened marginally in her hair and tugged her closer before he kissed her softly. His erection pressed against her center; it throbbed between her thighs, and she knew he was becoming impatient. He wanted her, but she wasn't quite done with her questions, so she pulled away with a soft moan. His eyes pulsed, his fangs peeked out from behind his lips, and he snarled softly before lightly wrapping one of his hands around her throat.

The pressure was nowhere near tight, yet the fist in her hair caused her toes to curl as he watched her silently. Her pulse leaped beneath his palm as her hands wrapped around his wrist. "I wasn't done asking my questions." She glared, but there was no genuine anger behind her stare.

"Then ask them as you ride my dick...if you can." He smiled, showing sharp fangs that made her pulse thump harder against his palm. "Now climb onto the balls of your feet and sink down on me, princess."

She could tell by his expression that he was deadly serious, and a part of her wanted to see if she could keep asking her questions while she rode him. The thrill was there. The excitement of making him unhinged ran through her, yet there was also some hesitancy. She wasn't experienced in pleasure. She knew it didn't take much to excite him, but would she hold out?

Na'tori climbed onto the balls of her feet, her nails dug into the skin of his wrist as a deep moan parted her lips, and his cock slowly began to fill her the farther down she went. Alaric's groan rumbled in her ear and filled the space of the room when her ass touched his balls.

"Fuck!" His eyes brightened, and his hands loosened their death grip from her hair and around her throat before he pulled her in for a drugging kiss.

She could barely formulate words, let alone catch her breath, as his tongue battled with her own in a fight for dominance. Her legs shook; the feel of his length filling her and throbbing uncontrollably was nearly too much as she moved to grip his shoulders. Her mind scrambled to remember her next question as the hand around her throat dropped to her breast and cupped the globe gently. Alaric kissed his way down her throat until his lips wrapped around her nipple and sucked gently.

"Ride me," he whispered against her flesh.

She gripped his shoulders harder and rose gently before coming back down on a gasp. Her eyes nearly rolled into the back of her skull as she rode him softly, the water sloshed around them. His hand dropped from her hair to hold the back of her neck as his hips jerked beneath her with every downward shift.

"GOD!" Na'tori screamed as an unexpected orgasm slammed into her when he went deep enough to feel him in her gut.

Alaric groaned as his mouth released her tit. His eyes locked onto her face, and his smile was infectious as her cunt rippled around his cock. "I thought you had more questions, princess. Are you now incapable of speech?"

The bastard knew she could barely formulate words as he continued to guide her movements. She wanted to slap the smile off his face as he fucked her deeply. Her moans filled the bathroom and echoed off of the walls as her body spiraled out of control from the sensations that hit her from all sides. The glide of his skin against hers, the sound of his groans, and the sight of ecstasy that filled his gaze had her once again creaming on his cock before he stilled her movements. Her legs shook like a leaf as her breath panted between her lips, and her heart slammed against her ribs. His hands ran soothing circles into her back as he watched her attempt to catch her breath.

"The water is cold." He stated before lifting her easily after pulling the plug in the drain.

He didn't bother grabbing a towel off the rack before stepping up to the bathroom sink and placing her on her feet. The tile was cold against her skin, sending a shock to her system as Alaric turned her to face the foggy mirror. He wiped the condensation off of the glass as he gripped her dripping wet locks and slid back into her warm depths. Na'tori moaned as her fingers grasped the porcelain sink, and her eyes locked onto the Eternal that fucked her with a brutally that made her heart pound in her chest. There was no give in his thrusts as her hips snapped into the sink. With a hand holding her ass open and another pulling her hair, Na'tori could barely catch her breath as his eyes drilled into hers over her shoulder. The sound of her cream and cum coating him could be heard over her soft moans and his harsh groans, and it still wasn't enough. She needed something more.

Na'tori wanted the fangs she could see within his mouth piercing into the flesh of her throat, yet she knew for whatever reason that he was incapable of doing so. The thought of those fangs in her made the walls of her pussy flutter as her clit throbbed in anticipation. Alaric read her body like a man that knew her better than she knew herself as his hand on her ass slid around to her front and held her clit hostage between his pointer and middle finger. His hips paused as a tremor ran through her body, and her impending orgasm withered away at his sudden stillness.

"W-w-why'd you stop?" Na'tori stuttered as her body twitched and throbbed continuously.

"Ask me anything?" He replied as his fingers rubbed at her clit gently. It wasn't enough to grant her that orgasm, but it was enough to send her onto her tippy toes. "Distract me from the fact that I can't fuck you the way I want to. Give me that, and I'll give you more orgasms."

She hadn't been expecting those words, and her brain had turned to mush the moment he'd sank into her body. What the hell was wrong with him? Any other given time, and he would be fucking her into oblivion. They'd been on that path, and now this. She wanted to reach around and scratch her nails down his chest to get what she desired, but something in his gaze gave her pause. It was a look she wasn't sure she knew how to decipher. The arch in her back was beginning to ache, but there was no way to move. His body kept her pinned effectively as his fingers continued to tease her clit, but his eyes were telling her something. Was that red around his irises? She opened her mouth to ask what she was seeing, yet it was gone the second he blinked. Had she imagined it? His finger tapped her exposed clit.

"Fuck, okay, okay," Na'tori moaned, and her fingers ached as her hands and body tightened. "W-why can't you read m-my m-mind?"

His smile turned feral. "Who says I can't?"

"You told me you couldn't."

She wanted to face him because now her interest had peaked along with an emotion she didn't want to voice. If he could read her, then why hadn't he said anything? Did he know what she'd discovered from the blood tests she'd run? Did he know what she was thinking of doing? Her heart raced for an entirely different reason as his eyes narrowed on her and his smile dropped from his face. God, was he reading her now?

Alaric released her, only to turn her around and lift her onto the counter. His hips slid between her thighs as his eyes scanned her face, and his hands slowly lifted her legs around his waist. Her nails bit into his biceps when he guided his dick back into her warmth. They moaned in unison, and when she attempted to close her eyes against the intensity of his stare, he gripped her chin and snarled.

"Eyes on me, princess."

Her eyes found his again on a breathless moan as he began to fuck her once more.

"Now, tell me why you don't want me privy to your thoughts."

She wanted to scream at how unfair it seemed that he was so unbothered and unmoved by the spasms that caused her core to clench and tighten around his erection. Instead of ecstasy, there was a look of measured calm on his face as if he was holding himself back from honestly taking her. She wanted to scream at him to fuck her as he usually did, but her mind was still trying to wrap around his words as his hand moved to rub at her clit. Now she wanted to scream for an entirely different reason as her legs tightened around his waist, and her body fell back into the mirror as he fucked her deeper.

How did he expect her to answer him through what amounted to sexual torture? It seemed that every time she was close to the edge, his hips would slow to a snail's pace, and his fingers would fall still against her clit. Sweat had beaded along her skin. She could feel the drops perspiring between her breasts as his eyes dropped to them and held. Na'tori's moans turned to whimpers as he pinched her clit and held incredibly still as she dug her nails deeper into his skin. Her breath stalled in her lungs when her impending orgasm once again came to a standstill, and his chest rose and fell harshly. That was the only real sign that he seemed to be struggling with something. Whether that was control or something else was another matter entirely.

"What don't you want me to know, Na'tori?"

His voice caused her to shiver, yet he still remained stiff within her. She wasn't beyond begging. Her clit and core ached more than ever before, and she wanted the orgasm that seemed to elude her more than she wanted her next breath.

"Please," she gasped when his hips ground into her.

"Fuck, you're pretty when you beg." He pulled her until her ass hung off the edge of the sink, the edge of the porcelain digging into her back as he pushed his cock deeper until he caressed her womb. "Answer me, baby."

Na'tori saw stars as her pussy convulsed, and still, her orgasm was out of reach. Tears sprang in her eyes as every cell within her trembled and clenched beyond her control. Alaric gripped her thighs and spread her wider, his balls touching the globes of her ass as his eyes moved to focus on their joining. His fang nicked his bottom lip and drew blood. Finally, a look of barely restrained need filled his face, but so did that unusual red glow before it disappeared again.

"Fuck it." He groaned before he pulled out, only to slam back into her with a brutal thrust. "Cum on my dick, princess. Give it all to me."

She screamed as her orgasm hit her like a bolt of lightning. Na'tori's control splintered as a jet of pure liquid coated Alaric and dripped to the ground along with her cum. She knew she'd just squirted all over him, but she couldn't formulate thoughts enough to care as he continued to fuck her until his cum began to fill her with a burst of heat that had her breath shuddering in her lungs. Her eyes opened when Alaric slowly pulled from her sore pussy to watch as their shared release slowly dripped from her. Her body was sated and loose, yet he still looked stressed and tight. She opened her mouth to question him, but his gaze stilled her.

His eyes were like molten lava, not red but burning with that same intensity that had her questioning what the hell was happening. His need still stared back at her as if he hadn't just fucked her like a man starved as he pulled her into his arms and walked her to his bed, and tucked her beneath the covers.

"Ala—"

"Don't," he snapped, "I need to… I'll be back." He stared down at her and stepped back hesitantly as his hands shook at his sides. "Sleep, princess. Please."

He kissed her forehead and pulled away before she could convince him to join her. Thanks to his added speed, he dressed quickly and left the room before she could stop him. She tried to process what was happening, but nothing came to mind. He was keeping something from her. That was evident but she couldn't really blame him. She was keeping something from him as well.

She had one chance. One chance to save his life, and she felt like she'd found something. Whether it would work was another matter entirely but she couldn't tell him and give him false hope. Not again. She needed to be sure.

CHAPTER
THIRTY

Alaric felt anger so fluid and consuming that he feared his next actions enough to head for the only person who might be able to help him. His fist pounded against the bedroom door that separated him from the sounds he chose to ignore beyond the wood. A furious snarl rumbled from within before Rome opened the door, chest bare and pants barely hanging onto his hips. His bottom lip carried a drop of blood, and his eyes were light blue neon beams as he met his stare without a word.

"I need you to go into my thoughts," Alaric stated. His eyes never wavered from Rome's intense stare, but the need to do so was there. "Something's wrong, and I nearly...Fuck Romulus. I almost hurt her."

That sobered Rome up quickly. "Give me two minutes."

The door slammed closed in front of his face, and he refused to listen to the conversation taking place between Alara and her mate before Rome appeared again, but this time fully clothed and with a severe expression on his face.

"We'll need Silas," Rome commented as he entered Silas's room without knocking.

Silas sat on the floor, legs crossed and hands sitting relaxed on his lap before his eyes flew open and his milky white gaze stared back at them before his color shifted to their normal state. "What's wrong?" He questioned as he came to his feet swiftly.

Alaric rubbed at the nape of his neck as he began to pace. It was his attempt to calm down, but it wasn't working. Something had happened while being intimate with Na'tori, something he was terrified to name because then that would make it real.

"Alaric?" Rome spoke and placed his hand on his shoulder, stilling him. "You told me you almost hurt her. What happened?"

Like a child, he didn't want to meet Rome's eyes when he spoke. He didn't want to see the disappointment or possible anger. "Ever since I was shot with the virus, I've been fighting this sort of darkness within my mind that drives my obsessions to new levels."

Silas frowned. "What obsessions?"

"My obsession for Na'tori...and blood."

It was Rome's turn to look at him wearily. "Explain."

"Having her. Fucking her is driving me insane because I can't do that one thing I'm dying to do." Alaric moved away from Rome's hold as the need he spoke of took hold of him, causing his muscles to tense at the thoughts that flew through his mind. "I want to tie her to me so that she's incapable of ever leaving me. The fear of her being snatched from this world because of that sick family of hers is driving me to insanity. I want to brand her with my bite and tie her to me in the only way I know that would protect her from even death. I know sharing our blood with the mate that completes our souls is what keeps them from dying by natural means. I can't do that and sometimes the intimacy isn't enough. I crave blood and death."

Silas couldn't believe what he was hearing. "Hers?"

Alaric glared at his best friend. "Never her death, but the death of our enemies is a very tempting thing that I'm finding hard to ignore. You saw what I did, Si. You know I'm close to the edge of no return if I keep going down this path of destruction, but I don't know how to stop it." He looked towards his brother-in-law, his eyes pleading with every part of his mind open except for the wall and door that held back the darkness within. "I need you to go into my mind and tell me what the hell is going on because whatever this blackness is, it's starting to consume me."

"Alright, but Silas and I need to go together because no matter how open you try to be to our mental probes, your mind rebels against us, so I'll need him to hold back your blocks as we walk through." Rome admitted with a blank stare.

"Do it."

Alaric moved to sit on the chair in front of Silas's desktop computer before he closed his eyes and lowered his mental shields. The only thing he kept in place were the barriers holding back the inky blackness that had begun to send a stab of fear into his heart. He felt it the moment Rome and Silas stepped into his mind. The sensation sent fire racing through his brain, and the urge to shove them out was more vital than ever before, but he held the urge back and clenched his hands into fists as he attempted to calm his breathing and racing heart. He was terrified of what they might find and what it would do to him if the answers were devastating.

He heard their groans and frowned. What the hell was happening? He could feel them moving around his thoughts and memories, yet there was a cloak around just what they were seeing and possibly experiencing. Alaric opened his eyes and watched as both Rome and Silas's bodies shuddered as if in agony, as their mouths hung open with silent screams before he shoved them out and rebuilt every barrier within his mind again. Silas bent over and clutched his knees as he resisted the urge to throw up while Rome stared at him as if he had several heads. Beads of sweat covered each of them, and Alaric desperately wanted to dive into their minds to find out what they'd seen and learned because their reactions told him it was bad. He decided against it.

"What did you see?" Alaric questioned as he came to his feet.

Rome watched him wearily and wiped at his nose just as a drop of blood began to trickle down. His voice was like granite when he spoke. "Why the fuck have you been hiding this from us? Your mind is like a dark tunnel with barely any light, and that barrier you're trying to keep in place isn't working. Whatever is trapped behind that wall is slipping through the cracks and infecting your mind like an opioid. You're barely holding shit together."

"Nah...fuck that." Silas spat as he whirled on him with a snarl, his fangs bared and his eyes blazing with a warning. "You should have told me it was this bad, Alaric! That damn darkness nearly strangled us and tore into our minds like a ravaging beast!"

Alaric shook his head in denial. "No. I have it locked up. It shouldn't have touched you at all."

Silas scoffed. "Then you've got some piss poor locks for someone who's supposed to have stronger mental blocks than Rome and I because it definitely fucking locked us in a chokehold strong enough to kill. At least you had the decency to notice we were in serious trouble to get us out before that shit could actually kill us."

It didn't make sense.

Alaric took Rome's continued silence as an indication that Silas was speaking nothing but the truth, and that terrified him. They didn't know what this dark hole within his mind was doing to him other than what he already knew. It was corrupting him, pushing his obsessions, and driving him insane. He stepped back and turned away from their judgemental stares. His skin was beginning to itch as the need to get back to Na'tori arose, but he could also feel the need to sleep as the sun started its slow climb into the sky.

"Do you feel that you can be trusted?" Rome questioned unexpectantly.

"No," Alaric replied honestly, reaching up to grip the strands of his hair as he sighed heavily. "I don't think I can be trusted to act rationally around her, but I don't know Romulus...I can't be around her, or it makes this urge I have a thousand times worse."

"Go to the cells, lock yourself inside, and drink a few bags of blood. I'll check on you periodically as the day progresses. I'm sorry we don't have more for you, but Silas is right. Trying to sift through your thoughts was hard when we could hardly see through that blackness. It was more about the sensations brought on by whatever that virus has done to drastically blacken your mind, but we won't give up. I'll help you get answers one way or another."

Alaric didn't bother replying; he simply nodded his head in

acknowledgment and left the room quickly. What else was there to say? They hadn't failed him, but they also hadn't been helpful in the slightest, unless you count learning that the barriers within his mind were failing and the darkness was still finding a way through. He headed into the cells without speaking to anyone else but made sure to grab at least six packs of blood before he locked himself behind silver strong enough to hold him back.

The moment he took a seat on the small cot, he sank his fangs into the plastic pouch and tried not to barf when the tangy metallic blood hit his tongue. He didn't know what Na'tori's blood tasted like, but Alaric knew without a doubt that it would be sweeter than heaven itself, and it would be something he would struggle to resist. When he finished the third bag, Alaric could feel his eyes becoming heavy as the urge to sleep struck him. He should have explained to Na'tori why he wouldn't be with her when she awoke, but the temptation to fuck her would have hit him like a freight train the moment he took in her scent. He couldn't risk what had nearly happened early.

He tossed the pouches into the trash before sinking into the covers atop the cot and closed his eyes to sleep. He would figure something out when he woke up, or he'd ask Silas for the favor that was owed, because he refused to hurt the woman who was taking over every aspect of his mind, body, and soul.

CHAPTER
THIRTY-ONE

Na'tori listened carefully as she gently pulled open the front door and slipped through the crack before closing it softly behind her. Everyone was asleep except for Alara and Rome, but they were otherwise occupied and busy entertaining each other. It gave her the perfect opportunity to slip out without being seen.

The sun was out, and a chill in the air made her tug her jacket closer to her neck as she rushed down the sidewalk. It wasn't hard figuring out where she was. After years of studying the roads of Van Scive, Na'tori could close her eyes and make her way out of any neighborhood she found herself in. By the look of things, it seemed that Rome lived in the suburbs but in the rich part, which meant there was a library several miles from them.

She quickly cut through the neighborhood and walked until she reached the library's parking lot. She didn't pay close attention to the other stores in the area, but she took notice of the number of cars in front of her destination. What she was doing wasn't wise, but she needed to see if she could find Evan and get him as far away from their brothers as possible. She wasn't sure if Evan would pass

Alaric's mental probe, but she hoped he wasn't corrupted like their older brothers.

She knew it wasn't wise to be out, especially after Titan attacked them, but she needed answers. Her brother had gone missing before all of this happened, and that wasn't like him, but maybe he had done it for a reason. She would breathe easier if she could contact him and ensure he was safe and willing to return with her. She headed into the library before she could talk herself out of it. It took her less than ten minutes to get unfettered access to a computer before logging into her work email, hoping to find something from her brother, but only work emails greeted her. She tried not to let disappointment fill her, but it was hard.

She should have just stayed home. Being out like this made her paranoid, so she shifted through her email contacts and quickly sent one to Evan. Only forty-five minutes had passed since she'd walked out of Rome's home, yet it felt like hours had passed as she logged out of the computer and quickly made her way to the front door. A small smile pulled at her lips as she thought of returning to Alaric. Since meeting him, her life had shifted entirely to a life she still couldn't believe was possible. She was free from her family; she was appreciated, thought about, and, dare she say it...loved. Na'tori felt loved. Even if those words had never left his mouth, she felt them in his every action towards her. A particular memory resurfaced in her mind when she exited the library and came to a stuttering halt at what she saw.

Ezekiel was leaning against a large black Humvee; the back passenger side door was wide open, and he was cleaning his nails out with a sharp blade as he stared at her with his dead-eyed gaze. A smirk tilted his lips in an unfriendly manner that caused the blood in her veins to slow to a snail's pace even as her heart raced in her chest and the need to flee slammed into her like a fist to the gut. She could make out the murderous rage in his eyes even through the calmness he was trying to present. There were people around. Which meant he wouldn't hurt her in front of the eyes of many, but that didn't mean she was safe either. He could hurt her without so much as touching her. She knew that from previous experiences.

"Get in the car, Tori." He ordered and finally put away the blade he held, only to flash her the handle of a gun that was tucked into his pants.

"Just let me go, and you'll never see me again." She tried to reason with him, even knowing it wouldn't work.

A part of her wanted to turn and find another exit from the building, but if she knew her brother at all, then she knew he already had the place surrounded by his men. There would be no escaping from him and returning to Rome's place. There was only one natural choice she could make because anything against what Ezekiel wanted would end with someone in pain, and as her eyes scanned the lot and stores around her, Na'tori knew that he would hurt any number of people to get what he desired. Did Lukas even realize he had found her?

"You know it doesn't work like that." Ezekiel commented, "You're coming back with me. Or must I hurt one of these bystanders to get you moving?"

She knew the answer immediately. She didn't need to think about what she was doing as she loosened her hold on the door and slowly descended the library steps. The moment she was arm's length away from her brother, his hand lashed out, gripped her bicep, and yanked her forward as he snarled into her ear.

"I know you helped that bastard Alaric escape, and for that, I've got something really special waiting for you when we get back, but first, let's go say hi to Big Brother, shall we?"

He shoved her into the backseat of the Humvee before he climbed in behind her and slammed the door closed. She moved to slide across the seats but found herself being pulled into Ezekiel's side as the muzzle of his gun dug into her side.

"I'll keep you nice and close until we're safely behind the company walls. I don't need your new friends just popping in and stealing you away now, do I?" He chuckled as his fingers dug deep grooves into her arm.

She winced and tried not to tense up even though she wanted to lash out and, for once, fight against him. There was no telling what he would do to her once she was beyond Titan's walls. What would

Alaric and the rest of them think once they found her missing? Her heart pounded harshly within her chest at the thought because she knew without a doubt that Alaric would come for her, and when he did, he might not leave anyone standing. But would they think she'd left them because she wanted to or that she had left them against her will?

"I bet you're wondering how I knew where to find you."

He broke the uncomfortable silence within the truck's interior, and she tried not to tense up even more beside him. She didn't need to guess how he had located her; the only answer was that he'd been waiting and watching for the moment she would use her company login information to gain access to her emails. Ezekiel was a madman, but he was also a great security asset to Titan, who always had eyes on the comings and goings of everyone within the company, especially after the recent events that had happened to them. Na'tori had known it would be incredibly dangerous to sign on, but that need that refused to rest after speaking to Alaric wouldn't stop pressing against her. She needed to know how Evan was and if getting to him before her brothers was possible. Or had they already located him?

"I know how you found me," she finally replied, "I don't need a play-by-play on just how smart you are, Zeke. Just tell me one thing, have you located Evan? Before, Lukas told me he was AWOL. Is that still true?"

His chuckle sent chills down her spine, not the good kind of chills that she had begun to get used to because of Alaric. No, these chills told her that whatever he knew wasn't good, and Evan was possibly hurt. Or worse, he was dead. His fingers loosened and released her, although his other hand still dug the gun into her side as he reached forward to tap the headrest of the driver.

"Tell me, Mark, have you seen my brother Evan lately?"

The large man behind the wheel peered through the rearview mirror; dark brown eyes settled onto her, and the same evil in her brother's gaze lurked within the guards as he smiled before he spoke. "Baby brother was a screamer."

She didn't react. Na'tori knew that's exactly what they wanted from her. They wanted her to respond, even to raise hell, but she would do nothing. She dragged her gaze away from Mark's to stare out the windshield as they turned onto a familiar street and drove up to the Titan corporation gates. She remained calm even as she cried internally and forced herself not to look towards the door or attempt an escape. She would never make it far enough before Ezekiel or any of his guards took her down, so she remained beside her brother even when the vehicle stopped. She calmed her racing heart and, for once, wished that her mental barriers weren't as strong as they were so she could reach out to Rome and tell him what had happened. Maybe if she had just asked, she could have used anyone's device at home to access her email, but the thought of them saying no kept her from taking that leap.

"Shall we go see Lukas?" Ezekiel smiled and opened the back door before he climbed out. He continued to point the muzzle at her as he indicated that she should climb out.

She did so without much fight as her eyes scanned the parking lot. There were fewer cars than usual, the patrol was light, and the outside door was open when they approached. Sweat began to bead along her skin as they headed down hallway after hallway until they approached Lukas's office. She was shoved forward; her sweaty hand gripped the metal handle and opened the door before Ezekiel could prod her back even further with the gun. Her brother looked up from the desk and frowned.

"Where the hell have you been?" He questioned, his piercing green eyes narrowed in anger as he moved around his desk.

The moment his wheelchair came into view, Na'tori's mind drifted to what she knew and how he'd ended up paralyzed. Anger surged through her, and now she knew without a doubt that she would have let him die had she known just what he was capable of. Her eyes turned to take in Ekeziel's relaxed form as he leaned against the door at his back. She'd never heard him close it, but that didn't matter. By the look in his eyes, it was apparent that he'd never even told Lukas that he was coming after her or that he had found her. It made her wonder.

"Do you know that he killed Evan? Or if not him, one of his

guards surely did." She stated in an attempt to change the subject and shine a light on the fact that Ezekiel was clearly doing things without their older brothers' knowledge.

Lukas's gaze shifted to Ezekiel. His brow rose in silent question as his fingers began to steadily tap against the arm of his chair. "Is that true, Zeke?"

Na'tori stepped to the side, keeping both her brothers in her sight. She attempted to look around Lukas's office without being noticed. She needed a hint to tell her what staying here would look like. Now that she knew they tortured and killed people, there was no telling if she would be safe from that torture because of her relation to them or if that wouldn't matter. Based on the conversation from the truck, she knew that Evan was dead. What would that mean for her? Was she next?

"Ezekiel!" Lukas slammed a fist against his chair arm and glared. "Fucking answer me. Did you kill Evan?"

Ezekiel tilted his head in that predatory manner of his and smirked. "He was planning to leave us, you know. He was going to empty his accounts and disappear somewhere across the world with all of the secrets we harbor here. Would you have liked that, brother? Or is it a good thing I stopped that shit from happening?"

"So you fucking killed him instead of bringing him to me!? When do you operate and move without my say? Since when is it okay to kill family?" Lukas thundered.

"That's rich coming from you, considering you killed our mother in cold blood."

There was no way Na'tori had heard that correctly. Lukas couldn't have killed their mother, right? Her eyes swung between them, trying to figure out if what Ezekiel had stated was true, and by the look in their older brother's gaze, she knew that, for once, he hadn't lied. She hadn't always liked her mother, but she'd loved her even through the moments of her life when she'd been looked over in favor of her brothers.

"Oh god, you really killed her," she mumbled, her hand covering her mouth as she fought to hold back the urge to vomit.

She knew her brothers were fucked up individuals, but this level of unhinged she hadn't been expecting. She would die here if they weren't happy with whatever they wanted from her, and she had a good idea what that something was. She wouldn't give it to them. Anything they wanted to know about her time with the Eternals would never come to light. She would take Alaric and his people's secrets to her grave before she ever allowed them to be hurt by her family again.

Lukas's gaze whipped toward her, his eyes blazed with anger. "None of that matters now. I know you were with Alaric and his merry band of Eternals, and I know you've turned against us, so if you want to get back into my good graces, then you know what to do." He snapped, "So what are they planning, and what are their weak spots? You'll tell me, or I'll let Zeke deal with you."

Na'tori had a bad feeling that if Ezekiel was left to deal with her, then she would die today because she would never tell them a thing. She stepped back until her back pressed against the wall, all the while, her heart raced in her chest like a racehorse. They studied her. Waited patiently for her to speak, but she knew it was an illusion. They weren't being patient; they were simply amping her up for the inevitable. She'd be punished regardless if she told them a thing or not, simply because she'd left them. It was a slight to the corporation and to her older brothers, who would never see her as anything more than a traitor.

"I won't tell you anything." She finally spoke, and this time, when she scanned the office, it was in search of something that would help her fight against them.

That evil smirk that Ezekiel had perfected over the years flashed across his face, and his words sent fear tumbling through her. "I can easily get the words out of you, little sis, so please, I insist. I want you to put up the fight of your life because I don't plan on going easy on you."

She thought Lukas would stop this madness, but with a simple nod, her eldest brother wheeled his way behind his desk as Ezekiel came for her. Na'tori rushed him when he reached for her and caught him off guard when she slid under his arm, sent a swift punch to his ribs, and raced for the door before yanking it open and sprinting down the hall in search of an exit. His raspy chuckle followed behind her, but she didn't risk glancing over her shoulder to see if he was on her ass or not. Adrenaline was racing through her bloodstream as a million and one thoughts filled her mind with what she should do. She knew she couldn't just run through the hallways of Titan, especially not with them having guards at their disposal.

Na'tori turned a corner that was sure to lead her back towards the closest exit and came to a stuttering halt when she found Ezekiel leaning casually against the door, the door that could grant her her freedom. He twirled his switchblade in his hand as he watched her closely. Her fear began to turn her stomach as the urge to vomit arose. The desire to run was strong, yet the look in his eyes told her that her escape attempt would never work. She would be tortured. Shit, she would probably die here. The fact that Lukas had clearly given their unhinged brother the green light to handle her told her everything she needed to know.

"Come on now, Tori, let's not prolong the inevitable." He stated with a smile, stretching his lips. "I let you deliver that nice little hit, and I see you've been practicing on your swing, but it just wasn't as effective as you thought. Come easy, or I'll make this so much worse for you than it needs to be, although…I do love the thrill of the chase."

Her limbs locked up. She knew she should just run, but he was right. The guards would never let her leave even if she made it to an exit, but she couldn't just go willingly. There was really no telling what she would reveal if he got his hands on her and tortured her for information. She could reveal things she didn't mean to, and as badly as she didn't want to reveal a thing, she might not have a choice.

Na'tori tried to reason with him. "You don't have to do this, Zeke. Just let me walk away."

"We've already been over this, my sweet, naive little sister." He prowled towards her with a slow gait. "Do you really think we can just let you leave here to return to our enemy? Do you think we're seriously that weak within this war to not see you as the threat you really are?"

By the time he finished speaking, he was within her space, not even touching her, and yet she felt his evil aura surrounding her like a predator stalking its prey. No matter how hard she tried, she couldn't slow her heart and nerves. Na'tori should never have allowed her feelings to get the better of her. She should have found another way to find out if Evan was truly okay because now she might never feel the sun's rays on her face or feel the breeze from the wind as it brushed against her skin. She might never see Alaric again. There was no telling what was in store for her, but whatever it was, it was clear by Ezekiel's psychotic gaze that she might never walk away from his particular brand of torture.

His hand whipped out and gripped her by the chin; his blade lay inches from her right eye as she stared into eyes that fed on her fear. She barely breathed from terror of accidentally stabbing herself with the pointed tip of his knife.

"We should start easy," he whispered, "I don't want to hurt you too badly when we've barely even started, so tell me, Na'tori, was it worth it? Was turning on us worth it, or do you regret the part you played? Will you seek redemption in the hopes of us allowing you back into the fold? Should I convince Lukas that you didn't really mean it and, instead, you plan to give me everything on those blood-sucking fiends?" He tapped the blade against her skin and smirked, "Think long and hard about your answers before you reply, sweet sister."

God, she hated her fear. She hated how it settled deep in her marrow and choked off the oxygen that she needed to breathe. She knew her brother was dangerous. She'd known it all her life, but to feel the tip of his blade now against the nape of her neck and to feel the animosity and pleasure at seeing her fear is what stabbed the realization through her heart that she truly wasn't safe. Tears threatened to fill her gaze, pain slashed through her throat as she swallowed her spit roughly to dispel the dryness that had begun to take place, and Na'tori couldn't tear her eyes away from the brother that now held her life within the palm of his hands. Even as terror flowed through her veins, she stared directly into his green eyes as she spoke whispered words that would indeed have her killed, but she didn't care anymore. She would probably die here anyway.

"I don't regret a thing." She paused when his stare hardened, and the pleasure that had previously been there withered away within the blink of an eye, yet she continued. "I hope Rome and his people tear down everything our family has built, and I hope both you and Lukas are crushed beneath the rubble!"

"We'll be dragging you along with us if that's the case!" He snarled as he gripped a fistful of her hair and yanked her head back to press his blade more firmly against her throat. "I'm sure you thought that by angering me, I would try my hand at torture before killing you swiftly, but I'm telling you now, Tori, that death would be too sweet of a reward for you, so you'll suffer and watch as I eradicate every single one of them from this earth; saving Alaric for last."

"Not if he kills you first!"

Ezekiel's expression soured before he glanced over her head and nodded. Na'tori felt it the moment a needle was plunged into her throat and felt it the moment the drugs began to pull her under.

CHAPTER
THIRTY-TWO

Alaric came awake with his fist wrapped around his cock and the mental image of Na'tori orgasming so intensely that his balls tightened and a load of cum splashed against his lower stomach. He groaned in annoyance, wiped his release off with the edge of the blanket that had somehow ended up on the floor, and glanced toward the cell door that should have been closed and locked. Instead, the door was open, and the house was eerily silent except for the soft sounds of his sisters chatting quietly in the kitchen. Thank Christ, no one had witnessed his morning wood and, even worse, the release that still echoed throughout his body. He came to his feet as thoughts of Na'tori filled his thoughts even more and pulled up jeans he couldn't recall pulling down.

Why couldn't he hear her as well, and why was the house so quiet? There was no way the Eternals had already begun their hunt. Something within his body was telling him that the sun had only just set, so what the hell was going on? He reached out with his mind to locate Rome or Silas and winced when a stabbing pain forced him to slam down his shields. Alaric used his supernatural speed to race upstairs and take in the sight of Alondra and Alara as they spoke and sipped tea around the kitchen island.

Alondra's gaze clashed with his, a frown pulled at her lips when she spoke. "Where's the fire?"

"Where are the others?" He questioned as he forced himself not to express pain when that stabbing pain once again slashed at the barriers within his mind.

Alara rounded the counter to stand before him. Her face was filled with worry as she looked him up and down. "You're the first one awake. Are you okay?"

"And Na'tori?"

"She's in your bedroom; she hasn't come down yet. What's wrong, Alaric?"

He peered in the direction leading to his room and inhaled sharply. Na'tori's scent was stale, almost as if it barely registered. Was she really in there? A nagging feeling pulled at him, but before he could investigate, Alara grabbed his hand, and the sensation of her healing energy sank into his skin and banished the pain that was radiating throughout his skull.

"Why are you in so much pain?" She questioned after slowly removing her hands from his skin to take a seat at the island table.

Alondra quickly passed her a glass of water as she looked her sister over before her penetrating gaze fell on Alaric and held. He could see the silent question within her eyes, but he knew she wouldn't voice it. At least not in front of Alara. Alondra was more perceptive than their younger sister. She was possibly witnessing the cracks within his foundation and seeing how poorly put together he really was. His mind was a swirling mess of thoughts, and his obsession with blood and sex was rearing its head as the itch to locate Na'tori pulsed through his blood. He needed to get control over this and fast.

He smiled softly and looked into Alara's concerned expression when he spoke, hoping to dispel her worry. "I'm okay, Angel, I'm just worried about Na'tori. She's normally up before me."

"Go check on her then, I can see that it's really bothering you."

Alaric wasted no time and swiftly left the kitchen to hunt down his woman. That nagging feeling at the back of his mind kept poking, prodding, and screaming at him that something was wrong, and by the time he approached his bedroom door and swung it open, he knew exactly why that was. Na'tori wasn't there. It looked like she hadn't even slept in his bed. Her scent still lingered, but it was obvious that it had been hours since she'd been inside.

Sound ceased to exist for him as his heart took off at a gallop in his chest, and his blood roared through his veins. Alaric could feel his fangs dropping as his lips peeled back in a snarl, and his eyes began to brighten and pulse as the darkness within his mind slammed repeatedly against his mental barricade. The sound that emanated from his chest could only be described as animalistic in nature as he prowled through his room to search the closest, only to find them just as empty as his bedroom.

Where the hell was she? Had she left him and run back to her family? Had everything between them been a lie? Had she been sent to spy on his family, and now she planned to return to capture them and fulfill her role within Titan? His thoughts wouldn't stop spinning with the possibility of her working for his enemy and simply using him for answers and insight into the Eternals. Alaric grabbed the lamp on his bedside table and launched it across the room without even processing what he was doing. The lamp slammed into the wall and broke on impact. The sound of glass and metal filled the space, along with a scream he'd hoped to hold back, but it was too late. The guttural sound caused Rome to appear moments later; a look of concern filled his expression before he placed a large hand on Alaric's shoulder to keep him grounded and still. His voice was full of authority when he spoke.

"What happened?"

"She isn't here," Alaric snarled through his sharpened fangs, "Na'tori isn't here. She fucking left me. God Dammit Romulus, she left me!" He clenched his hands into fists and forced himself to stay still under his King's heavy hand, but all he really wanted to do was hunt his wayward mate down and demand answers.

Fuck, they weren't actually mates, though, were they? He still couldn't bite and bind her to him for life, and he'd definitely tried. She was a mate to him in all the ways that mattered, but now she was somewhere without his scent marking her, which terrified him.

"Alaric!" Rome snapped impatiently, "We'll have Akio look over the cameras throughout the area to see where she could have gone. I don't like that she left without a word, but she wasn't a prisoner here. You do realize that, don't you?"

"And if she's been secretly working with our enemy this whole time, then what, Romulus? Why would she leave if not to go back to her brothers with a report on everything she's learned here?"

"Do you really think she's capable of doing that? She's done nothing but apologize for the atrocities of her family and help us fight this war against them." He dropped his hand and headed for the door as he continued to speak. "Let's find out what really happened before you allow whatever thoughts you have to fester and grow."

Alaric followed him from the room and wasn't at all surprised when they went downstairs into the meeting chamber and found Akio already at the computer, pulling up the video footage from that morning. They watched as Na'tori crept from the house, glancing every few seconds over her shoulder as she walked down the street and cut her way through the neighborhood. Alaric stepped closer to the monitors when she entered the library several blocks over before Akio hacked into the cameras inside and followed her to a bank of computers, where she sat down. It took her less than thirty minutes to do whatever she'd done on the computer before she stood and headed for the exit.

"What the hell is she doing?" Alaric questioned with a frown.

"I couldn't zoom into the footage without making it grainy and impossible to see, but I think she reached out to someone or responded to a message," Akio responded as he continued to type furiously as his gaze scanned another monitor that was filled with a jumble of words and numbers Alaric didn't understand. "The library gave her a login to use, but when she signed on to a site with more firewalls than I've ever seen, I lost her electronic signature. She could have been talking to someone across the world, but I wouldn't know. It would take me several hours to crack the encryption that was used, and I'm guessing we don't have hours."

"Show me what happens when she leaves. Where does she go next?"

Akio pulled up video footage from three different angles outside the building, and Alaric's breath came to a stuttering halt when he saw Ezekiel's smirking expression as he spoke. He couldn't read his lips, but he knew the bastard was telling his woman to come with him or suffer the consequences. He could see the fear in Na'tori's gaze and knew that she didn't want to go with him, but in the end, she did as she was told. He watched her slide into the backseat of the vehicle and drive off with his enemy, but the thoughts of betrayal he'd been harboring dissipated.

"He took her." Alaric glanced towards Rome. "We need to go after her. They could be torturing her even now."

Rome shook his head in denial as he continued to watch the video until she was behind the walls of Titan. "We can't just storm the building, Alaric. We need to plan this out and not go in like savage beasts. By the look on your face, I can see that you disagree."

Of course, he didn't fucking agree. "If this were Alara, we would already be slamming through the gates!" He exclaimed.

Rome leveled him with a look as he crossed his arms over his chest. "I didn't risk my people when I went after my mate, and you won't be risking my people for your woman. Is that understood?"

"Then I'll go on my own." He moved for the exit and growled in frustration when Silas appeared from the hallway to block the door with his larger frame. "Move, Si."

"You know I can't do that, brother."

"You'll do it if you know what's good for you."

Akio chuckled from his position in front of the monitors. "My money's on Alaric."

"Zip it, Akio!" Rome chastised him and stalked forward until he was a breath away from his brother-in-law. "This is exactly what they want, Alaric. They want you to go barreling in there without a plan and then the next thing you know you'll be another hostage who needs saving. We need to be smarter. I know what it's taking just to keep you here, but going in there blind will do nothing but get you killed. I can't have that. Your sisters would murder me in my sleep. Let's give Akio a little bit of time to see if he can find something that will help us get her back. No running off half-cocked, do you understand?"

Why did he have to be right?

Alaric nodded in understanding and moved for the table in the room before taking a seat in the exact spot where he'd taken Na'tori's innocence. That memory barreled into his mind and sent his thoughts careening, but he forced himself to close his eyes and focus on the now instead of the sex. He remembered the facility's layout and tried to think of where they might hold her, but there were so many options. She could be anywhere behind Titan's walls, but they couldn't risk searching everywhere for her. That could get her moved or even killed.

"Akio, I need you to pull up the blueprint of the building. It should be included in the public city records. We need to figure out where they would hold her so that it's a straight shot when we go in for her."

"Good idea." He replied.

The only sound to be heard for several moments was the clacking of the keyboard keys as Akio worked tirelessly to get him answers. Alaric's eyes were still closed, head tilted back in the chair as he continued to plot and plan within his head. It took him less than a second to feel Silas standing directly in front of him before he opened his eyes to find his best friend holding a blood bag.

"You look like you're starving, and you know Rome isn't going to let you leave this house unless you've properly fed, so drink up." He ordered.

Now that he mentioned it, a gnawing hunger was clawing at his insides, demanding sustenance. He took the bag and quickly sank his fangs into the pouch before he could somehow talk his way out of it. The cold taste of coppery blood slid down his throat and settled into his stomach. It took him less than a minute to drain it before another one was shoved under his nose. Six bags later, he finally found an even balance with his erratic emotions, but now he felt starved for real food and the touch of his woman. Rome had disappeared somewhere upstairs, Akio was still working at the monitors, and Silas sat beside him at the table, his eyes glued to the side of his face as he observed him.

He turned to stare into Silas's mismatched gaze and frowned. "Why are you just sitting here staring at me? Nothing better to do?"

He shook his head softly and ran frustrated fingers through his waist-length hair. "I'm still seeing your death, and I don't understand why. You're immortal now. My visions of you aren't making sense, and now I can't stop myself from ensuring you stay alive. I need to change your fate because I can't risk losing you. We can't risk losing you."

"Should you even be telling me this?"

"Do you think I give a damn about that? Alaric, I just told you I'm still seeing your death, and that's all you have to say about it?"

What did he want him to say? Yes, he was shocked by the revelation, but all his mind and body could focus on was that Na'tori was with his enemies, and the darkness within his mind had punched a hole in his mental barrier the size of Texas. He had felt that break the second he'd finished his third blood bag. Darkness was pouring into his every thought and memory, twisting and corrupting him as his mind rebelled, but it was useless. The fact that he was strong enough to hide the battle going on with him said enough. Maybe Silas's thoughts were trying to tell him something. Perhaps the darkness he'd been fighting for well over a year was finally winning, and death would be his reprieve, but then where would that leave Na'tori?

"We need to locate Na'tori, and once we get her, you promise me that you'll protect her even if I don't make it out." Alaric watched his closest friend blanch and immediately shake his head in disagreement before he spoke again. "You once promised to take me from this life if I ever went too far and lost my fight against the darkness that's infecting my mind. Well, I'm telling you now that I will no longer hold you to that because I know I'll have to do some unsavory things to get to her, but I'm willing to risk myself for her. Just protect her, Si, please."

"If I say yes to this, then I'm just as responsible if you do die, and she might never forgive me for that." Silas glared. "I won't be her enemy."

"Then I suppose you'll just have to ensure I live through this."

At first, Alaric thought Silas would continue to ignore his ask, but when his head dipped in acknowledgment and agreement, he knew without a doubt that Silas was someone that he could always depend on to have his back in any situation. Relief filled him, knowing that no matter what happened next, Na'tori would always be protected by someone he trusted without question, but first, they had to get her back.

"Akio, how's it going over there?" Alaric questioned as he stared at the back of his man bun.

"It would go even better if you two would shut up and come look at this." He snipped back.

Alaric tried not to chuckle at the annoyance within his voice but failed as he stood, crossed the room, and peered over him to view the monitors. A blueprint of the Titan facility was blown up on the screen, but what he saw and remembered about the building meant that these blueprints were a lie. From what he remembered, this print was missing multiple hallways, doors, and even levels. This was a front.

"I'll draw out what I saw while I was there and what I picked up within the memory of some of the guards." Alaric offered.

Akio pulled up another screen and continued attempting to hack into the Titan facility as he commented again. "Once I'm in, we can move on this and get your girl back."

He clapped Akio on the back and headed back to the table to get started on his own blueprint. He was getting his woman back. He was getting Na'tori Titan.

CHAPTER
THIRTY-THREE

Na'tori wanted to pass out again just to escape the pain
that was tearing through her entire body, but she knew
that even if she did, that reprieve wouldn't last nearly as
long as she needed it to. Her face was covered in snot, tears
drenched the cotton fabric that had been tied tightly over her eyes,
her body was no longer cold against the metal table she was
strapped to, and she was slowly beginning to lose feeling in her
hands and feet with how tightly she'd been tied down. Every time
she took in air, she struggled to catch her breath, and every sound
she heard made her jump in fear. How long had the torture been
happening? She wasn't sure, but whenever she yelped, cried, or
screamed in absolute terror, her brother's soft chuckle would fill the
space around them.

His voice broke the silence and caused her to tense. "Tori, I
need you to tell me how Alaric is still alive because he should be
dead, according to Dr. Salazar. He should be six feet under the
ground with his body corrupted by the virus you created. So tell me,
sweet sister, and I promise to ease your pain."

He was lying.

She knew he was lying, and yet the urge to escape the pain that was coursing through her veins was tempting enough to part her lips as if she intended to answer. She couldn't, though. She wouldn't betray Alaric's trust. Not even to save her own life.

"Nothing?" Ezekiel tsked softly. "I'm not sure how much more of this you can take but I'm willing to continue for as long as you can handle it. Would you like to know how long Evan lasted? How he begged me to stop?"

She shook her head as more tears leaked from her eyes before a hot poker was pressed against the flesh of her inner thigh. Her scream echoed through the room as pain flared through her leg, and her hands clenched into fists as the urge to get away forced her body to go taut. Bile churned in her gut, her vision swam, and Na'tori was on the verge of getting what she wanted and passing out before he removed the rod and chuckled darkly. She had lost count of just how many burns and cuts were now etched into her skin. She felt them everywhere, and each time the edge of a blade or the heat from the branding rod sank into her skin, her mind and body rebelled as her heart cried out for someone to save her from the pain.

"Evan wasn't as strong as you. He cried like a bitch and told me everything I wanted to know." He paused and began to run his fingers through her hair as she whimpered in fear. "Granted, he didn't know that no matter what he said, he would still die. You see, he knew too much. He'd figured out things that he shouldn't have, and he had plans to ruin things for me. I couldn't allow that, right? He couldn't continue to live while having blackmail on me. That just wouldn't do, but for you." His hand became a fist that practically tore her hair out from the roots before his lips caressed her ear with his following words. "For you, I'll let you live as my toy to take out and torture whenever I please, but first, you'll tell me what I want to know. Tell me about Alaric."

"F-fuck you Z-zeke!"

Her blindfold was ripped from her eyes, light seared her vision, and when she finally focused, she found herself staring down the barrel of a gun, but this she refused to fear. The weapon was now becoming familiar territory for her, but he'd already played his hand. He wouldn't kill her. He needed her for his sick, twisted pleasure, so instead of cowering in fear, Na'tori released a pain-filled laugh that made her body ache. She laughed through the pain and licked the blood that had somehow appeared on her bottom lip as Ezekiel's expression turned murderous. He snarled and jerked away from her to cross the room.

She took that opportunity to check around as much of the room as she could see and shuddered at the sight of a wall that carried every type of torture device that she had only ever seen in movies. Her brother moved out of her periphery and returned carrying the scorching poker that had been the bane of her existence since she'd awoken. He didn't cut her nearly as much as he burned her, and she was seriously beginning to hate the smell of her burning flesh, but she refused to beg. It wouldn't work.

Na'tori tried to sink into the table when he laid the tip of it against her ribcage. She screamed inside of her mind instead of allowing him the pleasure of watching her scream aloud, but that only seemed to anger him more. The poker was heated and pressed against her several more times before she screamed her throat raw and passed out from the agony.

"Please," Na'tori *whimpered into the darkness in her mind.* "Please make the pain stop."

She figured she was alone in her head for a moment until a warm presence bled into her thoughts, and a familiar voice reached out to her. "Na'tori? Damn, am I glad to hear your voice." *Silas's voice was a calming balm in the storm of her mental state and pain.* "I heard your psychic scream but I don't think anyone else heard it. Are you alright? Where exactly are you in the facility? We're developing a plan to get you out of there, but we need to know exactly where you are."

"Silas!" *Shock filled her.* "How are you in my head?"

"You must have unintentionally dropped your shields."

"Then why can't I hear Rome or Alaric?"

The warmth turned to a searing heat as Silas moved around her mind. It was like he was searching for something, but what that something was, she wasn't sure, and quite frankly, she didn't care. She was just glad to finally talk to someone who wasn't Ezekiel, and now that she had reached the people who cared about whether she lived or died, it gave her hope that she might actually get out of there alive.

When Silas spoke again, his voice was softer, almost as if it were farther away. "It's possible that they couldn't hear your psychic cry because they don't keep their mental barriers cracked open. I do it for moments like this, but my clairvoyance assists me greatly in that regard, and I never take in negativity, but for them, it's a toss-up because that negativity can slip between their cracks and drive them to lash out against it. The only reason why I didn't simply avoid your cries is because of a vision I experienced. It expressed my need to stay open. Now tell me where you are."

"Ezekiel has me in a torture room somewhere within the lower levels of the facility, or at least I think I'm still here. He drugged me."

"Fuck, okay." He paused; his voice took on an even softer tone, as if he were barely speaking. "Dammit, Tori, fight to keep your mind open. If you're asleep or knocked out, then that would explain why your shields are down, but I need you to focus now. Keep your shields down. Let me try to walk you through this."

NA'TORI ATTEMPTED to respond and instead found herself sucked into light and awareness as she came awake. Her mouth was wide open on a strangled scream as electric currents slid through her muscles and caused every inch of her to tense in agony.

"Finally!" Ezekiel exclaimed as his face came into view. He hovered over her with a cattle prod grasped within the palm of his hand. "If not for the heart monitor I attached, I would have thought you were dead and that my fun was cut short. I haven't quite perfected bringing someone back from death, but we'll get there in time." He stepped away and moved for his wall of torture devices.

She tried not to react to his words. He was only hoping for a response from her, and she refused to give him one. Instead, she focused on breaking down her shields to return to Silas. Her mind and mostly her body rejected the idea as she thrashed against the steel bands that held her down. They would surely leave deep grooves and marks in her skin from her rough movements, but the second she felt the noose around her shields loosen, she breathed a sigh of relief and welcomed the voice that followed into her mind.

"Na'tori, If you can hear me, then you know you need to play this out exactly as I have planned. I've informed Alaric and everyone else that we're communicating. Only a handful of us are coming for you, but I need you to give your brothers some information to help us execute this. Can you do that?"

"Yes. Of course." She didn't need to think about her answer. She knew she would do whatever she needed to get out of there and take her brothers and their company down.

"I'm sure he's trying to get information out of you. I need you to tell him that you were kept a prisoner and forced to give up crucial information on Titan. To sell him on the idea, you'll tell him we found the device that prohibits telepathic communication and that you tweaked it for us so we would keep you alive. When he asks, because we both know he will, you'll tell, instead of blocking, that you've enhanced it and made it possible for every Eternal or Kindred to communicate with one another. From there, you'll lead him to believe that we are coming for you right now because we've been communicating with you this entire time. We are coming for you, Tori. Just give us at least three hours. Can you hold on until then?"

Her breath paused for only a moment as she processed his words. Could she wait that long? Would her torture become worse once she passed along the message, or would she be left alone while Ezekiel helped Lukas plan for an attack? She wasn't sure, but she would trust Silas.

"I'll convince him." She responded to Silas before focusing on her brother as he continued to look over the assortment of weapons on the wall. "Zeke?" She whispered through lips that felt like sandpaper from how dry they were.

Ezekiel glanced over his shoulder and pinned her with a questioning look that chilled her to the bone. His eyes were dead orbs that she couldn't believe she'd never noticed until now.

"What is it?" He asked, and his voice was flat and unemotional. "Have you decided to tell me what I would like to know?"

"I can't tell you why Alaric is still alive, but you have to believe me, I didn't want to be there! They dug into my head and got the information they needed. They used me, but I did it to gain their trust. I know it may not seem like it, but I promise you that I did it with good reason."

He approached the table carrying a hunting knife until he hovered over her once more and pressed the tip of the blade against the flesh of her throat. "Just hours ago, you told us, your family, how you couldn't wait to see us ruined and buried beneath the rubble of Titan. Has that all of a sudden changed? Is it no longer fuck you, and I wish you dead? If so," he chuckled darkly, "then your pain is about to elevate to new levels because you're lying to me and not well enough. So which is it? Did they force you to reveal things and help them, or do you wish me and everything our family built would burn in the pits of hell?"

She controlled her expression, ensuring her hatred didn't glow within her eyes before she licked her dried-out lips and swallowed harshly. The tip of the blade pressed more firmly into her jugular, causing her to hiss softly as her blood beaded up and trickled down the side of her throat. Ezekiel grinned softly, and she knew without a doubt that the only way he would believe her was if she fed into his sick, twisted fantasies.

"You want to make me your torture toy, right? Well, what better way to hurt Alaric than to hurt me in front of him?" She whispered. "I can help you do that. I only pretended to spew hate at you because I figured Romulus would have me watched closely. I wasn't supposed to be at the library. I was never supposed to leave their home, but I knew if I could just reach one of you, I'd be okay."

Ezekiel's grin morphed into a frown. "And why exactly would Alaric care if anything happened to you? You're nothing to him."

"I mean way more than you'll ever know." She swallowed harshly as she attempted to keep up with this new lie she was weaving, hoping to get him to believe her. "You know how strong his mental powers are. He'll want me back just to ensure that the supplement I created to boost his powers continues to work, and I know how much you hate him. Zeke, you have the person he desires most in his miserable life. He'll come for me; in fact, I'm sure they're already on their way."

"How do I know you're speaking the truth? And if they dove

into your mind before, then what's stopping them from doing so now as they tell you exactly what lies to feed me?" The pressure against her throat built before he reluctantly pulled the blade away and sighed heavily as he ran a frustrated hand down his face.

He began pacing beside her table, and Na'tori knew he was second-guessing everything she'd said. If he wanted Alaric as badly as he claimed, then he would do everything within his power to make it happen. She waited and watched for several moments as he continued walking the room's expanse. He was mumbling to himself while he caressed the blade of his knife in what could only be described as a loving touch before he paused and pinned her with a look.

"If I leave this room and talk to the group monitoring Romulus's house and they tell me nothing about an imminent threat, then know that when I return, you'll be losing toes or fingers, maybe even your tongue, for your deceit, but I'll let you pick what you prefer to lose most. Are we clear?" He questioned with that dead look in his eyes.

"Yes." She replied, "I understand completely."

He stormed from the room with one more hard look before she released a sigh of relief. Without thinking too hard about it, Na'tori focused on the shields within her mind in an attempt to lower them and reach out to Silas, but she was still in shock when his voice easily slid through her mind.

"I never left you, Tori, and miraculously, you didn't push me from your mind as I thought you were doing. You simply woke up, and I strengthened our connection, so I was privy to the entire conversation with your brother. Ezekiel will find that we are, in fact, heading for Titan, but we won't come for you until the sun is cresting in the sky. That will give us the element of surprise since your brothers will assume we've retired to our 'coffins.' Be ready when we arrive."

She chuckled softly in her mind, afraid that the possible hidden cameras would catch it if she expressed it outwardly. *"I'm not going anywhere, Si, I'm strapped to a table in my bra and panties."*

"Is it bad? Will you need extensive healing?"

Tears poured from her eyes at the thought of what her body now looked like, covered in cuts and burns. Would Alaric even still want her as she was now? The idea of him not wanting her now because of the marks that now covered her gave her tunnel vision as her mind went into a tailspin.

"Na'tori!" Silas snapped, *"Focus on my voice and tell me how bad the damage is. I can't see what you're seeing. You're effectively blocking me from whatever images are causing your panic and fear."*

"Can Rome heal branding marks?"

"Fuck." He paused momentarily, but she could feel his anger filling her before he spoke again. *"Rome will heal you. I just need you to focus on Alaric and keep him calm. We don't need him ripping everyone's mind open and leaving husks behind. We'll be there, Tori, I promise."*

She closed her eyes and sighed heavily, even as every inch of her body throbbed and ached in pain. All she could do now was wait.

THIRTY-FOUR

S ilas couldn't dispel the foreboding feeling clawing at his insides as he stood with Erick, Romulus, and Alaric in the alleyway directly across from the building they planned to infiltrate within the next five minutes. He couldn't tear his eyes off of his best friend as he watched him fiddle with the 10-inch blade strapped to his bulletproof vest. Although he was Immortal now, they didn't want to chance Titan learning that Alaric was now an Eternal, which meant keeping him as calm as possible for Na'tori's extraction, but now that he knew somewhat of what they would be walking into, Silas wasn't too sure if they'd be successful. He hadn't told Alaric about her condition, but Rome knew what they were heading into. Rome knew that Alaric might very well lose his shit and get them into a deeper situation than they were prepared for.

Rome looked them over before his gaze turned to watch as the beginning rays of the sun began to creep along the horizon. "I know the sun's pull will be strong, so I'll attempt to shield you all with my shadows. We should be in and out in less than seven minutes if we time this accordingly. I don't need any fuck ups, and I damn sure need to know if anyone weakens too quickly so I can get you the fuck out of there. Are we clear on what we're doing?" He questioned before his blue orbs focused wholly on Alaric. "I need you to keep it the hell together when we get inside because no matter what you see, I will fix it. Know that I'll fix it."

Alaric simply nodded, never taking his eyes off of the building ahead, and Silas could swear he saw a flash of red within his eyes. Before he could question his best friend, Rome gripped him by the shoulder as Erick and Alaric touched some part of their King before darkness engulfed him.

Seconds later, they were inside the building, in a broom closet too small to hold them all comfortably before Rome cracked open the door and pushed a telepathic thought into their minds. *"Based on the research and information provided, Na'tori should be locked behind the third door to our left. She has no guards on her, and this hall seems reserved for upper Titan management, so it's loosely guarded."*

"How did you get past the silver within the wall?" Erick questioned, *"I can feel it all around us, and it's throwing me off. It's weakening me."*

"Alara's blood has been strengthening me with every interaction we have. Silver hardly fazes me. Now let's focus."

Alaric released a frustrated growl before he spoke. *"Then why couldn't we transport into the room? Dammit, Romulus, we don't have time for this!"*

"Because we don't know the setup in the room. We don't know if it's being monitored, and we don't know if there's a trap lying in waiting for us. We need to do this correctly. Now, do you plan to argue with me or get to your woman?" Rome snapped.

Silence stretched through the telepathic bond between them before Rome slipped through the crack of the door, and they each followed behind him. Silas took the rear and watched their backs as they crept down the hallway. Their long strides ate up the distance between them and the door they intended to reach. The moment they slipped into the room Silas took in the sight of Na'tori strapped to the table in the middle of the room with only her underclothing covering her. Burns and cuts covered her body in a way that spoke of several hours of meticulous torture. Her opalescent eyes took them in before they landed on Alaric and stilled. Seeing him seemed to convince her that she would be finally saved as tears began to pour freely from her eyes as she whimpered and struggled to move.

The moment Alaric tensed up and a furious snarl filled the room, Silas and everyone else knew without a doubt that every plan they'd devised for the night was now ruined. It was cemented even more so when a searing pain tore through his mind and caused him to wince.

"Dammit, Alaric, don't do this." Silas moved for him, intending to knock his best friend out so they could grab Na'tori and get the hell out of there when the pain increased, and he felt his legs give out.

Rome and Erick were frozen in place as Alaric crossed the room and snapped the straps holding his woman down with a simple yank. He could smell Alaric's burnt flesh, yet it didn't seem to register with the man himself. Silas tried to fight against the compulsion to stay put as his mind continued to pulse with pain. He knew what Alaric was doing. Those tendrils of blackness that he'd glimpsed only twice before were penetrating his thoughts, so he knew without a doubt that his friend was slipping beneath the barriers of everyone else's minds in an attempt to harm the one who'd hurt his woman.

"R-Romulus," Silas gritted through clenched teeth as he forced words past his lips, "we h-have t-to s-s-stop him!"

His eyes were glued to his King, yet Rome remained still as a statue, his eyes fixed on his brother-in-law. It looked as if he were fighting for control over his body, yet when he opened his mouth to speak, no words came out. The lights within the room flickered, energy swelled around them, and time slowed when Erick reached out abruptly and grabbed his hand. Without prompting, a vision slammed into his mind.

ERICK GRIPPED his hand and moved for Rome while time slowed around them. Na'tori and Alaric were motionless, his face filled with anger and sadness. His eyes burned a deep red that shouldn't have been possible while she clung to him like he was her lifeline.

"I have to stop him," Erick stated. "He'll die if I don't, and we need him in this war. I don't know what makes Alaric so special, but his blood revealed his

death. Only she can save him. She doesn't know that I'm aware, and I know she's afraid. She's afraid to test her theory and fail, but I know he'll live as long as she initiates the bond. Na'tori has to be the one to initiate it."

"What the hell are you talking about?" Rome questioned. "Just grab them both, and we can be done with this. No one has to die today, and even Titan will remain standing. At least for now."

"It's not that simple, sir. You'll hate me for what I must do, but you'll forgive me in time. In time, things will make sense to each of you. Just know I did this to give our people the best chance they'll have in this life and within the next."

No one could have prepared for what followed next.

Erick released them, and time stopped, yet somehow, Silas could still watch everything unfold. The pain in his head ebbed, and the door was kicked inward as several guards, along with Lukas Titan, strolled into the room, firing tranquilizer darts that struck each of them in either the throat or the chest. Rome and Alaric were fired on repeatedly, causing them to fall unconscious before anyone else. Na'tori's scream was earth-shattering as she launched from the bed and grabbed the blade strapped to Alaric's chest.

"You won't hurt me." Lukas stated, "You don't have what it takes to do what needs to be done in this world. You're weak, just like Ezekiel said. You want to join them so badly, then I'll gladly make that happen, and you'll watch their deaths when they come." He snapped his fingers and pointed at his sister. "Grab her and secure them."

SILAS WAS SUCKED out of his premonition the moment Erick released his hand. What he had just witnessed within his mind slowly unfolded in front of him before he could voice anything to warn them. The door was kicked in, a tranq dart pierced his throat, and he could do nothing but watch as Rome and Alaric dropped like stones to the ground before they passed out. He fought the effects of the drugs as Erick struggled to hold himself up with the table, and Na'tori stood with Alaric's blade in her hands.

Lukas's words fell on deaf ears but he didn't need to hear them to know what was being said. The world swayed beneath his feet while Erick gave him a pointed look and allowed his power to flare within his gaze. It caused his red irises to brighten more than he'd ever seen before, just as Silas dropped to the ground on his knees. He could feel the poison of the drugs flowing through him as pain pierced his wrist, and three guards moved in unison to grab Na'tori. With a glance down, Silas could make out Rome through his blurred vision as he greedily sucked at his wrist before his gaze whipped back towards his best friend's woman to find her throwing that knife with everything in her. Shock blossomed through him when the blade pierced her brother's throat just as darkness pulled him under, and he face-planted on the cool tile floor.

CHAPTER
THIRTY-FIVE

Several hours later, after the sun dropped from the sky and the moon rose again, Erick found himself sitting on one of their hospital beds, his eyes firmly fixed on Alaric's unconscious form as Silas occupied the third bed and everyone else stood around them. Some wore strained expressions; others held anger, fear, and sadness. The woman they'd saved was the only person who sat motionless and calm. Na'tori had yet to speak since the events of that morning. Her eyes wouldn't leave the monitors that watched Alaric's vitals, and she refused to address or respond to anyone within the room. Although she'd allowed Rome to heal her, she had yet to say a word.

Erick remembered the events of the day and how he'd pushed his body beyond what should have been possible, and he knew what he had done by doing so. He didn't regret his actions, but now he had to come clean. Rome was hovering over him; the feel of his ice-blue gaze staring at the side of his face as he attempted to breach his mind was a telling sign that he didn't have long before his King threw caution to the wind and simply broke down his shields to get to some answers.

"Can someone just tell us what happened?" Amirishka snapped

from her seated position on one of the tables Erick typically used for his medical tools.

"I'm waiting for Erick to come clean. You told me I would understand and forgive you? We're all here, no one but that sick fuck Lukas died." Rome looked him over with a frown. "Silas should wake as soon as his blood transfusion is done and we'll heal Alaric as soon as we figure out why he isn't waking. So what am I missing?"

Erick finally looked away from Alaric, but it wasn't to look at his King; it was to meet the eyes of the woman that this was all centered around. "I saw the results, Na'tori. You know what you need to do if you truly wish to save his life. He doesn't have long on this earth if you keep avoiding what needs to happen."

Na'tori's voice cracked when she spoke. "What if it doesn't work?"

"He was pumped with so much of the tranquilizer drug that I'm surprised he's even still breathing. Giving him your blood won't hurt him any more than he already is, so what are you really risking?"

"Okay, seriously, what the hell is going on?" Alondra questioned from her position near the stairs. "I thought my brother couldn't bite her. Not that I should know that information, but it's pretty well known that he hasn't been able to mate her, so what's different now?"

"Wait," Alara stepped away from her brother's unconscious body and approached her mate with a frown as tears began to gather in her eyes. "Is he really dead?"

Rome glanced around the room before focusing on his woman and speaking. "Yes, little flower, Lukas is dead." He pulled her into his arms and kissed her head before sighing heavily. "There's a lot going on right now, and I think the most pressing matter is figuring out what we can do to help your brother."

"I've already told you what needs to be done. Na'tori has to initiate the bond." Erick pressed a hand against his head when a bout of dizziness struck him suddenly. He brushed it off. "Her blood will heal him completely; he needs her blood and the bond. I may not be a geneticist, but the tests aren't lying."

Na'tori placed her hand on Alaric's cheek as tears began to trek down her face. "This is all my fault. If I had stayed put, this would have never happened. Ezekiel never would have gotten a hold of me, and Alaric wouldn't be lying here dying once again."

Maverick shrugged his shoulders and frowned. "He was always dying, Tori. You can't put that on yourself."

"I created the damn virus in the first place!" She snapped, "Or did you forget? I caused all of this. If not for me, none of this would even be happening. I should heal him and just leave; give you guys some sort of reprieve from the madness my family and I keep creating."

Erick shifted atop the hospital bed as another wave of dizziness struck. They didn't have time to discuss this. Things were progressing too fast for him, and Rome needed to know what would happen now that things had unfolded in a way he hoped they wouldn't. At least not until he'd found answers to his own problems, but it was too late for that now.

"Romulus." He cleared his throat and met the eyes of the man who had helped him in more ways than he knew. He couldn't meet the eyes of everyone gathered around without allowing his armor to crack. "Can we speak privately?"

Rome gave him a stern look. He could feel him pressing against his mental barriers once more and pushed back. Erick knew his King wouldn't tear down his walls, but he wouldn't put it past him to try to slip beneath them. Rome wasn't a man used to waiting for answers but he steeled his spine and gaze against his King and kept his expression clear even as pain continued to flow through his entire body. He noticed it the moment Rome decided to give him a solo audience when he kissed his mate again, crossed the room, and gripped him by the shoulder before the room disappeared around them.

The cool night breeze brushed against them from their position atop a rooftop that didn't look familiar to Erick at all. Snow coated the ground, and he knew they were no longer in Van Scive or even New Jersey, for that matter.

"Where are we?" He questioned.

"Alaska," Rome replied dryly. "I figured I could kill two birds with one stone once you tell me what's happening."

Erick sat on the cool brick of the building with his back to the city behind him as he met his friend's unwavering gaze. He already knew that no matter what he told Rome, he wouldn't care. He would try to fix what couldn't be fixed now that it was in motion. He smiled through his pain before he forced words past his lips that Erick thought he would never have to speak. "I'm dying, Romulus. Whatever Alaric did when he entered my mind did damage that I didn't even know was possible. My abilities spiraled. Using them meant taking centuries off my life. Whenever I manipulate time, I feel my insides burning and dying off. Last night was it for me. Stopping time for as long as I did cemented my future. Sometime within the next few days or even hours, I'll breathe my last breath."

Rome didn't speak for several moments, although his eyes betrayed his mood when they brightened, and his hands balled into fists. His voice was rough and angry when he chose to speak. "Allow me to try to heal you."

"You'll find that there's nothing to be done, but you can try if it will make you feel better about the situation."

Rome reached forward to hold Erick's head between his palms. Silence stretched between them before Rome growled furiously and paced away from him with a snarled fuck that echoed around them, along with a crack of thunder before the sky opened up with a downpour.

CHAPTER
THIRTY-SIX

N a'tori paced the floor of Alaric's bedroom as a million thoughts flew around her mind. After Rome had returned with Erick, she'd asked if they could be moved into Alaric's bedroom to grant them privacy. Rome had teleported them without a word and made sure to keep him connected to the machines that were currently keeping him alive. She wasn't sure what Rome and Erick had discussed when they'd left, but the energy around them when they returned told her there was more bad news on the horizon. However, the beeping of machines kept her from trying to pry for information. Alone with the man who made her heart pound faster, Na'tori had no choice but to focus on the now and what she would have to do. If only she could decide what to do.

She remembered what the test results had read. Her blood would help him; it would give his already crazy strong immune system an actual fighting chance against the virus that was robbing him of his immortality, but in return, the mating would begin. That initial drive to tie her to him would resonate in him, and he would attempt to tie them together for eternity. Na'tori wanted nothing more, yet fear held her back. The fear of tying him to someone who constantly brought war into his life terrified her as her mind raced with how much of a burden she had been since they'd met. Did he really want to be saddled with her for the rest of his immortal life?

She wiped away tears that had begun to creep down her cheeks and jerked around when Alaric's heart rate abruptly plummeted. Rushing for the side of the bed, Na'tori watched as all of his vitals dropped, and she knew that her decision had already been made for her. She was out of time. She reached for the blade on the night-stand and hissed in pain when she cut across her wrist and watched as beads of blood swelled from the wound. She parted Alaric's dry lips as the machines continued to scream at her and watched, heart racing in her chest as her life bled into his mouth before his fangs punched into her wrists.

Pain seared her before ecstasy replaced the sensation and sent her heart soaring for an entirely different reason. Her clit pulsed in tune with every pull and suck from her bleeding wound. Alaric's hands snapped out quickly and yanked her forward as he released her wrist with a slow lick that caused her toes to curl in absolute pleasure.

"Princess," he whispered against her lips with a rough exhale, "where are we, and why am I so weak?"

"You tried to overexert your ability, and you were dosed with more of the tranq drug," she whispered back, "Now I'm trying to heal you. How is my blood making you feel?" She watched as he licked his lips, and allowed herself to smile softly when his eyes brightened and a soft growl rumbled from his chest. His hands had moved to her waist as he attempted to pull her even closer until she was flush against his side, lying across the bed with him.

"You gave me your blood..." He licked his lips once more, closed his eyes on a groan, and reached down to adjust the erection pressing against the fabric of his pants, "I don't know what this means."

Na'tori placed her hand over his now racing heart as she struggled to gather her thoughts. He wasn't the only one affected by the change taking place. Her body was an erogenous zone waiting and willing for him, but she needed to ensure that she wasn't taking his choice away from him. Did he still want her? Rome had healed her of her burns and cuts, but that didn't erase what happened, and a part of her had wished to keep at least one mark to show that she had survived what her brothers thought would be her breaking point. In the end, they didn't win. Especially Lukas. That only left Ezekiel, and her anger towards him was more profound than any emotion she could feel. All except for the emotion Alaric elicited from her.

With grey-blue eyes that swam with want and need and her body clenching in anticipation, Na'tori reached up to caress the side of his face as tears began to slip once more from her eyes without prompting. Speaking was hard, and her throat was constricted with emotion, but she pushed through. "I never thought I would find what we have. Honestly, I don't even know what we have, but I do know that no one could make me feel as you do. I've known for some time that by giving you my blood it might be the answer we needed to heal you, but a part of me was terrified. A part of me thought that in doing so, I would be taking you away from the woman who is meant to be your mate because, clearly, it can't be me. By all accounts, Eternals are the ones that initiate this bond, and I'm not one of you. I gave you my blood anyway because I couldn't lose you, not if I could stop your death somehow. Allowing you to die is something that was never in the cards for me."

"You think I want someone else?" Alaric's eyes narrowed in anger, "Whatever gave you that impression?"

"I just don't want to keep you from being with the woman who is meant to be your true mate. If I have to, I'll just give you blood every few weeks until she comes along to heal you completely. I truly believe that only a mating can right the wrongs within your cells, but my blood fights the virus off enough to keep you alive and hopefully without pain."

Alaric's expression remained furious, yet his hand was gentle when he took her by the chin and pulled her closer until his lips brushed against hers as he spoke. "Do you remember what I told you when I first took you into my arms and filled the sweet heaven between your thighs? I told you then what I'll tell you now. The fact that I was incapable of binding you to me changed nothing! You are mine, princess. Or did you forget?"

"I needed to make sure this is what you wanted," she replied.

"When I fought the Gods for you, I knew then that you were my end game. There would be no other woman. Even before I felt it, I knew I was in love with you, and there would be no other woman to rob me of all common sense. I love you, Na'tori, and I hope you figure that out in the next ten seconds because completing the bond with you is all I can think of, and these jeans are becoming incredibly uncomfortable."

He loved her.

Na'tori smiled softly. "I love you too."

She kissed him while her heart raced in her chest, and her hand gripped the fabric of his shirt. His fingers threaded into her hair and tugged gently until he looked into her eyes with the softest expression he could probably muster. She wanted to keep kissing him; in fact, she wanted to do so much more than kiss him, thanks to the essence from his fangs that were sliding throughout her bloodstream. When she attempted to get another kiss from him, Alaric held her still and shook his head slowly before allowing his eyes to caress every inch of her face.

"I need you to undress and come take a seat right on my face. Can you do that for me, princess?" His thumb rubbed against the wetness of her bottom lip, and he smiled softly as a look of shock crossed her face. "Don't act shy now, my love; give me what we both need."

Her ears felt like they were on fire, along with her cheeks, as she climbed from the bed and slowly undressed. This was really happening. She couldn't look away as he removed the IVs from his arms and carefully discarded his clothing. She could see the strain on his face and knew he still wasn't at a hundred percent. The urge to give him more blood sang through her veins when he motioned for her to climb onto the bed with his legs spread and erection waving in the air like a flag blowing in the wind.

"Come sit on my face." He instructed with a smirk.

"How?" She whispered.

"Climb up, knees on either side of my face, but I want you facing my feet."

The heat on her face spread throughout her body as she did as she was told. Embarrassment churned in her gut as the feeling of the wetness between her thighs slid down her inner thigh. Alaric simply snarled with pleasure and grabbed her thighs; his fingers dug into her skin and sent sparks of need through her body as she slowly lowered herself onto his face and felt that first slow lick to the lips of her pussy that caused a moan to spill from her. His tongue slid through her folds languidly, as if he had all the time in the world as her legs trembled and her abdominal core clenched in preparation for an orgasm. Now that he knew how to work and play her body like it was his own, it didn't take long to bring her to completion. Na'tori's nails dug into his chest, and she screamed in ecstasy when he sucked her clit into his mouth and grazed it with his fangs. His groan of pleasure matched her moan until he released her and whispered against her wetness. "Lean forward and wrap your pretty lips around me, princess."

"Fuck," she whimpered before doing as she was told.

Leaning forward, she put her mouth over his dick as it leaked precum down to the base of him. She could see it dripping and sliding along his balls and couldn't resist the urge to run her tongue along the mess to taste him. It was sweetness mixed with something she couldn't decipher, but that didn't even matter when he moaned hoarsely and gripped her ass to spread her wider as he began to fuck her with his tongue. Na'tori sucked the head of his dick into her mouth until she swallowed him whole. His hips jerked beneath her, ramming him into the back of her throat repeatedly as she loved him with her tongue until his fist gripped her hair and pulled her away.

"Enough!" He snarled breathlessly. "I need you."

Na'tori found herself flipped around, hands digging into his shoulders as Alaric gently eased her body down until she was enveloping his erection into her warmth, and they were moaning in unison.

"This is going to be so satisfying." He murmured. "I can feel your blood mixing with my own throughout my veins, and for once, the urge to bite you isn't just an urge. We'll be mating this evening, and you'll be mine completely, wholly, and without question."

"I know." She replied with a smile as she began to work her hips against him.

The smooth thrust and glide of their bodies joining was like a symphony fighting to reach its peak. Alaric's hand dug into her waist and the back of her neck as he pulled her forward to kiss and suck along her throat. Her moans were cries of passion as their hips fought to be in charge, and although she was on top, Alaric was winning their battle of wills when her legs began to shake, and her abdominal core became tense with the need to cum. Na'tori cried out when his hand tightened marginally around her throat seconds before the feeling of his fangs slid into her jugular and robbed her of speech. The moment he sucked and his essence filled her, stars burst behind eyelids she hadn't realized she'd closed and caused an orgasm so intense that she could hardly catch her breath to spear through her.

Alaric's groan vibrated against her throat as their bond clicked into place before he slowly retracted his fangs and continued to fuck her at a brutal pace. Her nails dug into his skin, the smell of blood, sweat, and sex filled the air, and their eyes swirled with color. Na'tori watched as his aura changed before her. Before, it had been weak and tainted with a twinge of red, but now it pulsed just as brightly as Rome's did with a streak of red that made her wonder just what the hell it meant. She couldn't form the words to ask him because his lips took hers in a brutal kiss before the feeling of his cum bathed her walls and sent another orgasm crashing into her.

As their hips slowed to a stop, Alaric kissed along her throat and face before he spoke. "Thank you for giving me the greatest gift of becoming my mate. I hope to continually please you and keep you happy for all the days of our lives."

Na'tori smiled against his cheek and leaned back to search his expression. "You're everything I didn't know I needed, so thank you for choosing and wanting me." She slid off his body and cuddled into his side as she ran her hand lazily across his chest. "Maybe this isn't the right time to bring it up, but I need you to know that ever since meeting you, you have changed my mindset on life and opened my eyes to the bigger picture of the world. With you by my side and the family that we've gained within the Eternals, I pray that everything we're fighting for can one day see the light of day without war and death following us. I have ideas and plans I want to bring to fruition, but I can't speak about them yet. I don't want to get anyone's hopes up."

"Whatever it is, I'm sure you'll do your best, and the results will be promising."

Alaric buried his hand within her hair and kissed her forehead just as she felt him go lax beside her in sleep. Na'tori's mind began to run with ideas that only the light of day would confirm. She settled into her mate's side and planned for their future and what her brother's death might mean for the company. Ezekiel was still out there, and Titan still stood, which meant the threat was still very real. There was no telling what would happen next, but she would do everything within her power to see that the people she loved and the new family she'd gained would remain standing in the end.

CHAPTER
THIRTY-SEVEN

Zeus stormed through the doors of Hera's bedroom chamber and grabbed her by the throat before she could react or even speak. Lightening and thunder streaked and boomed throughout the heavens when he slammed her up against the wall and practically spit words of anger and revulsion.

"I know what you've done, and it ends now. Your meddling will cease to exist, or your life will be forfeit, and I will throw you to the hellhounds where you will suffer endlessly. Defying me or ignoring to heed these warnings will make the punishment I once delivered upon you look like child's play. Do you understand me?"

Her hands fought against his hold, yet she was no match for his strength. The burning gaze of his fury made her realize her mistake. Hera was sneaky and manipulative, but Zeus always saw beneath her guise. He could always sense foul play when it was her doing. It's what he always expected of her, but she had been careful. The only way he could have known of her tampering with the Eternals was if that bastard Hypnos had spoken against her. Only he had sensed what she had done.

"I asked you a question, dear wife," a bolt of lightning slammed into the pillar beside her head, causing her to tense. "Answer me, now!" He demanded.

"I will never interfere again," she whispered back hoarsely.

He continued to watch her for any signs of dishonesty before he released her and watched her crumple to the ground, hand rubbing at her throat as she watched him warily. His robes billowed around his body as anger and fury still churned within him. He had thought that her rebellious stage was over and that she had come to accept their Eternals.

Oh, how wrong he had been.

"Let this be your last and final warning, Hera. Interfere with the lives of our Eternals in any capacity, and I will torture you for the rest of your miserable existence. You know better than to play with the strings of fate. Do not let your jealousy hold you in a death grip so tight that you can't even see what your actions will grant you in the end because I promise you, whatever ending you receive, it will not be pretty, and your meddling will have been for naught."

He walked away before she could voice a word. His thoughts churned with all the different ways he could make her pay for her deceit, but he would give her one more chance. It was a chance she didn't deserve but a chance he was willing to give nonetheless. If she should fail him again, he would have no choice but to punish her for her insolence. Once, he had loved her. In fact, he still did, but he would not let her play him for a fool or allow himself to grant her leniency in defying him repeatedly. It had to end somewhere and somehow. They couldn't continue on this way, or there would be another war in the heavens that most would not walk away from.

CHAPTER
THIRTY-EIGHT

The following morning, Na'tori was up before anyone else. She was down in the infirmary monitoring Ericks' vitals and racing against time to figure out what she could do to keep him alive, but at every turn, she met negative results. There was nothing she could do, and with each passing hour, his vitals looked even worse than before. He was dying just as he'd said.

After her mating with Alaric, Rome had told them what Erick had said and how Alaric's mind tampering had condemned him to a slow death that couldn't be stopped. Regret and sadness had filled her mate, and he'd stormed off before she could voice a word or soothe him for that matter, but with their mating, she felt a tether between them that told her he was still alive and well. Alaric had returned a few hours ago, bathed in Rogue blood and refusing to speak. She'd granted him the silence he seemed to need and had waited until he'd showered and fell into a slumber before she'd come downstairs to work.

Tears of frustration gathered in her eyes as Na'tori flung her hand across the desk, causing the paperwork and beakers to scatter and shatter onto the floor. She couldn't bring herself to care as she slumped in her seat and threw her head back with an exasperated groan. She unclipped her long hair and allowed it to flow down before she massaged her scalp and turned her gaze to the man lying across the hospital bed. Erick's vitals continued to drop, and she knew that by today's end, he would be dead, and the Eternals would be mourning the loss of a warrior. She couldn't even begin to think of how her mate might feel, considering he was the reason for Erick's demise.

Na'tori was closing her eyes again but paused when someone's presence registered at her back before a familiar hand curled into her hair and pulled her head back gently until she was peering into gray/green eyes that swirled with worry. Alaric's weary expression tugged at her heartstrings, but what confused her most was the fact that he was awake while the sun sat heavy in the sky. He should be in a sun-induced coma like the rest of the Eternals, and yet here he was, shirtless, covered in sweat, and watching her with a curious expression.

"What are you doing awake?" She exclaimed, even as she remained motionless within his grip.

She'd been right in her assessment. Finally, something was going right for them, and this new discovery would give them a significant stepping stone in the war against her family.

His fingers began to massage slow circles into her scalp as she had been doing as he continued to watch her quietly. His gaze shot to Erick's prone body and held. "I could feel your emotions in my sleep. Your frustration and anger woke me, and so I sought you out. I'm guessing you've still found no answers as to how you could help him?"

"I'm sorry, but no." She replied.

His expression dropped even more before he released her hair and perched himself on the edge of the desk as he brought his gaze back to her. Remorse stared back at her. "I never meant to hurt him this severely. I never wished him dead."

"Trust me, everyone knows you never intended to harm him." She placed her hands against his knees and stared into his face. "It isn't your fault, Alaric."

"But it is. If I had just embraced what I associated as darkness

316

within my mind, then maybe none of this would have happened. Maybe Erick wouldn't be lying there dying because of me."

"Wait, what are you talking about? Embrace the darkness for what? Being injected with the virus caused that entity to fester and grow within your mind. It was killing you."

"Yeah, that's what I thought as well, but in reality, it was helping me; I just didn't see it. Ever since I was infected with the virus, I'd developed a type of shadow within my mind that seemed to feed and crave the harsher parts of reality. I put blocks and barriers in place to hold that darkness at bay, but all that really did was hurt me. Darkness has always been a part of me. The virus just brought it out more. It wasn't until we mated that it fell quiet, almost dormant, but that didn't stop the urges I felt. Now, I just have a better understanding of how I should have handled things. Starting with embracing all sides of me, even the more shameful aspects and desires within me. Erick is like this because I was angry and hurt, and I wanted to make someone hurt as badly as I did. He was in the crossfire and didn't deserve what I did."

"So now that we've mated, the darkness is what? Just gone?"

"No," he replied, gripping her chin in his hand as he rubbed his thumb across her bottom lip. "Look into my eyes and tell me what you see."

She watched as his eyes brightened before she froze when his gray-green irises flashed with a red hue that looked too familiar to deny. Her words were a whisper when she spoke. "The red matches your aura's hue. Is that your darkness?"

"I'm assuming that's exactly what it is because it wasn't until recently that the color in my eyes changed. The weaker my barriers became, the more red shone through, at least until last night. When our bond clicked into place, something within my mind did as well. I can't explain it, and I don't know exactly what this means for me, but I feel more whole than I've ever felt in my life, and there's no longer a war going on within my mind on what I should or shouldn't do. I'm at peace within myself, but my actions bore consequences I don't know how to accept." His focus turned to Erick when his vitals began to plummet once more.

She watched as her mate pulled away before balling his hands into fists. Na'tori gripped him by the wrists before he could stand and shook her head vehemently. "There's nothing to be done. I've tried everything within my power to save him. I've looked over his blood front to back, and I've found nothing that can reverse the effects on him. Every one of his vital organs is shutting down. There's nothing to be done for him. Beating yourself up won't change the outcome, and Erick wouldn't want to see you like this. He sacrificed himself for our future. He did something he wasn't obligated to do, and beating yourself up about it is granting him no favors."

Alaric opened his mouth as if he planned to speak but paused to look towards the stairs just as Rome descended them with a look of confusion.

"How are you withstanding the effects of the sun right now?" The King of Eternals questioned with a frown.

Alaric shrugged his shoulders in response and stood as his brother-in-law approached. "I felt Na'tori's emotions through our bond and could no longer rest. I simply woke up and sought her out."

"No, I don't think you understand," Rome looked him over quizzically. "You're a newly turned Eternal. Nothing should be able to wake you from sleeping once you succumb to the sun's rays. Not even my eldest Eternal can withstand the effects unless I shelter him from them as I did for us when we went against Titan to get your mate back. You struggled then. But now I do not sense weakness in you where there should be."

"I think I can explain why." Na'tori interceeded and blushed slightly when their focus turned to her. "I'll need to collect a blood sample from him, but I believe my blood has given him the ability to withstand the sun. For how long? I'm not sure, but I can figure that out with more testing."

"Why with your blood? What makes it so special?"

"I have RHNull blood, also known as golden blood. When I mixed my blood with Alaric's, something happened that I hadn't expected. It mixed perfectly, and beneath a microscope, it seemed to glow like everyone's auras when I look at someone, but it was different. It changed on a molecular level, but I need more research now that I see him up and walking around. When I tested it before, it was only studied within a test tube, but now I see it works. I had an idea that he'd be able to walk in the sun from how it glowed, but I wasn't entirely sure."

"Can you do this for the rest of my Guardians?"

"I won't know unless I do some more testing."

Rome nodded in understanding, as he stared at his brother-in-law with a look of hope. "I suggest you head back to your room after she collects your blood before anyone sees that you're awake. We don't want to give anyone false hope if she can't deliver. I never would have thought this was possible, but here we are." He pulled Alaric into a hug before moving to Erick's bedside. "I'll watch over him."

Na'tori wanted to agree yet argue against his words when Rome suggested looking after Erick, but she could do nothing for the man lying in bed. All she could do for now was search for more answers within Alaric's blood to find a solution for all Eternals. After taking several vials of blood from Alaric, she ran them through a battery of tests as he disappeared upstairs. The itch to follow him was there, but the desire to find answers within his DNA pressed against her even harder until Rome crushed the silence with softly spoken words.

"I remember what it was like when Alara and I first mated. The need to be with her was a pull I could hardly resist. I still struggle with it daily." He glanced over his shoulder and smiled softly. "I'll yell for you if your monitors print out the results. Go to him. He might need you just as desperately as you need him, if not more so."

Na'tori didn't need to be told twice. She looked over her paperwork and machines one more time before she booked it up the stairs in search of her mate.

CHAPTER
THIRTY-NINE

Alaric stood before the open window in his bedroom and felt the sun's rays as it caressed his skin. He hadn't been an Eternal long enough to miss the feeling, but he had figured that he would never feel the sensation again, but because of his mate, he was capable. He untied the man bun on top of his head and allowed his curly black hair to flow down to his shoulders just as the sound of the bedroom door opened and closed behind him. He didn't need to turn around to know who it was. The scent of honey and elderberry surrounded him, and the sun's warmth couldn't even compare to the heat she pulled from him.

"Rome told me that maybe you would need me as much as I need you." Her voice calmed him in a way that nothing else could. "I'm hoping that's true."

He turned to face her, eyes taking in the knit sweater and leggings that hugged her curves and the fact that her hair still hung down to her lower back, free of restraint. The itch to grab all of her locks within his fist was strong enough that he found himself stalking across the span of his bedroom before pulling her into his arms where she belonged. She wrapped her arms around his waist and pressed her lips against his chest before her head tilted back, and he found her eyes sparkling with excitement and love.

He didn't want to ruin whatever moment this could have been with talks of her family, but they needed to discuss the elephant in the room. No one had told him what had happened after he'd passed out from being tranqed by that damn brother of hers. All he knew was that Lukas was dead, Ezekiel was still roaming freely about, and Erick was dying because of what he had done to his mind. It was great that one Titan tyrant was no more, but he had been nothing compared to that sick fuck Ezekiel, and Alaric needed to know what he had done to his mate. He remembered the smell of her burnt flesh and recalled the precise cuts that marred her body, but Alara or Rome must have healed her because the evidence of what her brother had done to her was no longer evident.

"Princess, I need to know what happened to you." He pushed his fingers through the hair at the nape of her neck and held her steady as he watched her expression for any shift of negative emotion. "We've been so worried about me and everyone else, but has anyone spoken to you about how you're doing and if you're okay?"

Na'tori's opalescent eyes filled with tears, and he watched as a wall fell and all of the pain she'd been holding back showed itself within her gaze. "I was so scared I would never see you again, terrified that I would die on that table and never get the chance to tell you I loved you. When you came for me, I knew everything would be okay, but when Lukas and his men attacked, every hope and dream I had of getting out of there nearly vanished in the blink of an eye." She paused to brush her tears away as her expression turned fierce. "It took me seconds to decide what to do. Seconds to realize that Lukas couldn't walk out of there alive, so I took matters into my own hands and threw your knife without thought or remorse. He died so that you all could live, but Zeke is still out there, and he's so much worse than Lukas could ever be. We have to find him, Alaric, and do it quickly before he has time to plan."

"You killed your brother Na'tori. Are you sure you're okay?"

"That's what you focused on?"

She attempted to shake her head, but he held her steady and frowned. Why was she taking this so lightly? For him, killing was as easy as breathing. It was inconsequential and something he'd been used to since the age of sixteen, but for her...she shouldn't be this okay. This should bother her. His mate wasn't a killer.

"You aren't a killer." He stated.

"You're right, I'm not," she replied, "but I'm fine Alaric. I promise."

He studied her closely but found no dishonesty in her expression or body language. He began to massage the back of her skull and watched as her eyelids slid shut and her lips parted in a soft moan before he leaned forward to suck her bottom lip into his mouth. She went even more pliant within his arms and turned their kiss up by several notches when she returned the favor. Alaric felt his heart racing within his chest at the thought of how much further they would take this. Now that they were mated, everything was heightened for him. Her scent, taste, and every bit of skin he could touch amplified his attraction and need for her by several degrees. He leaned back to look into her eyes but instead watched the top of her head as she leaned forward to kiss along his chest. Alaric inhaled softly, took in the scent of her arousal, and released a rumbling growl that shook his chest as his erection began to press heavily against his pants.

"What are you doing, princess?" He questioned when Na'tori dropped to her knees, unbuttoned his pants, and pulled the zipper down.

She glanced up at him, her hands steadily pulling down his clothing as she replied. "I think you know."

He had a strong feeling that he knew exactly what was about to take place, especially when she wrapped her small hand around his erection, looked deep into his eyes, and slowly ran her tongue over the slit of his dick where precum steadily leaked from it. He groaned roughly and watched as her lips wrapped around the head and slowly sucked him in. He couldn't look away even if he wanted to. He clenched his hands into fists, watched as her head steadily bobbed up and down, and listened to the slurp and suck that produced from her mouth. He knew that if he reached out and wrapped his hand into her silky hair, he wouldn't just hold her steady. He would end up fucking her throat, but he wanted her to have her fun before he took back his control because with every lick, suck, and sound from her, he found his balls tightening to dangerous degrees with the need to cum. She'd just started. He didn't want it to end too soon. Alaric was beginning to slide his eyes closed in ecstasy when her tongue moved in a pattern that caused his fangs to drop and his hands to grip the soft strands of her hair into his fists.

He watched as Na'tori looked up and into his eyes before sucking him even deeper into her mouth until he was grazing the back of her throat with his dick. His moan was deep and raspy; the look in her gaze spurred him on and sent his hips flexing as he slowly fucked her throat. "Fuck," he groaned.

Her nails dug into the skin of his thighs when she began to choke around him, yet she never pushed him away. The smooth back-and-forth glide of her mouth over him was causing him to see stars, and he hadn't even cum yet. She moaned around him, the vibrations causing his balls to tighten that much further as he cursed under his breath. The urge to fuck her was intense. The need pulsed and thrummed through his veins as she stared deep into his now glowing eyes. Spit ran from the sides of her mouth, and the sight of her mouth so full of him had him coming down her throat before he could process what was happening. He threw his head back with a deep groan, loosened his hold on her hair, and shuddered when she swallowed around him and sucked down his cum without pause.

Na'tori sat back on her heels; he dropped to his knees before her, kissed her deeply, and pulled back with a questioning smile. "What did I do to deserve that?"

She returned his smile with one of her own. "I just love you."

"And, I you, but now I feel like reciprocity is in order." His smile turned wicked as he crowded her with his body until she was lying flat against the floor, him hovering over her as his larger hand drifted up her body and captured the fabric of her sweater before he pushed it up her body.

With the sun beating against his back and his mate lying

beneath him with a look of wanton surrender on her face, Alaric couldn't help but marvel at his luck. To survive the darkness that had been plaguing him, to beat the odds that the Gods had indeed stacked against him, and to learn that the woman he'd been obsessed with since day one, was in fact, his mate had him feeling like he could walk on air. As the skin of her stomach came into view, he moved to kiss along her ribcage before hooking his fingers into the band of her leggings and panties. She lifted her hips to assist him in pulling them down and spread her legs to him even as a blush spread across her pale, freckled skin.

"You want me to devour you, don't you?" He sat back and peered down between her legs, where her wet center sat open and waiting as he ran his fingers down the inside of her thighs.

Na'tori's legs trembled beneath him. The closer he moved towards her center, the more her breath passed through her lips in whispered gasps, and her body shifted uncontrollably beneath him. With his thumbs on either side of the lips of her pussy he used them to spread her until her clit was peeking out at him from the hood that generally covered it. He watched as her core dripped slowly and slid his tongue over his lengthened fangs before looking up to find his woman staring back at him with lust in her eyes.

"Your pussy looks like it's anticipating me. Was this your plan, princess? Were you hoping to have me on my knees to grant you the same climax you've given me?" He questioned.

Na'tori shook her head softly and raised her hands above her head. With her hair fanned out around her, shirt raised to bare the curves of her breasts, and cunt spread, she looked like his wettest fantasy come to life. He didn't believe her for one second, she had to have anticipated this, but that didn't matter. He refused to make her wait long. Leaning forward, Alaric gently sucked her clit into his mouth before releasing it slowly to slide his tongue as deep into her depths as he could get. Her moan, followed by a gush of her cream, caused a growl to stir from his chest as he devoured her as if she were the last meal he would ever consume. Her hips rocked uncontrollably in an attempt to dislodge him, but he gripped her thighs in a rougher hold and used his broad shoulders to spread her even wider before shoving two thick fingers into her warmth. Her scream was music to his ears, and yet he needed more from her. With a curl of his fingers and with his fangs sliding into the femoral artery of her thigh Na'tori moaned as her pussy squirted and soaked his fingers. The taste of her blood, the scent of her release, and the feel of her fingers digging into his hair caused his dick to harden painfully.

"Please," she whispered brokenly as he continued to drink in her blood as the essence from his fangs continued to flow into her.

He released her thigh, licked around the wound, and watched as it healed before his eyes before Alaric rose over her body. He gripped his erection within his hand and stared into the eyes of his mate as he eased into her warm center. His groan matched the look of ecstasy that filled her expression before he bottomed out inside of her. Her thighs gripped him like a lifeline, but that didn't stop the slow thrust of his hips. The sound of his balls slapping her ass, the scent of her, and the feel of her beneath him were heaven and hell wrapped in one. Alaric felt like he couldn't get deep enough, yet it was as deep as he could get.

"Tell me again." He demanded, "Tell me you love me. Let me hear the words, princess." He cradled the back of her head and searched her eyes for the look that always caused waves of need to hit him directly in his solar plexus.

"I love you, Alaric," Na'tori gasped between thrusts that caused her breasts to jump and her pussy to flutter around him.

He used his free hand to force her legs even wider and plowed into her like a man chasing relief that seemed just out of reach. He watched as her eyes widened before another orgasm dragged her under. He went right along with her, feeling every pulse and throb of her core as his cum filled her to the brim. When he pulled from her body, he looked down and watched as his release slowly fell from between her lips before glancing up to meet her eyes.

"I love you too, princess; now, let's get some sleep before tonight, shall we?"

He lifted her into his arms without waiting for a response and carried her to the bed before making them comfortable. He was sure that she probably wanted to wipe away the excess fluid leaking from her. Still, the primal side of him said to keep her full of him, so with them spooning, her ass firmly pressed against him, Alaric reached around her to slide two of his fingers back into her cunt and chuckled when she groaned and shifted almost uncomfortably.

"Problem?"

"Do you have to do that?" She questioned.

"It's either my fingers or my dick, Na'tori, and considering if I slide my dick back into your pretty pussy we won't be finding sleep anytime soon, I opted for fingers. Did I choose poorly?"

She shook her head against his arm and relaxed into his hold. He kissed along the column of her throat before curling tighter around her body and allowing himself to drift to sleep.

CHAPTER
FORTY

Three days had passed since killing her brother, and earlier that day, Erick had fallen asleep and never woken again. He was currently downstairs in the infirmary, Alaric sitting vigilantly at his side as guilt ate him alive. Na'tori had been by his side for several hours until Alaric had begged her to eat and relax. He'd wished to be alone, so she'd granted him that.

No one blamed him for what had happened, but her mate refused to accept it. According to Rome, they were waiting for a Guardian who was usually in charge of the burial of their kind. Some things had to be done to ensure the discovery of the Eternals was never found out. She understood that. Na'tori even understood why Rome had requested each of them to stay inside, at least for the night. Emotions were high, and doing something reckless didn't seem too far off for any one of them.

Maverick brooded in the corner of the couch with Alara sitting and murmuring to him as Rome stood behind the sofa, his eyes constantly watching his mate. Cairo sat in the recliner, his gaze fixed on the floor in deep thought while Akio, Amirishka, and Silas sat around the kitchen island, Akio steadily tapping away on his laptop while Amirishka played with her knives and Silas sat with his eyes closed as if he were meditating. Alondra had yet to descend the stairs to join them, but Na'tori knew what the rest did not.

Her mate's sister wasn't doing too well. The drugs she'd been providing her in secret were no longer working, and Na'tori was clueless about what she should do next to help. Telling the others seemed like the intelligent route, yet Alondra was adamant against it. Apparently, she didn't want their sympathy, but could they risk not doing anything? She would die if they didn't take measures soon, and hadn't they seen enough death to last a lifetime?

Rome spoke abruptly, "Azriel will be here in seconds; do not attack him when he arrives."

Everyone came to attention as Alaric appeared at the entrance leading to the lower levels. It seemed he wasn't comfortable having an unknown Eternal near his mate without being present as well. He moved to take a position behind the sofa where Na'tori sat just as a tall figure teleported into the room.

The male's skin was a medium brown with tribal tattoos decorating his entire chest, back, and arms; only a pair of thin cotton pants covered the lower half of his body, along with open-toed sandals that looked older than everyone within the room, including Rome. His Egyptian features were easily spotted, including his pointed, narrow nose, wide, thick, plush lips, sculpted high cheekbones, and thick eyebrows, giving him an ethereal beauty that defied man's logic. Like a chiseled art piece that had taken form in the body of a six-foot-five male, his wavy black hair was pushed back into a low ponytail. In contrast, eyes the blackest color of midnight held pinpricks of iridescent that made his gaze almost terrifying to meet. He scanned the room, his gaze pausing only once when they reached Amirishka before he met the eyes of their King and nodded silently. He was gone just as quickly as he'd come. Never ushering a single word. Na'tori's mind raced as she tried to piece together the male who'd appeared just as quickly as he'd left. Azriel's aura was nonexistent. If not for seeing him with her own eyes, she would have assumed he was a human with no soul, if that even existed. She'd never seen another living being with no aura. What did that mean?

"Mind telling us what the hell that was about?" Akio spoke first.

"I can't be the only one that thought he was a little off. And come on..what century does he think we're in, wearing that shit? Where's his shirt?" He lifted his foot in a mocking jester and chuckled. "Where the hell are his shoes?"

Maverick burst out in a full belly laugh, his golden eyes taking on a sheen as if he planned to cry from laughing so hard before he smiled wide. "I can see why the man prefers to stay to himself, but damn Romulus, Akio is right; what's with the silent act?"

Rome narrowed his gaze at his two Guardians and snarled. "He's deaf and only communicates telepathically. So unless any of you decided to learn ASL in the last few centuries without me knowing, there was no need to broadcast his inability to speak. Now, can we move on to more pressing matters? Like the fact that he's collected Erick's body and intends on laying him to rest in the new home we plan on moving to within the coming weeks."

"We're moving?" Silas frowned, "Since when and why are we just learning of this?"

"Akio has found an abandoned military base that we've purchased from the government under the pretense of being a newly formed military operation sanctioned by the president. The fewer questions asked about that particular matter..., the better. The move is because while living here, we've been attacked within a neighborhood where humans can stumble upon our world and learn things they shouldn't. Where we'll be going, we'll have enough ground to see the enemy from miles away and no civilians within the surrounding area to notice anything suspicious." He paused to look down and ran his fingers through his mate's hair, almost in a calming gesture, before he sighed heavily. "With the move, I'll expect you all to work with the two Eternals I've decided to place within our group. They'll be here any moment to introduce themselves. They are struggling with losing their group, and putting them with others hasn't worked well in my favor. At least with us, I can monitor them closely and see exactly what the problems are."

"Wait, more Eternals are coming into the fold?" Na'tori frowned, "How many more of you are there?"

Rome's piercing gaze seemed to look right through her as he

spoke. "I have many Guardians around the globe, men and women, that need just as much protection in life as humans and Kindred do, but keeping up with them isn't exactly the easiest feat. Maybe with Kai and Linc, I can divide my time more evenly between the Kindred we discover and the Eternals, who don't always have my watchful eyes within their group."

"And if they don't fit with us?" Maverick asked what everyone else was too afraid to voice.

Something changed. She wasn't sure what it was, but the energy within the room changed, and the temperature dropped several degrees as every Guardian tensed. Only Rome and his mate remained relaxed before Na'tori's eyes caught on the corner of the room, closest to the front door, and held. It was like seeing the sun's rays refracting off a body of water to create a mirage. Everything was still within its place, and yet something was different. Amirishka was the first to react as she threw several throwing stars in rapid succession. The sound of metal hitting metal rang through the room before the mirage dropped to reveal Lincoln and Kai with amused and annoyed expressions, along with swords clutched in their palms. The throwing stars Amirishaka had thrown were now embedded in the wall, inches from their bodies.

Snarls rippled throughout the room. Na'tori watched as Maverick and Cairo stood while Akio, Silas, and Amirishka rounded the kitchen island with equal glares that would have reduced most people to tears. She looked back towards the two men and chuckled when she found Alaric blocking her view of them both.

"Seriously?" Alara looked between the people she considered family and chuckled, "As much as I'm sure you guys wished they were your enemies because they snuck up on you, they aren't, so can we speak like civilized adults and not try to intimidate those that don't seem too bothered by your displays of anger?"

Akio sighed heavily and went back to his laptop with a shrug. "At least they're wearing this century's clothing."

Lincoln and Kai looked confused while everyone but Maverick rolled their eyes in annoyance. Maverick, on the other hand, was once again laughing before Rome spoke.

"Kai is the shorter male, and Linc is the male to his right with the resting bitch face. Kai has an eidetic memory, and Linc can cause illusions as well as pick up any residual memories or info from any object he touches. They'll join our ranks here, and I'd like you to welcome them and not be children about it."

Alaric shifted in front of Na'tori, his eyes steadily watching the new males with a look of distrust as he spoke to his brother in law. "Erick dies, and now we're taking in strays?" The venom in his tone made even his mate wary.

Rome simply stared back at him, and Na'tori knew that they were now speaking telepathically. She reached out to take hold of his hand. She could see his aura darkening in a way that reminded her of a time when the darkness that used to fill him had nearly broken him. At her touch, he glanced down into her face; his features softened, and the red that had begun to leak into his gaze fell away.

Kai chuckled. "I've seen the red discoloration before. It's interesting to know you have it under control and don't need a swift and painless death."

"What do you mean you've seen it before?" Alaric frowned, "I developed the red with the progression of the virus that was created to infect Kindred and slowly kill them as well as Eternals."

"Maybe that's what you believed because you knew nothing else, but I've been around for centuries, and with a memory like mine, I forget nothing and retain even the smallest of details." He sheathed his sword and stepped forward, his honey-brown eyes steadily watching Alaric's every movement. "The red discoloration is due to latent anger that triggers your abilities to act negatively. It's why you notice a strength in your powers that goes beyond what should be possible. It's a corruption that comes from the darkness that already resides in you. The difference between you and the Guardian I killed several centuries ago is that he didn't have a light keeping him grounded." His stare turned to Na'tori and held. "Maybe the mating between you solidified that. I suppose time will tell."

"We'll speak more on that later. For now, let's discuss the plans moving forward." Rome interceded yet paused when the sound of

Alondra groaning in pain penetrated the air as she came into view from the hallway leading to the bedrooms.

Na'tori came to her feet at the sight of her condition. Alondra had sweat through the light sleep shirt she wore, her face was pale as death and her eyes were devoid of any emotion but pain as she used the wall to hold herself up. She seemed to look around the room before her gaze fell on the two newcomers. If her complexion could become paler, it would have.

"L-linc?" Alondra questioned softly before her expression shifted from shock to agony.

Alaric used his supernatural speed to vault forward and catch his sister just as her eyes rolled into the back of her head, and she fell forward. "What the fuck?" He cursed as he cradled her body close to his chest and bared his fangs at Lincoln. "How the hell do you two know each other?"

Na'tori's gaze swung between the two men, yet Lincoln remained silent as he stared at Alondra's unconscious body. She didn't want to wait around to find out just what other secrets her mate's sister held. She moved for the infirmary and yelled over her shoulder as she went. "Bring her down. I'll do blood work and see what's happening."

It was time she told her mate the truth about his sister and how they knew each other, especially if she wanted help saving the woman who might hate her afterwards.

EPILOGUE

E zekiel locked the door behind him before crossing the office that had once belonged to his brother. After taking a seat behind the long oak wood desk that he'd envied to be at for so long, he leaned back as the high-tech computer rebooted itself. A smile stretched his face wide even as anger ate at him with a hunger that shocked him.

He wished for the death of everyone involved in the rescue of his sister, but most of all, he wanted to have Na'tori beneath his blade once more. Her cries had been more satisfying than any sound he'd ever heard before, and the Eternals, with their need for saving lives, had taken that from him. Seeing them on an examination table with their insides exposed to his gaze was now a sight he needed and wished for more than his next breath. His hatred for the Eternals was growing to new heights and levels with every hour that passed, and he was still unsure of what move to make against his enemies.

He wasn't a biochemist like Na'tori or a hacker like Evan had been. He wasn't even a leader in the way that Lukas had strived at. What Ezekiel was was a killer with a mind for death. He was proficient in corrupting those around him and pushing others to commit acts that would go against their very character. Torture, Blood, and Death were his forte. With Lukas dead, he was now the leader of Titan and the many men and women who followed the command of the one who wrote their checks, but with the way the Eternals kept winning every battle set between them, he wasn't sure where his footing would be within this war. One thing he refused to do was be on the losing end of the stick.

The moment he leaned forward to hold his eye to the biometric scanner beside the larger monitor screen, a red alert and a video message from several weeks ago appeared. He clicked the link and watched his brother's smug face fill the screen. Lukas was seated behind the desk where he sat in what could only be a three-piece navy blue suit with a tie practically choking off his airway as he began to speak.

"Zeke, if you're receiving this message, it means that I'm dead, and my special project has now been without food for several days." He cleared his throat, adjusted his tie, and brushed imaginary lint from his shoulder. "For several years, I've kept something from the entire facility. It has the potential to put Titan on the map, and only Dr. Salazar is aware of what I've kept secret, yet the man himself has vanished from the face of the earth. If you can find him, he'll also have answers, but once he's provided those answers, you might as well kill the bastard. He no longer serves a purpose now that we have younger, more efficient doctors and chemists.

The being I have kept detained for several years now has been uncooperative, combative, and silent. No amount of torture has gotten me the answers I seek. With eyes as red as blood, I'm heavily convinced that they are a Rogue with their vicious, bloodthirsty nature and inability to see reason, and yet they give me the impression that they're something more. It's entirely possible that I may have an Eternal locked within my arsenal, yet I have been unable to break them. Nothing I do works, and nothing I say will convince them to join my ranks and fight against that asshole Romulus and his merry band of Eternals.

Maybe you can achieve what I was incapable of doing. In five minutes, this message will be erased from the servers, but once it does, the door behind you will release, and down the hall, you will find my most prized possession. We have never really gotten along, but I wish you well, brother. Good luck!"

The screen went black several moments later before a latch clicked behind him, sending Ezekiel spinning around to look down a dark hallway. With a slight smirk, he came to his feet, removed the long blade from his knife sheath, and proceeded to walk down the hall even as every cell in his body told him that he might not make it back out alive.

When he approached the lone door at the end of the hall, there was a light switch, a window looking into the room, and a slot large enough to fit his entire arm. He flicked on the light switch and stilled. The room was essentially a jail cell with what looked like silver lining the perimeter of the room. A bucket sat in the corner, along with a roll of toilet paper and a jug of water that was nearly empty. The only other object within the room was the full-sized bed devoid of any sheets, but none of that mattered to him. What mattered was the woman glaring at him from her seated and stilled position on the bed. With blood-red eyes that caused goosebumps to cover his skin, Ezekiel wondered if this was what fear felt like.

She came to her feet. Dirty blonde waist-length hair hung around her five foot nine lithe form like a shroud of malice as her pale complexion made the red in her eyes look that much brighter. She smiled wickedly and revealed sparkling white fangs as she continued to approach the door. Her face was rounded with small pert lips beneath a button nose, giving her a look of innocence that he was sure most people had fallen for. Ezekiel could make out the leanness within her body. The tiny slip of clothing that covered her form kept nothing to the imagination. Large 32DD breast pressed against the cotton fabric along with wide hips. Her toned legs were bare to his gaze, and her feet looked like they had seen better days.

He dragged his gaze back to her unsettling eyes and simply watched her tilt her head to the side like a predator might watch its prey. The hair at the nape of his neck stood on end, yet he opened his mouth to speak anyway.

"My brother made me aware of your existence only moments

ago. I can't deny that I'm intrigued by what I've found, but I'll tell you now so you know. I am nothing like the man that has kept you caged for however long you've been here. I'm so much worse. I can be your biggest blessing in this life or the reason you'll wish for death, so I'll ask you this once and once only. How you reply is how we will operate moving forward." Ezekiel stepped closer to the door, never taking his eyes off the alluring woman inside. "I've been told that you refuse to speak, but in order to leave this room and have the freedom I'm sure you seek, you'll respond, or you will be left here to rot. Is that clear enough to understand?"

She smiled wickedly, licked her lips, and nodded as she twirled her finger through her knotted hair.

He knew this was a gamble, yet he was willing to risk anything to get back at Alaric and his sister Na'tori. He would see them burned alive before he would ever accept defeat. "I'll release you from this prison and grant you your freedom, but in doing so, you'll agree to work with me in building an army of beings that will wipe my enemies, as well as yours, from this earth. So what do you say?"

She scanned his face and smirked before her soft voice filled the space between them. "What if I decide to remove your head from your shoulders as soon as you release me?"

He smirked back. "I've always been a gambler."

"In that case, you may call me Lasandra, and we have a deal."

ABOUT THE AUTHOR

Tasha M. Taylor is a self-published author with ambition, drive, and excitement to create other stories for readers to dive into and become lost in. Writing has always been a desire and a passion, as well as reading, spending time with Eros, her European Maine-Coon, and seeing her friends and family. She has a full-time job as a telemetry technician and occasionally models in her free time.

www.ingramcontent.com/pod-product-compliance
Lightning Source LLC
Chambersburg PA
CBHW051231260626
47162CB00002B/382

Crossed Circuits

A SCI-FI SHORT STORIES

VOLUME IV

GAGE AXTIN

BLUE M PUBLISHING - CHICAGO

Library of Congress Cataloging-in-publication data
Name: Gage Axtin
Title: *Crossed Circuits*
Sci-Fi Short Stories - Volume IV

Description: First edition | Blue M Publishing (Paperback), Chicago, IL [2020] |
Contents: Crossed Circuits | Summary: A collection of sci-fi short stories that tell of
technology and its effects on people. | Audience Note: Recommended for readers
seventeen and older | Language Note: mildly offensive language.
Identifiers: ISBN 978-1-945385978-27-8 (Paperback)
Subjects: LCSH: sh85118629 science fiction| BISAC: FIC028040 | GSAFD: 00000cz
a2200037n 45 0 155 Classification: LCC PZ 370-380 | DDC 813-55/--dc23

by Gage Axtin
Contents: Multiple Parts

ISBN 978-1-945385978-27-8 (Paperback)

Printed in the United States of America
www.blueMpublishing.com
Book Cover Design by Allendorf-Vignere

Blue M Publishing
Chicago, IL